Praise for these other novels of delightful contemporary
romance by *USA Today* bestselling author
**Kieran Kramer**

## YOU'RE SO FINE

"Kieran Kramer writes a sexy, sassy Southern romance
with heart."
　　　　　—Jill Shalvis, *New York Times* bestselling author

"Kramer dishes up another delightful contemporary
romance that is deftly seasoned with sassy Southern wit,
snappy dialogue, and plenty of smoldering sexual chemistry. Readers who fell in love with Susan Elizabeth Phillips's
*Dream a Little Dream* (1998) or *Ain't She Sweet?* (2004)
will definitely want to add Kramer's latest sexy, sparkling,
spot-on love story to their reading lists."　　　—*Booklist*

"Filled with smart, believable characters and fresh, witty
storytelling. A sexy, poignant romance wrapped in Southern charm and lightly accented with Hollywood glamour."
　　　　　　　　　　　　　　　　　—*Kirkus Reviews*

"A superbly written, powerful, and touching book."
　　　　　　　　　　　　　　　　　—*Fresh Fiction*

# SWEET TALK ME

"The perfect combination of good-natured sass, sultry sexual tension, and hint of Southern crazy. I loved this book."
—Tracy Brogan, author of *Crazy Little Thing*

"A sweetly sexy love story that is everything a romance should be . . . a knockout!" —*Booklist* (starred review)

"The banter between these characters was fun to read and I loved the tension that flowed between them . . . a great read to lose yourself in for a few hours."
—*Night Owl Reviews* (Top Pick)

"Readers who enjoy works by Nora Roberts and Luanne Rice will want to give Kramer a try. This reviewer predicts that the beaches this summer will be covered with copies of *Sweet Talk Me*."
—*Library Journal* (starred review)

## ALSO BY KIERAN KRAMER

*A Wedding at Two Love Lane*
*Christmas at Two Love Lane*
*Trouble When You Walked In*
*You're So Fine*
*Sweet Talk Me*

### THE HOUSE OF BRADY SERIES

*Loving Lady Marcia*
*The Earl Is Mine*
*Say Yes to the Duke*

### THE IMPOSSIBLE BACHELOR SERIES

*When Harry Met Molly*
*Dukes to the Left of Me, Princes to the Right*
*Cloudy with a Chance of Marriage*
*If You Give a Girl a Viscount*

# Second Chance At Two Love Lane

## KIERAN KRAMER

St. Martin's Paperbacks

This is a work of fiction. All of the characters, organizations, and events portrayed in this novel are either products of the author's imagination or are used fictitiously.

SECOND CHANCE AT TWO LOVE LANE

Copyright © 2018 by Kieran Kramer.

All rights reserved.

For information address St. Martin's Press, 175 Fifth Avenue, New York, NY 10010.

ISBN: 978-1-250-11108-1

Our books may be purchased in bulk for promotional, educational, or business use. Please contact your local bookseller or the Macmillan Corporate and Premium Sales Department at 1-800-221-7945, ext. 5442, or by e-mail at MacmillanSpecialMarkets@macmillan.com.

Printed in the United States of America

St. Martin's Paperbacks edition / September 2018

St. Martin's Paperbacks are published by St. Martin's Press, 175 Fifth Avenue, New York, NY 10010.

10 9 8 7 6 5 4 3 2 1

# PROLOGUE

"So what did you think?" Papa Mancini asked his oldest daughter, Ella.

They were on her first-ever trip to a Sunday matinee at a Broadway theater, which Papa decided he would give her as a present every year around her birthday. Ella was five, and after the show he took her to the most marvelous place in the world, a restaurant called Serendipity 3. It was pink and white, with fancy light fixtures and beautiful tables. It was on East 60th Street, between Second and Third Avenues in New York City, and seemed a world away from their home in the Bronx. They sat on the second floor.

Ella dipped her spoon into her frozen hot chocolate, Serendipity 3's specialty. "It's good," she said.

"I mean the show," Papa said. And smiled.

She loved his smile.

"I liked it," she said, and dug out a cherry from the whipped cream on top of her sweet concoction. "Especially Simba."

She roared.

"I hope you always roar, *mio dolce figlia*," Papa said

softly as he wiped some whipped cream off her chin with a napkin.

Papa loved all his daughters. Each one was special. Ella, he saw, had a spark in her eye that turned to a blaze when she and her sisters performed little plays and songs for their parents and relatives. The way she flounced across their homemade stage and sang songs so earnestly in her little girl's vibrato reminded him of his grandmother, who used to be a well-known actor in Sicily.

Papa didn't want Ella's creative flame to be quenched. Ever.

The server came by. "This little girl is so sweet, her dessert is free."

"Free?" Ella's eyes widened.

Papa chuckled. "See? Everyone knows you're special."

"So what did you think?" Papa asked Ella, whose feet now touched the ground at Serendipity 3.

She dipped her spoon into her frozen hot chocolate. "I want to be Mary Poppins," she said. "I want that big purse she carried, with the magic measuring tape. I know what it would say if I measured *you*, Papa."

"What?"

"The best papa in the world. Times a hundred million." A hundred million was a big number.

He grinned. "You know what it would say if I measured *you*?"

"No. What?" She couldn't wait to find out.

He leaned forward and whispered, "This little lady is one of the great treasures of her papa's heart."

She was treasure? In his heart? Like gold? And diamonds? She would be a ruby, she decided. A red ruby that gleamed always with love for her father.

Once again, a server came by and said, "No charge for this table."

Papa leaned back. "Why not?"

The server indicated Ella. "She's too cute. The frozen hot chocolate is on us."

Ella's mouth fell open. Serendipity 3 was a magical place.

"What do you think, my princess? How did you like the show?" asked Papa at Serendipity 3.

At age twelve, Ella decided no more frozen hot chocolate for her. She was going to have something called a Forbidden Broadway sundae. "I loved it," she said, and dug into a chunk of chocolate cake with hot fudge sauce.

"Why?" Papa was always persistent.

Sometimes Ella didn't feel like talking to him as much, and that worried her. He was her favorite man. She never wanted to hurt him. "Well," she said, thinking, and then knew what she was going to say. "I want to be an actor."

"You do?" Papa's eyebrows flew up.

Ella nodded. "Today Belle looked out into the audience, and I got goose bumps. She was looking right at me. It was like she was telling me, 'you could be me.'"

She had little tears in her eyes, which brought tears to his.

"Is that what you want, Ella?"

"More than anything," she said. "In fact"—she put down her spoon—"I'm trying out for another play at school. Do you think I'm too young to be serious about acting?"

"Absolutely not," said Papa.

She grinned at him. "I love you, Papa."

A handsome teenage boy carrying a bus pan filled

with dirty ice cream glasses and plates walked by the table, and she blushed.

"Just don't let anyone stand in the way of your dreams." Papa winked at her and grinned.

"Papa!" she said back, embarrassed. She wished he wouldn't say such silly things!

She hoped that boy hadn't heard.

Later their server came by with the bill. When Papa looked at it, it said, *No charge.*

"They really like us here," Ella whispered to her father.

"It's because of you," he said. "You must be their favorite birthday girl."

"So," said Papa, his eyes tired, a little bloodshot, too, from working a late wedding party in the Mancini family restaurant the night before. "What did you think?"

Ella had decided to get a frozen hot chocolate again, her first time in years. "I loved it so much, I won't be able to sleep tonight." She laughed.

"Me too." Papa smiled.

"Papa," she said, "I just want you to know something."

"What, *mio dolce figlia*?"

Her eyes filled with tears. "I can't believe I'm going away to college in less than a month, and I won't be with you on my birthday." She had to swallow hard. "I just want you to know our annual trip has been the biggest, most wonderful memory of my entire life. Thank you. I'm going to miss you."

"And I you," he said, "but you'll always be here." He placed his hand over his heart. "Even when you are away. And someday you'll come back with a degree in theater. And when you do, I'll go see *you* star in a Broadway play."

Ella laughed. "I hope so."

"I *know* so," said Papa. He laid his hand over hers. "Don't let anyone or anything stop you from following your dreams."

She sighed. "Papa, no one and nothing will stop me. I promise."

He smiled a little sadly.

"What?" she asked. "Don't you believe me?"

"Of course, I do," he said, and laughed. "You're just like your great-grandmother. Such sparkle and fire. Always listen to your heart. It won't steer you wrong."

"I will. I promise," Ella said, but she was still worried about that shadow that had passed over his face.

He picked up the bill. "No charge. *Again.*"

Ella grinned. "I really do think I'm their favorite birthday girl. I want to thank them before we leave. They've been so nice to me all these years."

"Good idea," said Papa. "I'll be right back. I'm going to buy you a Serendipity 3 mug as a souvenir."

"Oh, that's so sweet of you!"

Papa spoiled her. But Ella knew she'd drink out of that mug every day when she moved to Charleston.

He winked and left her to finish her frozen hot chocolate.

A handsome young man about her age walked by Ella to a nearby empty table, where a waitress was filling a bowl with sugar packets. He hugged her.

"You? You're back?" the waitress said, grinning. "From our favorite busboy to college student. We're so proud of you."

Ella couldn't help listening in. She remembered him. From a few years ago—he was that cute busboy with the cowlick. . . .

She'd seen him the next year, too, and the one after

that—but not last year. Somehow the cowlick was patted down now. Totally gone.

"Don't get too excited," the guy told the waitress. "I dropped out."

"*No.*"

He nodded. "I'm going to be an actor."

"An actor? Not a lawyer?"

"Sure? Why not?"

"I don't know." The waitress lofted one eyebrow. "Don't lawyers make a lot of money? And actors starve?"

The guy caught Ella's eye and grinned.

She turned beet red.

"Think I can be an actor?" he asked her, off the cuff.

Ella smiled and nodded. She was terrible with boys. Maybe someday she'd become more sophisticated.

He kept his eyes on her while he said to the waitress, "See? That beautiful girl thinks so."

"I do," Ella piped up, and didn't even have time to blush about the compliment he'd given her. "I'm going to be an actor myself."

*Actor.* Not *actress.* Ella wasn't going to enter any profession without pushing for equal say and equal pay. Papa and Mama had both taught her to fight for what was right.

The waitress shook her head. "Young people," she said, and sighed.

He kissed the older woman on the cheek and walked over to Ella's table. "What's your name?"

"Ella. Ella Mancini."

"I'm Hank Rogers. You've been here before, right?"

She was shocked he recognized her. "I come once a year with my father. Nice to meet you."

"You too, Ella." He paused a beat. "Hey, will I see you around at auditions?"

"No," she said, her heart fluttering in her chest, "I'm going to college first. Out of state. I'm majoring in theater. No one in my family has ever gotten a college degree. I want to change that and *then* start my big Broadway career."

"Good for you," he said. "Break a leg."

He was so cute! Her heart did a huge flip. "Break a leg yourself."

They looked at each other a beat too long.

"We'll meet again," Hank said. "I can feel it."

Somehow, she did too. But she was afraid to agree with him out loud.

"I'll look for you, Ella," he said, his hands in his pockets. "Four years from now, after you graduate. Back here in New York. This day. The day before July Fourth. Here in Serendipity 3. Mark it on your calendar, okay?"

"It's a date," she said, not wanting to break eye contact.

And that was when Papa showed up with a little shopping bag that contained her souvenir mug.

"Goodbye, Hank," she said to the boy over her shoulder as she wrapped her arm through Papa's free one.

"Good thing you're going to South Carolina," Papa said with a chuckle. "Hopefully, there are no boys there."

"Oh, Papa, I'll be fine," she assured him.

At the register on the first floor, Ella thanked everyone for gifting her with a free birthday treat each year. "You're very kind," she said.

They were all smiles. The manager said, "It's our pleasure. It's nice to see a father and daughter with a tradition."

At the door Ella said, "I wonder how they knew?"

"Do we not look very much alike?" Papa asked.

"Yes, we do," Ella said. She had his eyes and his chin.

"And they must have noticed us coming in, year after year after year."

"We're hard to miss. You're a beautiful young lady," her father said.

"Oh, Papa." She squeezed his arm.

When she walked out, Ella had no idea she and Papa would never go to Serendipity 3 together again.

# CHAPTER ONE

*Her show must go on.* That was what Ella Mancini told herself when she saw the flowers in her dressing room at the historic Dock Street Theatre in Charleston, South Carolina. The vase of her favorite hothouse blooms was from her old boyfriend, Hank Rogers. The (Former) Love of Her Life is what she secretly called him.

Ella was the star of her own life, and no ancient love affair was going to weigh her down, especially ten years after the breakup.

It had been an especially good night, the final night of the play's run, and an especially good audience, she thought as she inhaled the heady scent from the flowers. Maybe Hank hadn't appreciated her as much as she'd wanted him to, but tonight's audience certainly had.

She opened the card that came with the delivery, her fingers trembling a little. *Dear Ella,* the note read. *I hope you're well! I need a huge favor. Please call me. It's not an emergency or anything, but it would mean a lot if you could. Hank.*

He'd left a number she didn't recognize. Of course, he'd have gotten a new one since the last time she'd seen him, when he'd been penniless and had a flip phone. Now he was a big movie star and probably had a flip phone again—this time to protect his privacy.

Was he still single? He was in the tabloids all the time with different women, and yet he'd never been committed enough to one that rumors about an impending elopement or marriage had been passed around. Nope, every story was just about Hank loving life, a beautiful woman always on his arm, a new movie script in his back pocket.

Ella was a muddle of emotion, as she always was at the conclusion of a play's run and after each night's performance. She was spent, her vocal cords exhausted. But tonight she felt removed from the whole scene in a way she never had before. She didn't know what to think. She couldn't latch onto a single, clear feeling.

And it was all Hank's fault.

Why had he done this? Why had he contacted her?

Ella pressed down the hurt, the confusion, the simmering anger. He didn't deserve her attention. At all. Ever again. She refused to go back there, to the most painful—and yet the most glorious—time of her adult life.

The door to her tiny dressing room opened.

"You know the drill," the props master said. "Leave everything hung up in your dressing room."

"No prob," said Ella. "Are you going to come see me at Two Love Lane? There will be cookies, mint juleps, and sweet tea. Not to mention Miss Thing. She's always a hoot."

Miss Thing dressed like the Queen of England and was the office manager at the matchmaking agency Ella owned with her other best friends, Macy and Greer. They'd both recently married after whirlwind courtships—Macy to native New Yorker Deacon Banks, and Greer to Englishman Ford Smith. Miss Thing, Macy, and Greer were as close to Ella as her own sisters.

"I am," said the props master. "I promise." She'd broken up with her long-time boyfriend a year ago and told Ella she was thinking about becoming a client at Two Love Lane. She pulled the door almost shut, then pushed it open again. "Who are the flowers from?"

Ella forced herself not to roll her eyes. "An old friend."

The props master shot her an amused look. "That's cryptic. Is it something complicated?"

"Not anymore."

They both grinned, then the props master finally shut the door behind her.

Ella sank down on her castered vanity chair, closed her eyes, and took a breath. She pulled her cell phone out of her purse and saw that she had ten texts from ten different people, all wishing her well, including her sister Jill and Jill's new husband Cosmo, a famous tech mogul. Miss Thing had also texted. She'd seen Ella in five performances of the play already (Greer and Macy had come three times with various friends and family), but Miss Thing hadn't been able to come tonight because Pete, their dear friend from Roastbusters, the coffee house up the cobblestoned alley from Two Love Lane, had asked her to fill in at the shop while he was recovering from minor surgery.

Reluctantly, Ella put Hank's number in her phone. It was the polite thing to do. "But I won't call him," she said out loud to her reflection in the mirror, and entered *Ancient* as his first name and *History* as his last name into her contacts list.

What was that like for him, being famous? Ella would never know. But she was okay with that. She had a good life, a *great* life.

Inside, though, she felt a twinge. It sometimes came out in dreams about the old days in New York, when she'd been working so hard to make it as a professional actor.

*But it's okay*, she reminded herself. *It really is.*

She closed her eyes and tried not to think of "Bring Him Home," the most moving, tear-jerker of a song she knew . . . from *Les Misérables.* But it was there—in her head. Instantly, salty tears flooded her eyes, which she clamped shut to stave them off.

Why did that song come to her now, crashing into her brain like a runaway train? Of course, it was because before he'd left, Hank would lie with her on the couch, and wrapped in each other's arms, they would listen silently to "Bring Him Home." Their love of music, of theater, was what had drawn them to each other in the first place. They'd been two struggling artists in awe of the beauty of songs like "Bring Him Home." Those special moments felt more sacred to Ella than any spoken vows of love. Without a word, they'd known they were made for each other.

After Hank left, Ella used to hope beyond hope he'd come home. To *her.* She'd stand in the shower in their tiny apartment, tears pouring down her cheeks, "Bring Him Home" running through her head.

But that was ancient history.

"*Ancient history*," she stressed to her reflection. Now she put the phone down. Turned it all the way off. Really looked at herself in the vanity mirror rimmed with naked, round bulbs. Her entire body felt rigid with hurt, still. It shocked her that it did. She felt pain. And sadness.

*After all these years.*

And she'd thought she'd been so happy. She really had believed it. All the wonderful things she'd done in the ten

years since she'd dated Hank, things she could be proud
of . . . they did matter, but so did her heart.

And it obviously hadn't healed yet.

She swallowed back the lump in her throat, glad she'd
turned her phone off. In fact, she didn't know if she'd ever
want to turn it on again.

She stood. Slid out of the sleek wedding gown. Briefly
admired the old-fashioned corset in the mirror. She'd
never get to wear it again. And her legs—they looked
gorgeous in thigh-high stockings and garters, if she did
say so herself. Her underthings were important parts of
her costume. At one point in the story, a chorus dancer
slid Ella's skirt up and exposed one sexy leg all the way
up to her garter belt. And in the same scene, a chorus
member buttoned her up in her wedding gown, Ella's
back to the audience, her corset laces exposed.

Those scenes had happened before she'd known Hank
would have flowers delivered to her dressing room. Did
he remember all the times they'd made love and he'd run
his hand up her leg and told her how beautiful she was?
Would he think she was as beautiful now as he'd thought
she'd been then?

"I don't care," she said out loud to her mirror.

But the truth was, she did. Very much.

# CHAPTER TWO

The day after the play's last run was a Sunday, and Ella was in her mother's kitchen, where she often found herself on Sunday afternoons when she wasn't at rehearsal or performing in a matinee. Mama Mancini owned a 1930s bungalow on a residential street in Charleston's new tech corridor north of Calhoun Street. It was a neglected area of town that had been declining steadily for decades but was currently being revitalized. Older houses there could be picked up at decent prices but required lots of work.

The whole Mancini family had fixed up Mama's house together—painting, tiling, refinishing the hardwood floors. Uncle Leo and Uncle Sal had done all the rewiring. Cousin Vittorio had updated the plumbing. The older nephews and nieces painted the bedrooms and the living room. The aunts worked outside, sprucing up the front walk with some monkey grass and planting azaleas beneath the living room bay window. Out back, they made Mama a little herb garden and added a bird bath, a comfy garden bench, and a hammock for her to lie in and read the fabulous romance novels she loved so much.

And the sisters, amateur painters ever since Jill had gotten them hooked on YouTube videos about mural painting, had dutifully followed Mama's orders to paint decorative scenes wherever she demanded them.

In her mother's kitchen, a nearly naked Jupiter, artfully robed and surrounded by clusters of purple grapes, stared down at Ella from the ceiling while she prepared antipasti, which she could do blindfolded. Olives to the left, mozzarella to the right, peppers in the middle. A drizzle of oil, some good cracked pepper, and there you had it—the nectar of the gods.

Miss Thing called while Ella was scooping olives out of a Harris Teeter supermarket container. "I got your text," she trilled. "Hank Rogers had flowers delivered to your dressing room last night."

Ella braced herself. "That's right." She'd been about to give them away before she'd left the theater, but instead she'd brought them home to her mother and made something up about them coming from the Footlight Players' board of directors.

Something in her had not been able to give those flowers away, although she'd tossed the card.

"Sugar, I *knew* something was up," said Miss Thing. "Yesterday afternoon, I looked outside and I saw a cardinal looking at me on the branch outside my bedroom window."

Whenever Miss Thing saw a cardinal on the branch outside her bedroom window, that was her late husband come down from Heaven to let her know something big was going on. At least that was what she said, and Ella believed her.

Except that a cardinal landed on that branch at least once a week, so Miss Thing was in a constant state of high drama. But if that meant she felt closer to the man who'd brought her such joy, then Ella was perfectly happy to go along with her friend's excitement.

"Well, he wants a favor, but it's not an emergency, so I'm going to take my time thinking about if and when I'll respond," said Ella.

But she didn't need any trouble. And those eyes of his were trouble. So was his mouth. And his voice. Every time she heard it on the big screen or on television, it still sent shivers down to her toes—the good kind. But she didn't tell Miss Thing any of that.

"Don't you think for a minute he doesn't still have designs on you!" Miss Thing said. "He never would have asked you a favor if he was completely over you. Aren't you dying to know what he wants?"

"*Miss Thing.*" Ella strove to be gentle. "*No.* We were together ten years ago. I can't imagine I could help him in any way. The man's a celebrity. He's got assistants and agents and whatnot. Let *them* do him favors."

She tried to forget that this morning she'd woken up from a feverish dream in which he was making love to her on their old brass bed with plump feather ticking.

"But he left you when he was young and foolish and didn't know his own mind," said Miss Thing. "He's matured. As have you."

"We both made a very sensible vow to put our careers first," said Ella. "He wasn't being foolish. Look how it paid off."

"Yes, but when you had *your* shot, you didn't take it. Because of him!"

Ella sighed. "I was the foolish one then, wasn't I? Let's not talk about it anymore." It reminded her too much of her conversations with Papa.

She'd failed Papa. She couldn't stand thinking about it.

"All right." Miss Thing sighed. "Although I have to admit something. I'm glad you're here with us in Charleston."

"I'm glad too," said Ella. And she was.

But secretly, every time she thought about the choices she made in New York, she got furious. At herself. Which was why she didn't think about New York. She'd been happily free of any regrets for years now, except for one day a year—Papa's birthday.

And now, last night. Receiving those flowers had thrown her off her game.

"I'm a terrible person being glad you didn't hit the big-time like Hank," said Miss Thing. "But living in Manhattan or L.A. in a fancy penthouse, riding around in limos, wearing amazing designer clothes all the time, and making movies in exotic locations—that ain't nothin' compared to living in the Lowcountry."

Sometimes Miss Thing lapsed back into her super Southern voice, especially when she was bragging on the place she'd been born and never left.

"You got that right," said Ella, who was ripping open a bag of pita chips. They scattered across the counter, and she started scooping them up. What the heck, she thought, and ate a few right out of her cupped palm.

"What's that noise?" asked Miss Thing. "Static?"

"No," said Ella, "it's me chomping on pita chips."

"Oh, honey. You only do that when you're stressed."

"I know. Mama just told me today we're having eight cousins over seventy years old coming over from Sicily for the next couple of weeks. She's farming them out and wants to know if I can put up two at my apartment for the first week. They'll go to one of my sisters the following week."

"Well, can you?"

"Sure. But they barely speak English. And they're very loud. The neighbors won't be pleased."

"A week with you and then a week with your sister? That's a long time."

"Not in Mancini time. They only come over every five years or so. They try to get the most from their airline ticket."

"Poor you. Want to leave them the apartment and come stay with me?"

"I'd love to."

"But you'd have to share your room with my new guinea pigs. I have no other place to put their cage. They love to squeal. Do you like guinea pig squeals? They're adorable."

"I guess. Do they squeal at night?"

"Sure. Any time of day or night."

"Uh . . ."

"And do you care that I'm having painters come? They're painting the whole house. But they're hot, honey. College boys. Which is disgraceful of me to mention. I don't think of them like that, but *you* might. They told me they've just graduated, actually, and don't want cubicle jobs."

"*Miss Thing.* I'm too old for college boys who've just graduated."

"I don't think so."

"I *am* too old for them!"

"I understand." But she could tell Miss Thing still thought she wasn't. "They're only seven or eight years younger, though—"

"Enough of that. And I don't want to sound like a diva, but if I hear a guinea pig squeal at night, I might have a heart attack in my sleep. But thanks anyway for the offer to stay."

"No problem, sugar," said Miss Thing. "Back to that celebrity scene you're missing out on. Who needs caviar and endless pairs of designer shoes? Look at where you are. How many places can you put out a crab trap in the morning and have a feast that evening? Or ten months of the year, be able to jump off a dock for a good float down the creek? And then get gussied up and go to a white-tie ball? They're a dime a dozen around here, all year 'round. I have fourteen ball gowns. And I use 'em. Thank God for Goodwill during prom dress season. They've saved me many a dollar."

"I know." Ella started chopping olives. And then realized she wasn't supposed to chop the olives. She wasn't making pizza. So she ate the ones she'd chopped and spread the other ones on the antipasti plate. She rolled them around a little too much. Three fell off the side and landed on the floor.

"How many ball gowns do you have?" Miss Thing asked.

"Ten." It was true. Charlestonians loved black-and-white-tie events. You needed long evening gowns here all year 'round. Most of Ella's came from TJ Maxx or a good Macy's online sale. She bent down and went looking for the missing olives.

"Did you hear about the new movie they're making here? You should audition." Miss Thing slurped something up a straw. Probably an iced coffee from Roastbusters.

"Yes, I heard. But I'm not interested." Ella had a Screen Actors Guild card, so every time a movie came to Charleston, she was alerted via email. And they were coming way more often than they used to. Just about once a year now.

"Why don't you want to audition?" Miss Thing asked.

"Being a film extra is more trouble than it's worth," Ella said right away. Maybe she sounded like a diva, but it *was*. She had no desire to sit around eight hours a day and occasionally stand up and play a bystander in a scene and then get paid a pittance, all because you wanted to appear on-screen for a second or two or, more likely, have your scene cut.

"But what if you got a speaking role?" Miss Thing was always persistent. Like Papa had been.

"The only speaking roles they haven't filled yet are for a fifty-year-old male nurse and two teen girls." Ella drizzled oil over the olives, peppers, and mozzarella. She drizzled two big *X*'s over them. Done and done. Kind of like her professional acting career and her love life, and so what? She didn't care.

Most of the time.

Miss Thing clucked. "That's a shame."

"I don't mind. Movie work takes up your whole day." Now it was time for the pepper. Ella cranked the heck out of it. Probably too much. She was about to sneeze, but she caught it just in time. "I can't afford to indulge silly whims. I'm a matchmaker, and I have to pay my bills."

"And you're a damn good one. But Samantha Drake's in this movie. Why, she's more famous than Meryl Streep! Almost."

"No one is more famous than Meryl Streep," said Ella with a chuckle. "But Samantha's just as talented. In fact, I'm pretty much in awe of her."

"Me too. She's forty and looks thirty," Miss Thing said.

"It's not that. She's an amazing actor," said Ella. "She's racked up almost as many Oscars as Meryl."

"Then why wouldn't you want to work with her?"

Ella laughed. "I wouldn't get to be anywhere near her on set if I was an extra."

"Wouldn't you catch a glimpse of her now and then?"

"Probably. But she'd look right through me. It's too . . ."

"Too what?"

"Painful." Ella gulped. She thought she was over leaving her New York dreams behind! But seeing Hank had brought it all back to her. All her daydreaming about becoming a famous actor on Broadway, and maybe making a leap to TV or the movies. All Papa's excitement about her doing that too. . . . It used to fuel her when she had setbacks, like bad auditions.

"Aw, sweetie," said Miss Things. "You're a big fish in a small pond. And Charleston's not such a small pond, really. It's an international city. A very culturally rich place, right? You should be proud."

"Yes, it is, and I *am* proud." Ella stood back up. She'd accidentally kicked the olives she'd dropped under the fridge. She was in trouble now. She needed a broom handle. "But I have no desire to make any movies, with or without Samantha Drake in them. Or Frampton Cooke."

The male lead. Ella respected his work professionally but had never been a huge fan, personally.

"He's kinda cute, in a Shakespearean way, with those piercing eyes," said Miss Thing. "He's so intelligent. And English. Is he single?"

"No, he just married his publicist," said Ella. "And his piercing eyes would get kind of annoying after a while, don't you think?"

"No," said Miss Thing. "Frampton Cooke could stare at me all day, and I'd be happy. But speaking of another hot male celebrity, have you told Greer and Macy about getting flowers from Hank?"

"No," Ella said. She didn't like to bother them on Sundays. It was a good day for couples to get cozy—although sometimes Deacon and Ford played golf or did volunteer construction work with The Sustainability Project, Deacon's nonprofit, and the women all got together for brunch or shopping. But that was an exception to the rule. "I'll see them tomorrow. I'll tell them then. I'll be sure to mention this wasn't a romantic bouquet. It's a bribe, to do him some kind of favor."

"Still. It was *flowers*."

"So?"

"Ellaaaa! Ella-bella? *Ella Vittoria Maria Mancini!*" It was her mother's voice.

"Gotta go," Ella said to Miss Thing. "See you tomorrow."

"Bright and early-ish," Miss Thing reminded her. They never came into the office before 9:00.

"Come help your *nonnas* understand this show!" Mrs. Mancini called to her eldest daughter from the living room. It was heavy on purple accents, from candlesticks to pillows to curtains, a far cry from the drawing rooms of Charleston's more sedate, historic homes on the opposite side of the city.

Ella popped an olive in her mouth. Yum. *Really* yum. Better-than-sex yum? She squinted up at Jupiter. *No*, she thought, and wiped her hands on her mother's vintage apron, which she'd wrapped around her waist to protect her Armani suit. The *nonnas* liked her to dress up on Sunday when she came to visit since they didn't get to see her fashion choices as much during the week. The Armani was a gift from Jill, who owned a company called Erospace Designs.

At Erospace, Jill worked hard to make everyone's living space their erotic loving space on her own dime, and she was doing really well. Her very first client had been Greer, who claimed to this day that Ford showed up in her life at the exact same time Jill committed to working on making Greer's bedroom sexier to attract her soul mate. Jill's boudoir-design style had been labeled "deliciously, provocatively tacky" by *Home and Garden* magazine, and the PR had had nothing to do with her new husband's high profile. A *Home and Garden* magazine editor happened to have a second home in Charleston and stumbled upon Jill's business advertisement in that local hipster's delight, *The City Paper.*

Maybe Ella needed Jill's services too. Her own bedroom was boring. She had the same old blue paisley bedspread and walnut four-poster double bed Mama had given her after college, along with a mismatched bureau and nightstand. Her reading lamp sometimes turned on and off by itself because the wiring was bad, and she still had posters on the wall she'd had at her college dorm.

Her guest room, with its two prim twin beds with yellow spreads and daisy pillows, was no better. That was where the Sicilian cousins would have to stay. But she'd need to give them her TV, which was a shame. She loved watching TV in bed, especially the *Real Housewives* franchise. Now she'd have to read, which she also loved, but she'd been avoiding it lately because of her stupid flickering bedside lamp, which she really needed to fix. She'd been so busy at work and helping Mama with the *nonnas.*

Sometimes she just forgot to take care of herself at home.

*Whaddya mean? All the time, you forget! When are you going to paint your hallway sage green, like you wanted to? And when are you going to wallpaper the tiny kitchen? And don't you deserve a new rug in your entry-way? You got the money, Ella-bella!*

Who was that voice in her head? It was a little bit Mama, a little bit the *nonnas*, and a little bit dear Papa . . . and Ella's guilty conscience too. She had plenty of that. All the Mancinis knew they were only two steps from Hell, no matter how nice they were. It ran in the family.

With a little sigh, Ella strolled into the living room too slowly for her mother's liking. It was her silent protest at being talked to like a twelve-year-old, even though she was the perfectly mature age of twenty-nine and co-owner of a thriving matchmaking agency.

"Hurry," Mama said, her eyes glued to the TV.

The *nonnas* were sitting next to their Birkin bags that Cosmo had just bought them to try to win them over, which Jill told him would be difficult because he hadn't been born in Sicily. He'd given Nonna Boo a saffron os-trich Birkin. Nonna Sofia's was candy pink crocodile. The bags were stuffed with umpteen balls of yarn and knitting needles, and they were knitting away, watching their favorite reality TV show, which they'd taped from the night before (Ella had watched it that morning at her own apartment, avidly eating two Krispy Kreme dough-nuts and drinking tea while she did so). It was the show about the Hollywood women who walked around with Birkins just like the nonnas'.

"Why are they so unhappy?" asked Nonna Boo. She'd been called Boo since she was five years old and made the international news when she met the Pope at a church in Sicily and yelled "Boo!" at him when she presented him a bouquet of flowers. She'd been going through a ghost phase. "That one has the same bag I do. And a dot-ing husband. Who cares that he's ugly? He loves her!"

"Are you ever going to walk around with *your* Birkin, Nonna Boo?" asked Ella.

"Why should I?" Nonna Boo kept her eyes on the TV set. "It makes a perfectly nice yarn holder."

"*Esattamente*," said Nonna Sofia, who was quieter and more dignified than Nonna Boo.

*Exactly.*

Ella smiled to herself. The *nonnas* so rarely agreed, even though everyone except them knew they were almost like twins. Their little arguments were what kept them alive, Mama said.

On the screen, the women were promenading on Rodeo Drive in their spiky-heeled Louboutins. Ella said, "It's just a show about the rich, powerful wives in Hollywood. Most of them don't work, but some of them do. The ones who stay at home kind of have careers in charity work, raising money and awareness and such."

"They totter around in those ridiculous heels," said Nonna Sofia, who wore sensible—and very ugly—orthopedic shoes.

"So silly," said Nonna Boo, who also wore orthopedic shoes.

"But *nonnas*, look at *my* shoes." Ella stuck her foot out. She wore three-and-a-half-inch heels. "They give me height." She was five foot two. "I feel more powerful. And I think they're sexy."

Nonna Sofia gazed at them a moment. "I wore a pair like that in December of nineteen seventy," she murmured, then smiled in that far-off way Ella knew meant she was caught up in the past. "You don't want to know the rest of the story."

"I'll bet I know it," said Nonna Boo, and laughed. She winked at Ella. "Your *nonnas* used to wear gorgeous heels, and the men flocked to us like flies. We are now only jealous old women who wish we still could flaunt our sexy legs in supple Italian leather."

"Speak for yourself," said Nonna Sofia primly. "I don't miss those shoes."

"Hmmph," said Nonna Boo.

"Nonna Sofia, will you tell me the story someday? About December of nineteen seventy?" Ella asked her. "And those shoes?"

Nonna Sofia considered it. "Very well. Before I die, I will tell someone."

Mama put her hand on Nonna Sofia's shoulder. "You can tell *me* too. I'm your daughter, after all."

Nonna Sofia's brows came together. "A mother doesn't reveal everything to her daughters. Unless she wants them to call her a fool behind her back."

"I would never call you a fool," Mama said, "*ever*."

But Nonna Sofia didn't answer. She kept knitting and watching the television screen.

Ella and her mother exchanged glances. Nonna Sofia was very hard on herself. Sometimes Ella saw that same trait in her mother. And sometimes she wondered if she was following in her mother's and grandmother's footsteps that way. She worried that she'd been a fool with Hank—and that she'd pay for it the rest of her days. And it was because she hadn't listened to Papa. He'd told her not to let anyone or anything get in the way of her acting dreams.

But even worse than not listening to Papa—she'd disappointed herself. She'd given up on her dreams . . .

*Because of a man.*

Her history with Hank played into her decision to team up with Macy and Greer. When they'd started Two Love Lane, they'd each had had their own reasons for wanting to get involved in the love business. Macy had never been in love, so she wanted to experience it vicariously. Greer had broken someone's heart very badly, and she felt that she owed it to the world to bring people together. And Ella was the one who'd had her heart broken badly—by Hank. She'd become a partner because she decided she'd turn a negative into a positive. She'd help other people have their own happily ever afters.

"I'll bring out the antipasti," she said to the *nonnas*, "and we'll settle in. You go, Mama. Go to the quilting store."

"Only if you're sure," Mama said, her eyes bright with excitement. She loved machine quilting. It was a new hobby for her.

"Of course I am," said Ella.

Poor Mama. She so needed this break. Ella knew it made her mother very happy when she came over. Dealing with the *nonnas* was Mama Mancini's full-time job. Ella loved to provide her with a little relief, and she also loved being around her *nonnas*. So it was a win-win situation.

She kissed Mama's cheek at the door and watched her toddle off to the silver Dodge Challenger sitting at the curb and strap herself in. The engine roared to life (thanks to Mama's insistence on pressing too hard on the gas pedal whenever she started the car) then settled down to a quiet purr. Mama took off, waving from the window. Ella waved back, then shut and locked the door behind her, as she always did. She'd been brought up in the Bronx and wasn't naive. Crime could happen anywhere, even in sunny Charleston, where people you didn't know said hello to you and smiled when you passed them on the street. And she had the *nonnas* to protect, anyway.

She bent down and petted the two gray tabby cats, Max and Henrietta, who'd sidled up to her feet at the door. The *nonnas* had each bought an adult cat from the no-kill pet shelter in Charleston when they'd arrived separately from Sicily. Nonna Boo had been here the longest, five years, so Max had lived in the bungalow that long too.

"You're a sweetheart," Ella told each kitty in turn. Max preened at the soft voice and wrapped himself around Ella's leg. Henrietta sat back on her haunches and stared at Ella. Female cats were so much harder to read! But maybe Henrietta needed more time, just like Nonna Sofia did. Nonna Sofia had only been in the States eighteen months and still wasn't sure of herself. She refused to go to McDonald's or Starbucks. Minor league games at The Joe, Charleston's baseball stadium, scared her, with foul balls flying backward sometimes into the stands. The only part of the United States Nonna Sofia wasn't totally intimidated by was American television shows. She'd watched many of the older ones in Sicily, and now she had even more to choose from. She was obsessed with Netflix.

But before Ella could walk ten steps back to the kitchen, another knock came. Mama must have forgotten something. Ella quickly turned around and unlocked the door, then flung it open. "Sorry I locked it," she began.

But it wasn't Mama. A stranger stood there—a woman about Ella's age with a dark ponytail, torn jeans—really torn—and a sexy V-neck T-shirt with a word on it that was entirely inappropriate, at least according to Mama's and the *nonnas*' standards. She squinted at Ella through gorgeous almond-shaped green eyes surrounded by thick lashes. Her mouth was wide and pouty with a beautiful bow on her top lip. She was a woman you'd look at twice if you saw her walk by.

"Hello," she said, almost primly, although she looked

totally fierce in her street clothes. "I'm Pammy Lockhart, and you're Ella, right?"

"Y-Yes," Ella said. "Have we met?"

"No, but you're the closest thing to family I have in this town," the woman said without preamble. "I'm Hank Rogers' cousin. Can we talk?"

# CHAPTER THREE

At her mother's front door, Ella tried to take it all in. She remembered Hank mentioning he had family on the West Coast, including a cousin he adored but never saw. But that was ten years ago. She knew absolutely nothing about Pammy Lockhart.

"Hank said he was gonna contact you and let you know I was hoping to meet up." Pammy scratched the side of her nose, sniffed, and crossed her arms over her voluptuous chest. Then she proceeded to look anywhere but at Ella. For some reason, she found the edge of the roof fascinating.

"Oh, okay," Ella said, striving for cool. "He did get in touch last night. I-I just haven't been able to call him yet. Thanks for coming by to meet me. Are you visiting for a few days?"

"I live here."

"*Oh!*" Ella couldn't help sounding surprised. Every part of her body went on high alert—not because of Pammy herself but because of her relationship to Hank. "Welcome to Charleston," she tacked on, and tried to sound upbeat and warm, even as she wondered how Pammy had found her at her mother's house.

Pammy looked down and scuffed a boot on Mama's welcome mat. "Your roof's wonky," she said quietly, then looked up at Ella with those gorgeous eyes.

She looked lonely, which immediately touched Ella's heart.

"The roof is wonky?" Ella eked out.

"Yep. It's drooping on one side. When did you last have it inspected? The shingles look like sh—"

"Don't say it." Ella grinned and held her finger to her mouth. "My grandmothers can hear really well, although they pretend not to. And they get upset at bad language."

Pammy started to say something beginning with an *F*, but caught herself just in time. She nodded. "What the hey. I can go with that."

"Good," said Ella. "I don't know about the shingles. But would you—would you like to come in? I mean, please do come in. I'll make you some tea. Or coffee." She held the door wide.

"I could go for a beer," Pammy said when she walked over the threshold in military-style boots.

Ella could use a beer too. "Sorry, Mama and the *nonnas*—my grandmothers—don't drink beer. But if you'd like a good glass of wine—"

"Nah," Pammy said. "I've never developed a taste for it." She laughed.

Ella liked her for being honest.

By this time, they'd made it to the kitchen, Pammy stomping in her boots. She tilted her chin to the ceiling. "Interesting guy up there. He's hot."

Jupiter *was* pretty hot. "My sisters and I painted him," Ella said. "We used a *GQ* model as inspiration."

"Nice," said Pammy. "Oh, and tap water's good."

Ella got her visitor some water and wondered how the *nonnas* were going to take her. Maybe she and Pammy had better hang out in the kitchen for a little while first.

"Ella! Who is it?" cried Nonna Sofia.

"Ellaaaaa!" yelled Nonna Boo. "I heard the doorbell. Who was it?"

"We'll be right there!" Ella called to them, then said to Pammy, "We'll go in and meet them in a minute. First, tell me, how'd you find me here at my mother's house?"

"Easy," said Pammy. "I stalked you online."

"Okay, then." Ella was going to go with the flow.

"Didn't even have to pay. Found you right away. Lots of Mancinis in Charleston. And I think you're all related."

"We are."

"I checked your apartment first, then came here next. Hank said you were close to your mother."

"What else did he tell you?"

"Nothing. Except you used to date. I remember that from a long time ago. But just barely, as in 'Cousin Hank is dating some chick who acts too.' Sorry. I was West Coast. He was East. And ne'er the twain shall meet. Except through airplanes. And you know how that goes."

Pammy was warming up to her, which was good.

"No worries," Ella said. "So tell me more about stalking me then." She was trying to be flattered that Pammy had sought her out. She wondered if Hank, as a Hollywood A-lister, had to live with being incessantly stalked.

Of course he did.

"You can learn so much through Google," Pammy said. "Your mother is sixty. And you're my age. There's a picture of you lying on your side in a bikini with a big red balloon on your shoulder. How'd you do that?"

"Spring break, Tampa. Junior year in college. Duct tape."

"Why?"

"It was spring break. Don't you do that in Oregon?"

"Not me. I never went to college. I got straight into carpentry. While you were on spring break, I was probably building kitchen cabinets in Bend. I'm often surrounded by sweaty carpenter guys in tool belts, so that's kind of like spring break, isn't it?"

"I think so."

"I didn't check to see if you had any arrests—"

"That was kind of you."

"Your Uncle Sal owns a pizza parlor on Wentworth Street," Pammy said.

Which was one reason Ella had issues with her weight: Uncle Sal's calzones. "He does," she said, and wondered what else Pammy had found out about her family. "I'm glad you found me, but tell me more about what's going on with you?"

"It's a little embarrassing," Pammy said, her tone uncertain. "Long story short, I'm not supposed to be homesick at my age. And I've been doing really well here. But now that I have a regular routine and can look up from all the chaos that comes from moving someplace new, I feel a bit lost. I was hoping to connect with someone in town who at least knows of me, however distant the connection. That would be you."

Ella handed her the water and shot her a warm smile. "I'm glad you found me. I'm happy to help you settle in. Before you know it, Charleston will feel like home."

Pammy took a huge gulp of water then decided to

chug the whole thing. She gasped at the end and handed the glass back to Ella.

She put it in the dishwasher and hid a smile. Pammy wasn't polished. But she was interesting. Over the years, Ella had come to find that Charlestonians loved truly interesting people. "Where are you living?"

"In a converted carriage house behind a big mansion facing the harbor."

"Wow. That must be great." Those little historic homes that used to house servants and horses were adorable.

"The mansion and the carriage house are owned by Beau Wilder, the movie star. Hotter than hell but married. Sadly."

Ella grinned. "Yes, he *is* cute. And definitely off the market. His wife Lacey is awesome."

"He and his whole family are in England at the moment," Pammy said. "He's filming."

"I didn't know that." Ella wiped some droplets of olive oil off the counter.

"They won't be back for a month, and, well, every night we ate dinner together, and I played with their kid. I felt kind of part of a family, even though they're not as close to Hank as you used to be."

Ella tried not to sound pained about the "used to be." She'd focus instead on the fact that Pammy obviously needed some company. "Hey," she said in an assuring tone, "especially while the Wilders are gone, I'll be happy to try to fill in some missing social gaps for you."

Pammy grinned. "Thanks."

"Of course," said Ella. "Do you have a job here?"

"Yes, at the Charleston School of the Building Arts. I'm a professor of architectural carpentry. I teach student-apprentices historic-home renovation. I'm working on Beau and Lacey's house in my spare time."

"Wow, you must be really talented." The Charleston School of the Building Arts was the only place in the entire country someone could get a college degree *and* also become a master craftsman.

"Thanks. It's so exciting to be a part of it. Which is why—" Pammy hesitated.

"Why what?" Ella coaxed her.

Pammy sighed. "Why I don't like that I'm having trouble finding my groove. It's so different from Bend. I've never lived anywhere else. Until now." She hesitated. "I love the faculty at the building school, but they're all married or paired off. And I can't socialize with the students."

Ella smiled. "Well, we can hang out, okay? And I'll introduce you to a bunch of people."

"That'll be great. I think I've been relying on the Wilders too much, too."

"I get that. When I moved to Charleston as an eighteen-year-old college freshman, I felt weird, too, coming from the Bronx down to the slower, more sedate South. My roommate Macy's family took me in a lot. That helped a lot with the transition."

Pammy nodded. "And this place is *really* Southern. They all drink tea with tons of sugar in it. All day."

"Yes, they do." Ella chuckled. "Did you do historic-home renovation in Bend?"

"Some," Pammy said. "We have some nice Craftsman-era houses out there, but most of the stuff I worked on was in San Francisco. But only a month at a time. I plan to live in Charleston for years, not skedaddle home whenever the mood hits me."

Ella was nervous for Pammy. Excited for her too. And worried. *Very* worried. She didn't need to have her own equilibrium disturbed—her happy Lowcountry life—by

Hank. But now her former lover had a vested interest in Charleston, in *her* city.

There was room for Pammy in Ella's life. But not for him.

# CHAPTER FOUR

Ella and Pammy were still hanging out in Mama's cozy kitchen, but only because the *nonnas* were arguing about one of the *Real Housewives* in the living room—in Italian—and it was getting heated. Ella didn't want Pammy to have to walk into that.

"I want to make it here," Pammy was saying. "And Hank's always been so supportive. He flew me out to New York three or four times the last couple of years, and we had a lot of fun. He encouraged me to see more of the world, and let the world see me and all my talent."

Aww, that was very sweet.

*And Ella didn't want to hear it.*

She didn't want to fall in love all over again, with a guy who wasn't even there, a guy who'd walked away from her a full decade ago and had made no attempt to win her back. But inside, she was feeling all melty and daydreamy thinking about him. Her body was betraying her! She needed a date with a nice man from Charleston. One who wore khakis with little whales embroidered all over them, and a bow tie. Maybe a shy doctor who wore glasses. Not some random A-list celebrity with rangy good looks and a style that came off as sexy and outdoorsy and yet also museumy, as in "I can go to museums and like them, and hold your hand while we look at old paintings, then take you home and strip you naked."

*That* was Hank's look.

But Ella wasn't going to be anyone's doormat ever again. She always used to say she was Hank's cheerleader, but that was a delusion. She let herself believe love was a good reason to give up her dreams for someone else, but it wasn't.

And she wasn't blaming Hank. It had been her decision.

She pushed off the counter. "So, are you ready to come meet the *nonnas*?" They had quieted down again.

"Sure." Pammy made a face. "Old people scare me, kind of. They're way too honest. And whoever is out there was yelling pretty loud. Are you sure they're all right?"

Ella laughed. "Fighting keeps the *nonnas* young. And as for honesty, consider it part of the perks of being old. What are you afraid they'll be too honest about?"

"All their health problems," Pammy said. "Bodily functions are awesome, but hey—I can only take so much. And then they might say stuff about how I look."

"My *nonnas* are cool," Ella assured her. "They don't talk much about their health problems because they're in excellent shape. And they're too kind to comment on people's appearance, unless they want to compliment you. Then they'll say something nice. Here"—she grabbed a full-sized apron—"why don't you put this on so they don't have to read your shirt."

"Fine," Pammy said.

And it *was* fine. Pammy ate almost all the antipasti. And she got the *nonnas* to watch the Seahawks play the Eagles. They'd never watched American football. During a commercial, Pammy showed the *nonnas* how the fireplace needed some work.

"See?" She had her own pocket level and she'd propped it on the mantel. "It's off. You gotta do something about it."

"Like what?" said Nonna Boo.

"Like straightening it out," said Pammy, and rolled her eyes.

The nonnas weren't fazed at all. "A little crooked is good for the soul," Nonna Boo said.

"That's right," said Nonna Sofia. "Who wants perfection, eh?"

And they both laughed.

Pammy put her level back in her pocket. "I gotta go," she said.

"You go," said Nonna Boo serenely. "But you come back here every Sunday you're free and have supper with the family at six o'clock. I know we're boring old ladies, but you need some family while you're here. Maybe you can bring your cousin Hank around. Call him and tell him he made a big mistake with Ella."

Pammy's eyes popped. "Uh, Hank doesn't live here. And that's *their* business. Right?"

"Right," said Ella. "Don't listen to them, Pammy."

"You do what you want," said Nonna Sofia. "But we *nonnas* are only looking out for everyone's best interests. Yours too, Pammy. Be ready for some nosy questions about your love life."

"Yeah, well"—Pammy sounded doubtful—"it doesn't exist. But I guess I'll come back." She tossed them a grin.

"Look at that smile," said Nonna Boo. "It lights up the

room. By the way, Ella, we need to put two more Sicilian cousins in your apartment."

The *nonnas* always tried to squeeze outrageous demands into otherwise ordinary sentences, as if no one would notice.

"But Nonna Boo," Ella said patiently, "I'm already taking two."

"Two *more*," said Nonna Boo. "Cousin Julio and his wife Dorotea. Julio says Dorotea is very, very picky. She needs a nice queen-sized bed. No doubles. No kings. A queen. She needs him close enough to knock him when he snores, but not too close that he gets the wrong idea. She's too old for that kind of nonsense, she told Nonna Sofia. Once she hit eighty, she was done."

"Dorotea's done," Nonna Sofia said. "No more bedroom nonsense."

Ella didn't know what to say. "But where will I go? The sofa is so uncomfortable. It's got a spring jutting up in the middle. I need a new one."

"Yes, they want you out," said Nonna Boo. "Five people sharing one bathroom is too much, they say."

"I-I guess I could go to Miss Thing's," Ella said. "Or Macy's, or Greer's."

She hated to go to Macy's or Greer's and interrupt their honeymoon periods for an entire week.

"No one else in the family can take you in," said Nonna Boo. "We're all chock-full of Sicilian relatives."

"But we know you have lots of friends," said Nonna Sofia.

Ella looked at Pammy, embarrassed. "I have friends, but it's such an imposition staying a week. . . ." She shrugged. "I'll work it out." She would have to buy earplugs so she didn't hear Miss Thing's guinea pig. And then work around all the paint cloths that would be lying on the floors. Wet paint drying overnight wasn't exactly going to be great for her sinuses either.

"You can stay with me," said Pammy. "I've got plenty of room at the carriage house."

"Really?" Ella said. "You wouldn't mind? I wouldn't have to show up until tomorrow morning with my suitcase, and then I'll head to work. But it'll be a whole week. Are you sure?"

"It'll be great," said Pammy. "I'll get the spare room ready, and I'll see you tomorrow morning."

They exchanged phone numbers.

The *nonnas* exclaimed over Pammy's generosity and said she'd grow to love their granddaughter Ella—who wasn't the best cook in the family yet but someday might be if she tried a little harder.

"The way to a man's heart is through his stomach," said Nonna Sofia. "Just ask Ella's sister Jill."

It was true that Jill's carbonara played an instrumental role in capturing Cosmo's attention when they first met. "But we each have our own strengths," said Ella. "And I don't need a man to be happy, Nonnas. You have to join the twenty-first century."

"We know you don't," said Nonna Sofia. "But a good one is nice to have around."

"That's right," said Nonna Boo. "Especially a good one who knows his way around the bedroom."

"And takes out the garbage," said Nonna Sofia.

"*Nonnas*," protested Ella. "You can't talk like that."

"We just did," said Nonna Boo.

And they both laughed.

Ella gave them both a kiss and a hug. She was doing great as a single woman. She didn't need a man to feel good about herself. But she had to be honest: living with Hank's cousin Pammy for a week was going to be slightly rough. She'd put the past behind her, but she hoped she didn't have to hear Pammy talking to him on the phone— and God forbid Pammy FaceTime him with Ella in the room.

And then she remembered: she never called Hank about that favor he wanted, which was obviously for her to contact Pammy. She wouldn't bother. Pammy would tell him. No way did Ella want to talk to her old lover on the phone.

She'd moved on, no matter how her body and soul had reacted when she'd received those flowers. When she'd realized they were from Hank, it was as if her world was starting anew. As if none of the past ten years had changed the simple fact that she still loved him.

# CHAPTER FIVE

Hank was doomed. No, really. He didn't know how to get out of going to tea with his parents on Sunday at the Plaza, the famous hotel in Manhattan that chicks loved to go to and men had to dress up for to please the ladies in their lives. He wasn't a fan of scones and clotted cream and jam. He especially didn't like tea. It reminded him too much of Ella.

And his mom told him they were bringing along a birthday card for Aunt Sarah. They wanted him to sign it while they were together. She always got so mad at him when he paused for long stretches over cards, and then just wrote, *I hope you have a great birthday. Hank.*

"That's all you can come up with?" his mother would say. "You act for a living. I've seen you cry real tears in a movie when you picked a rose off a bush. And you can't say anything more meaningful and personal?"

No. He couldn't. He was unable to express personal feelings very well. He wasn't sure what they were, to be honest. He was too tired, too stressed, to recognize them. And even before he'd become tired and stressed—like when he was a teenager, pre-Ella (everything was pre-and post-Ella)—he'd had difficulty showing people his real face. Not that he was a phony. But he was profoundly shy beneath his confident exterior and wasn't quite sure what to do with that, especially since his parents and the few trusted friends he told didn't believe him.

After all, he'd been the friendly busboy at Serendipity 3 for years. He'd talk to anyone! As an employee at the fanciful, family-oriented New York eatery, he'd never been bored. The truth was, he liked watching people. He loved observing their gestures, overhearing the things they said.

The closest he came to figuring it all out was in English class senior year when his silver-haired teacher saw how sensitive his essays were. That was what she called them: "sensitive." No one had ever remotely associated him with "sensitive," not even the acting coaches he'd had later.

His high school teacher was an old hippy who encouraged him to take a gap year after he graduated and go travel the world. He wanted to, badly. He decided he'd read Kerouac along the way—it was almost required of teenagers who wanted to run off and have adventures—and maybe some poets, like Whitman and Wordsworth, and a few contemporary ones, like Elizabeth Bishop. She'd written his favorite poem.

Yep, "The Fish" was the best poem in the world, but the only person he'd ever been able to tell that to had been Ella.

He'd told her on their very first date, which was like out of a movie. He'd waited for her at Serendipity 3 four years to the day after he'd asked her to . . .

And she'd shown up!

He also told her he wished he'd taken that gap year instead of going to college—and then quitting—and then heading straight to Broadway auditions to prove his point that he wanted to be a professional actor. He wished he'd worked on a pineapple farm in Hawaii for a summer. Or bartended in Paris.

He'd really just wanted time apart from everyone who knew him and had pegged him with all their expectations. He wanted time to think about what he really, *really* wanted.

He wanted time alone.

On that first date, Ella had completely understood. She liked thinking, too, and she said she did it best when she was sitting with her tea at home, although sitting with a frozen hot chocolate at Serendipity 3 always made her think interesting thoughts too.

"How have the auditions been going?" she'd asked him.

"I love it," he'd said, "but I also want to know if I'd love anything else too. I'm on my fourth year of auditioning and getting small parts. But maybe something else is out there. Nothing hit me over the head in school."

And she'd understood. She'd also understood that he couldn't sit still, that he had to at least make the move toward a dream, even as he was unsure, and so she never made fun of him for his somewhat ambivalent acting ambition.

A guy had to do something, he'd said. And he'd rather act than sell insurance or real estate, or join the military, or drive a cab, or become an attorney.

All these years, post-Ella, things hadn't changed. Hank still pursued acting because it was what he did, and he would do it until he found out the thing he really wanted to do—or had he already found it? Was acting it? Did you ever really find something that was a perfect fit? Would he ever feel as if he'd synced with his purpose in the universe—locked in, like a rocket with the mother ship?

He wasn't sure.

But he was such a good actor, no one could sense this uncertainty in him.

The day Hank's parents invited him to tea was the afternoon after he'd sent the flowers to Ella's dressing room at the Dock Street Theatre in Charleston. He was in a limo heading to the Plaza. He hadn't gotten over the shock of telling the florist over the phone her name. He hadn't said it out loud in so long.

*Ella.*

*Ella-bella.*

He sang the name in the shower that morning while soaping his chest. He held the soap right up to his heart and stood under the sluicing hot water and thought about her. Ella was the only thing he'd always been sure about.

Their connection had made leaving her impossible for him. But he'd done it. He'd done it because the acting was panning out. He saw eventual success . . . he saw his parents' beaming faces. He saw money, and he saw that the stars could align there.

And he knew in his heart that there was no guarantee that stars aligned for lovers. There was always the possibility of a supernova. Or a black hole.

He couldn't afford to have the one thing in life he was certain about blow up in his face. He'd rather live with it in its potential state.

*What could have been . . .*

*With Ella.*

He tucked that possibility away in his heart. It was more important to him than his two Oscar nominations. It was what he'd look back on when he was an old man, that perfect love—

That he ended before it could end him.

"Do you ever just think?" he asked his driver.

"All the time," said the driver. "While I'm driving you."

"Hardly anyone has time anymore to think . . . to kick back, or hike, or sit staring out a window for no good reason."

"What do you do when you look out the window of my limo?"

"Hah. I look at my phone. And the few times I do glance up, I'm thinking about something else. Like a movie script. Or a contract. Not what I'm seeing."

"That's a shame."

"I don't know anyone who takes the time to really look."

"Maybe you're hanging out with the wrong people." The driver laughed.

Hank did too, but he loved his friends. He loved his family. He had two brothers and a sister, all older than he was, and they were terrific people with nice families and fulfilling careers. Hank was the golden boy of the family, but he could tell no one else at family gatherings wanted to be in his position: super rich and famous. They were all glad to leave it to him. He could tell they pitied him his lack of normalcy. And he appreciated that. It was rare to run into anyone in his life who didn't think he was the luckiest guy on earth.

Occasionally, his brothers would try to get him to go camping with them out in the Tetons or rafting down the Colorado River at the Grand Canyon. But he always said no because he was afraid he would get time to think— that thing he used to crave.

He craved it no longer because he was afraid of what he would find out.

So Hank stayed busy, busy, busy.

No surprise there, being a celebrity, of course. Everyone thought the busyness was what happened to famous actors who got lots of work. But no. Actors could carve out downtime if they wanted to. But he didn't want that. He hired people who would keep him moving.

And he'd never read Kerouac. As for "The Fish," he hadn't thought about it in years.

At the Plaza, he kissed his mom and gave his dad his usual one-armed hug. They'd changed a lot since he was younger. When Hank was a kid, his mom had always been wrapped up in her social life, and his dad had worked late all the time as an attorney. But these days, post-retirement, his dad was pretty laid back. They got along well, and he saw his parents at least once a month when he wasn't away on a movie set.

They were still living in the comfortable brownstone he'd grown up in on the Upper East Side. He'd never had to worry about money back then except for when he had lived with Ella and refused his parents' help. He was going to make it on his own.

And he did. It was a rough couple of years, but now he out-earned his dad and all his siblings combined. It wasn't fair because he saw how hard they worked.

But they didn't know what he'd given up. They didn't know that part of him, the slice of his soul that would always look at his own success from far away and never be quite attached to it.

"I'll take coffee," he told the server a few minutes later.

"Coffee at high tea," his mother said, and waved her hand at him. It was her typical gesture. She didn't *get* him. But she loved him.

"Mom," he said, "I'm finally going to admit to you

why I don't like tea. It's because it reminds me of Ella, my old girlfriend. She drank it all the time. Remember her?"

"Of course I do!" his mother said, almost defensively. "She was a very nice girl. Whatever happened to her?"

"She moved to Charleston. South Carolina." In case she thought he meant Charleston, West Virginia. "She's a matchmaker."

"Where Pammy is! Such a splendid town, so I've heard. Is she still single? Like you?" His mother always liked to remind him.

"I think so."

"You don't keep up with her?" His mother always acted so surprised about everything.

"No, Mom." But of course, Hank knew Ella was still single. He wasn't going to admit to his mother, however, that he checked the Internet every once in a while to see how she was doing.

His father only sat there, comfortable, immobile, enjoying the fact that he wasn't in the fray.

No one said, "You can't drink tea because of Ella? Why? Are you still in love with her? Is she the love of your life?"

Nope, his parents just moved on. That was how it had always been. He'd drop these massive hints, but no one picked up on them.

"Speaking of Pammy," Hank said, "I just talked to her. Sure, she's made a huge name for herself in historic-home restoration, and it's paying off with this professor position. But she's feeling a little homesick."

"Oh dear," said his mother in that faint voice she used when they talked about the Oregon branch of the family. They were too weird. A girl carpenter—that's what she called Pammy. And Oregon might as well have been the moon, it was so far away.

"So I lined her up with a project on the side," Hank said, "Beau and Lacey's house. They'll treat her like family. But right now they're out of town."

"Beau and Lacey," said his mother with a lot more energy. "What a lovely couple." She looked at him expectantly. She loved a good gossip, especially about his movie star friends.

But Hank wouldn't get sidetracked. "I did contact Ella to see if she could check in on Pammy."

His dad sat up a little higher, stirred his tea for no reason. *Clink, clink, clink.* "So what'd she say?" He put the spoon down and waited.

"I haven't heard back yet."

His mother placed her hand on her heart. "Why not? You're Hank Rogers!"

Hank restrained a sigh. "Being a celebrity doesn't merit everyone's instant attention, Mom. Especially from old friends. I'd rather they not think of me that way. It's a novel feeling being ignored, and it's probably good for me."

"My, my," his mother said, her usual reply when Hank baffled her.

"I always liked that girl," his dad said. Which was unusual for him. He didn't often comment on Hank's personal life.

"We barely knew her!" his mother exclaimed. "He never brought her home, except for that one time."

It had been during a pregnancy scare, and Ella couldn't go home for Thanksgiving because she knew she'd break down in front of her mother and father. So he'd brought her to his house, and she'd had no idea which bread plate to use or why she had two wine glasses—she didn't touch a drop—and after the meal, she sat stiffly in a wing chair in the den to watch football with the family, and she was miserable. Absolutely miserable.

"I liked her," his dad said.

Hank's mom stared at him, her mouth partly open, and said nothing. Her husband was the only person who could derail her drama train.

Hank repressed a chuckle.

"So what're you up to the next couple weeks?" his dad asked.

Hank's phone vibrated. He always ignored it in the presence of his parents unless it was his agent's home number.

It was his agent's home number.

He rose from his chair. "I normally wouldn't get this, but it's Tracy. She only calls from home when it's urgent. I'll be right back. And I'm not doing anything, Dad, except reading scripts. None of which are working."

His dad gave a brief nod. His mom nibbled a cucumber sandwich. Hank slipped away.

"Hey," he said into his cell. He was behind a column and near a potted fern. He was an expert at hiding in plain sight in public places. "I'm with my parents. How ya doin'?" He tacked that on because he knew she'd like it. Tracy was from Staten Island, a very nice person, and that was how she spoke to him. She refused to move out of her little house a couple of blocks from the bay, even though she could afford a very big one now right on the water. It was her stubbornness that made her such a successful agent.

"You believe in signs from the universe?" she asked without preamble.

"I don't know," he said.

"The job with Samantha Drake has come up again on

*Forever Road.*" A thriller/suspense movie written by the two hottest screenwriters in Hollywood. "Frampton Cooke's out. The royal dame's none too happy to be left hanging. They don't want to lose momentum and want you there tomorrow. What do you think?"

His heart thumped a little hard. Samantha Drake was an amazing actor. He and Ella had both thought she was the best in the biz—apart from Meryl, that is. Same league. Very few members. And now Samantha, a native Scot, was a dame of the realm, or some such title, thanks to the queen. Working with Samantha would be a huge feather in his cap and a personal dream come true.

But his heart was thumping about Ella, not Samantha. The truth was he'd been invited to audition for the movie, but he'd declined the first time around. He'd told them he had other commitments in the way. But that wasn't why. *Ella* was why. No way could he be in the same city as Ella.

He'd had to tell Tracy the truth at the time because she was the one who'd had to make up some fake commitments and tell the *Forever Road* people he was unavailable.

"They only just set up shop, and they're only in Charleston a week," Tracy said. "But Frampton dropped out this morning. His new wife is pregnant, and now she's having some complications. He doesn't want to be away from her."

"I feel for the guy. And I hope his wife and the baby are all right. But you *know* I don't want to work in Charleston."

"I still have an obligation to tell you about the opportunity. A potentially Oscar-winning opportunity." Tracy was an agent, and that was what agents did.

She was right. He couldn't be mad at her. "So who called?"

"Samantha herself."

That surprised him. He assumed it would have been the up-and-coming, Houston-based director, Isabel Iglesias.

"Samantha heard you were in Charleston last night and didn't stop by. She didn't like that."

"She's never shown me any particular interest before. Even when they wanted me to audition—"

"They hadn't chosen the female lead at that time," Tracy said. "She wants you now, and if you say no, Isabel is willing to throw extra money at you. But they do need you there right away for the week, starting tomorrow morning. Then you get almost a whole month off and finish filming in Montreal. Can't you make it happen? You have only three short scenes in Charleston. It's not like it's going to be hard work. Except for the minor stunt stuff. The script calls for you to jump over a railing."

"Yeah, into the ocean. You know I'm up for it. But I can't."

Tracy sighed. "You want to work with Samantha. The story is right up your alley. The money is good. They'll treat you like a king. *Stay busy*, and the girl won't be a problem."

"Her name is Ella."

"Fine. Ignore Ella."

"I know what I'm talking about," he said. "I can't *ignore* her."

"Okay." Tracy paused for a beat. "I'll tell 'em you don't want it. Again."

"*I'll* tell them," Hank said. "When I'm done with my parents, I'll call. Give me another hour."

"Fine by me." The good thing about Tracy was that she let him make the decisions he wanted and never second-guessed him. As long as he gave her an opportunity to state her case, she was good.

He told his parents the situation, leaving out any mention of Ella.

"That's not enough notice," his mother said. "Even if it *is* Samantha Drake. You're a busy man." She patted her mouth with a soft linen napkin. But Hank wasn't fooled by the ladylike move. Mom was a dainty eater until she came to high tea at the Plaza, and then she claimed all the good stuff with cream in the middle. He and Dad didn't stand a chance.

"I'm not ready to jump in," he said. "I'm finally at the point I can turn things down if I want, and it's not the end of the world."

"Right," said his mom.

His dad frowned. "Does this have anything to do with Ella?"

Hank paused, a lemon tart halfway to his mouth. "No," he said.

But of course it did. Hank might be a good actor, but he was a terrible liar.

For a brief second, his dad eyed him in a way he never had before. Hank went ahead and ate the tart and five tiny triangles filled with ham. For the next fifteen minutes, they made small talk about his parents' neighbors, especially the guy who had five dogs. But Hank had to wonder about his dad—and that look.

When they parted, Mom was her usual fluttering self, asking him to take good care of himself—he needed to eat better . . . and sleep more. And then she remembered the card for Aunt Sarah. She pulled it out of her purse. "Just sign it over there," she said, pointing to a table beneath a large mirror. "I'll be right back. Running to the powder room."

Luckily, so far, the general public had left Hank alone at the Plaza. No requests for autographs. No surreptitious photos from fans *or* the paparazzi. But when he was signing the card, someone came up behind him right as he was grappling with what to say.

People hovering were a fact of his life, and sometimes he felt like little more than a freak show in a gilded cage, but *blah blah blah*, no one cared. He could only occasionally whine to Tracy about it without looking like a self-obsessed ungrateful jerk. But it wasn't that satisfying because Tracy often scrolled through texts when he spoke to her, and went off on tangents—especially about the Yankees—as if she'd never heard him. And the plain truth was, whining was never satisfying.

*Argh*, back to Aunt Sarah . . . What should he write? He gripped the pen and scribbled, *Have a great birthday, Aunt Sarah. Love, Hank.*

It was the best he could do. At least he'd written *Love.* That was nice.

He took a secret deep breath and turned around, prepared to face an adoring fan.

But it was his father standing there. "Take the part in Charleston," he said, his hands in his jacket pockets. "You're avoiding the girl, and it might be time for you to confront whatever it is you're running from."

Whoa. Hank's father didn't often make those kinds of pronouncements. It threw Hank off, enough that he responded with equal bluntness. "She's a woman now," he said, "a very successful one. She was pretty much grown up when we were dating too. I just chose to act like we were kids. I didn't deserve her then, Dad, and I don't now."

He'd never admitted that out loud. And it hurt.

"People grow up," his father said. "Give yourself a chance."

"I *had* my chance."

"I don't buy that kind of talk." His dad rocked back on his heels. "You're making excuses."

"*Excuses?*" Now Hank was getting a little annoyed. His father certainly didn't mince words when he chose to speak up. "Dad, I'm way too old for lectures."

"And I'm too old to give them." His father's eyes flickered with challenge. "Live in the present, son," he said.

"I'm only there a week," Hank said.

"A lot can happen in a week."

Hank didn't know what to say, other than *No, a lot can't*, but he kept it to himself because his dad would have said he was wrong, and they would have gone around in circles talking about a week and how much one could fit into it.

"Do you want a second chance with her or not?" his dad asked.

Hank hesitated.

"It's a yes or no answer, son."

"Yes," Hank finally said. "Yes, I do. But I don't—"

"You don't deserve it," his dad finished for him. "Who does? We all make mistakes."

"Some mistakes are worse than others."

"True," said his dad. "But if we all held back from pursuing happiness because we're flawed, nobody would ever be happy. You have to learn from your mistakes. But don't let them hold you back."

"I'll think about it," Hank said. "Thanks, Dad."

Hank's mom came striding up on her high heels, an Upper East Side grand dame, and the whole conversation was necessarily over.

"All done?" She held out her hand for the card.

"Sure," said Hank, agitated and trying not to show it.

She read what he wrote and pecked his cheek. "It will do, sweetie. Can you come for brunch soon? I'll make blueberry pancakes. And spinach quiche. Your favorites."

His dad kept an enigmatic eye on him.

Hank scratched his ear. "I don't know if I'll be here, Mom. I've decided to think a little longer about the movie in Charleston."

She sucked in a breath over her newly touched-up red lips. "Really?"

"I'm thinking about it," he said. "Not saying yes yet, but I'll make a decision by the end of the day."

"Well." She blinked. "We just might have to have brunch in Charleston, then." She swiveled to face her husband. "What do you think? Haven't you always wanted to go see Charleston? There's a reality show about it: *Bless Your Heart*. I've never seen it. Maybe I'll start watching it."

"We'll see," said his dad—one of his favorite refrains. "He's only there a week, if he goes."

"Oh, that's a shame," said his mother. "A week isn't long enough to do *anything*."

Hank tried not to laugh and hugged them both.

"Let us know what you decide." His father was calm. Wise. A good guy. And today of all days, jabbing at Hank in a way he hadn't done since he'd encouraged him to go to college and then to law school.

Hank was mystified. And curious. And somehow grateful.

"Talk to you soon," he said, and watched them walk away, his square-shouldered dad and his birdlike mother. His heart squeezed at the sight of them hand in hand, and he recognized the emotion. It was love for each of them separately. And love for them both, as a pair, as one unit that took on the world together.

Family could be complicated. But all worthwhile things, Hank was coming to realize, came with their challenges.

# CHAPTER SIX

On Monday morning, Ella yanked a little harder on her suitcase and got it up Pammy's two brick steps to her front door. She'd packed as much as she could for a week's stay, and if she really had to go back to her apartment to get some other things, she would. But the elderly Sicilian cousins would be arriving in the next few hours, so she'd had to rush that morning and hope for the best.

Pammy threw open the door, an apple in her hand. It had a big bite taken out of it. "You're here," she said with her mouth full. Music blared behind her—crazy music, sounding like wind chimes mixed with electric guitars and someone whacking a cookie sheet with a spatula.

"I sure am," Ella said faintly, wondering what the heck she was doing there, but then she stepped over the threshold into a house that smelled faintly of cloves and sugar. The scent made the place feel homey and warm, and for the first time, her hopes rose that maybe she could manage this week with no problem.

Pammy grabbed her suitcase from her. "I'll put this upstairs. Make yourself at home."

"Thanks," Ella said, and barely had time to look at the collection of photos on the foyer wall before Pammy came bounding back downstairs.

"I gave you the room on the right," Pammy said. "Hank gets the one on the left."

Ella wondered if Pammy's strange music had messed with her head. "*Say that again?* And would you turn down the music, please?"

Pammy told Alexa to stop, thank God. Blessed silence reigned. "Hank's coming," she said. "He's doing a movie in Charleston. Only for a week. He just called me a few hours ago and wants to stay here. He could have had his own house, or even a hotel suite, but he said he wanted to hang out with me as much as he could when he wasn't filming because we're cousins and he'd not be here long. So that's cool."

Ella just kept nodding, over and over. "Right," she said. "Hank's coming." *Hank was coming?* "So"—nod, nod—"Pammy, would you please go upstairs and get my suitcase? I can find another place to stay."

A place with a squealing guinea pig and a very nosy friend who'd be asking her about Hank every moment.

*Hank was coming.* He was filming in Charleston. For a whole week.

A week wasn't much.

*A week was forever!*

Ella couldn't imagine being in the same place as Hank for a week. Her entire body was on meltdown. She needed to sit. But she didn't have time. She had to get to work. She had to escape Pammy's house before Hank showed up!

"Oh, but I *want* you to stay!" Pammy said. "Three's even better than two." A shadow passed over her face. "Hank . . . he probably won't be here much. He'll be busy working and going to parties, I'll bet, until pretty late at night. He's popular with the ladies. I tell him to be careful before he winds up married to someone who only wants his money. Or his looks. He's deeper than that, you know? He's smart. And he's a good actor."

"He's got a lot going for him, all right," Ella said.

Pammy looked at her with worry in her eyes. "I was really hoping you could stay and help, you know, with my settling in. You know all the Charleston haunts—the best restaurants, the best bars."

Ella sighed. "I honestly don't think you need me for that. You're going to be fine with Hank here. If I stayed here, I'm like a crutch. You don't have to try to meet people. If you really want to feel at home here—"

"I do."

"Then you have to explore. And you also have to give yourself time."

"I know," Pammy said. "But it would be more fun to explore and let time go by with *you*."

"I'm getting my suitcase," Ella said gently.

Pammy gave a long, drawn-out sigh. "This *sucks*."

But Ella ignored her and went upstairs. It was a charming little place. The bedroom with her suitcase in it held a queen-sized bed with a beautiful pink primrose quilt. A tall ivory-colored wardrobe stood in one corner. The whole effect was very shabby chic. She peeked into the other room, and it was just as lovely, but it was decorated in forest green and had heavier furniture.

*Hank's room.*

Over her dead body would she stay in a room next to Hank—in the same *house* as Hank! She didn't even want to be in the same *town* as Hank!

She grabbed her suitcase but then had to take a call. It was Macy at work. "Ella, Roberta Ruttle just showed up here at Two Love Lane and would like to speak with you in person."

Roberta was a sweet but very difficult client. "Is she listening to you right now?"

"I can't tell," Macy said.

"Okay," Ella said, "I'll be right there. Does she look angry? Or upset?"

"Not a bit."

Ella heard some rattling through the line.

"She's talking to Miss Thing," Macy whispered. "But she looks happy and is talking a mile a minute. We'll give her some sweet tea or lemonade and wait for you. Is something going on with her?"

"Yet another guy says he doesn't want a second date with her because she's not talking."

"I feel for you," said Macy. "This is a real problem."

It was true. Roberta was an enigma wrapped inside a riddle locked inside a mystery. Ella didn't bother telling Macy about the fact that Hank was coming to town. She'd do that in person. It was too big a deal to share on the phone.

Life was crazy, she thought, as she lugged her suitcase to the stairs. Usually, she was up for it. But as soon as she heard Hank's name—that Hank was coming to Charleston to stay for a while—she wanted to run for the hills. This was *not* going to be easy, having him around.

Not easy at all.

In fact—Ella swiped at her eyes—it had been a not-so-good day so far. First, the show was over, and she felt the usual exhaustion that came from it. She'd need time to recover. And she'd already been reeling from getting those flowers from Hank. Then she met Pammy, who simply showed up on her mother's doorstep, and then she was moving out of her own apartment into Pammy's for a week, and then Roberta was having dating issues, and now Ella was leaving Pammy's to live with Miss Thing and her guinea pig because—

*Hank was coming to town.*

*For a week!*

Oh, God. Ella needed a vacation. Or to hide her head in the sand.

*Bump, bump, bump* to the bottom of the stairs she went with her suitcase. And landed against a block of warm human. She knew before she turned around it wasn't Pammy.

It was Hank.

He smelled like Hank. Masculine. Sexy.

Dear God, what was she supposed to do? Ella closed her eyes, swallowed, and turned around. "Hank," she said, "fancy meeting you here."

That was *so* lame. It was a line straight out of her latest show—word for word, and he'd recognize it. But at least she'd said something.

He did. She could tell from that amused glint in his eye and his grin. "Ella," he said, as if he hadn't seen her in ten years, which was true. The flowers he sent to her dressing room didn't count for anything.

Was that just two nights ago?

"What are *you* doing here?" he asked.

He was still hard to look at head-on without wanting to swoon from lust and longing. Ella glanced anywhere but at him and noticed the front door was wide open.

Where was Pammy?

Ella smiled as if she didn't have a care in the world. "I was moving in with Pammy because I needed a place to stay for a week, and I was also going to keep her company. But now you're here, I'm moving out again. No big deal—I didn't even get a chance to unpack."

"Wow." His eyebrows flew up. His voice was scratchier than usual. Or maybe it had simply gotten deeper since they were together. "Pammy didn't tell me, but I didn't really give her a chance—I was on a private jet with no admin assistant. One's sick, and one's on vacation."

"You have two?"

"Yeah, and I think I need a third." He said it without bragging. Hank wasn't a bragger. Never had been.

"Oh," she said, thinking how different their lives were. Like worlds-apart different. She didn't even have the right to brush a speck of lint off his collar. She had no idea which bank he used, what his favorite TV show was, how his parents and siblings were, or whether he had a great car or valuable art.

He'd always wanted a Maserati and a Murakami. Did he ever acquire either?

"You never called me," he said. "Did you get my flowers?"

Do *not* blush, Ella told herself. But she felt heat creep up her cheeks. "I did," she said, "and I didn't call you. But the favor was about Pammy, right? She wound up finding me the next day. So I felt a call was unnecessary."

Neither were thanks. His reason for sending the flowers had nothing really to do with her.

"You're right," he said, "it *was* about Pammy. I was hoping to connect you two. I didn't know it then, but I'm going to be here this week. I'd love to have lunch. Catch up."

*Catch up?*

He had a lot of nerve acting as if they were old friends who only needed a breezy lunch to catch up!

"Oh." Ella didn't know what to say, so she said nothing else.

"So anyway"—he grabbed the reins of the conversation again—"this morning I was trying to set up my schedule here, and I didn't have time to chat beyond telling Pammy I wanted to stay with her this week."

"Where is she now?"

He pointed a thumb over his shoulder. "At Beau and Lacey's. Working on a wobbly stair bannister."

"Okay," said Ella. She gathered her courage to have a heart-to-heart with him. "I'm actually glad she's not here. We need to talk. Pammy's really sweet to offer me a place to stay, and I think it's because she's lonely. I told her she needs to give it more time. She also needs to explore her social options more. With Beau and Lacey gone for a while, she can focus on that."

"Agreed," said Hank.

"But even with you here," Ella said, "she wants me to stay. She thinks you'll be working—and partying—night and day." That was awkward to say, but she had to.

Besides, he could party all he wanted to. It was his life. She had hers.

"I *will* be busy," Hank said, not elaborating on Pammy's conjecture about him working and playing. "But of course I'll be here to hang out with her, every chance I get."

"Good." Ella pulled her suitcase down the last stair step, forcing him to step aside. "I have to go now," she said, trying not to hang onto this last, close-up look at him. Her plan was to stay as far away as possible from then on. "Best of luck with your movie."

"Thanks," he said, and his grin just about did her in. He still had that tiny scar near his left eye that he got surfing when he was thirteen. "But now that I know you were planning on staying here, Ella, I want you to stay too."

He said it so seriously. She was freaked out. A strange, silent tension hung between them.

"Please think about it," he insisted. "We can do a lot more catching up here than we could at a lunch at some restaurant. It's going to be really hard for me to break away from the set during the day. Besides, Pammy would be so lucky to have you as a friend."

He'd said that with such conviction. Such passion. But which "you" had he meant? The amazing girlfriend he'd once loved heart and soul? Or the new Ella, the successful woman he wasn't emotionally attached to anymore? The Ella he didn't even know?

She wasn't sure whether to be flattered or hurt. "Pammy and I can definitely hang out after you leave." She settled on sounding friendly and warm but professional with him. "I won't abandon her."

His handsome square jaw clenched just a tad. "Having you here at the house, though, would be great for her. I know I'm being overprotective, but she's my cousin."

"She's the same age we are," Ella reminded him.

"I know. But she's in a new place far away from home."

True. Everyone had their own little internal battles to fight, and who was Ella to judge Pammy? "Tell you what," she said, "you move out, and I'll stay."

"I can't do that," Hank said right away. "I promised her I'd live here. It's only until Saturday morning."

So not even an entire week. "Would you have stayed if you'd known I'd be here too?" Ella asked him.

"Not until I talked to you about it, to make sure you were okay with it."

Her mouth dropped open. "You're honestly telling me you would have considered living with me in this tiny house?"

"Sure," he said with a happy shrug. "We could have worked it out. And it's a *week*! That's nothing."

"Hank," Ella said, not a little frustrated, "I get where you're coming from. You're a loving cousin. But honestly, this is *not a good idea*. I don't want to live in the same place as my ex-boyfriend, the one I thought was going to be my fiancé, even for a week. Okay?" She'd raised her voice a little. She wasn't going to mince words. "It might not be hard for *you* to live in the same house as your ex-girlfriend. But I have some pride."

There was a half beat of silence. "Of course, you do, and rightly so," he said eventually. "I don't blame you." He didn't give a hint to how he was feeling, but at least he was being straightforward. "You have no reason to do this."

"Exactly," she said, her heart sore. She remembered holding his face in her hands, running her hand down his stubbly cheek when they made love. It hurt that she had meant so little. She *wanted* him to be freaked out at the idea of living with her. What had she been? A blip on his romantic timeline?

Apparently.

"Pammy will do great with you here this week," she said. "And I'll check in on her as soon as you go. I'll show her around my favorite places and I'll even have a dinner party and invite people over to meet her."

"That's so nice, and I appreciate it, but what if I could make staying here worth your while?" His tone was hopeful. "What if"—he paused and took a breath—"what if it actually benefited you?"

What was he suggesting? That he'd pay her?

"I'm not interested in your money," she said curtly, her heart breaking all over again. Where had her old, warmhearted Hank gone, the one she'd known when they were together? "Excuse me. I have to go."

"But I'm not offering you my money," he said hastily. "I'm offering you an opportunity. I can get you in the movie. *Forever Road*."

The movie?

Ella couldn't help it. She hesitated when she heard that. The actor in her always considered her opportunities.

And then she came to her senses. "I'm no ingénue," she reminded him. He might still think of her that way—the last time they'd seen each other, she was a bit naive, desperate to jump on chances to advance her career. Not all of those opportunities she'd taken had been particularly wise moves. "I'm beyond being dazzled by unlikely movie prospects. If I can't have a healthy speaking part where I can really practice my acting skills, I'm not interested. Plus, I have my own business, and it's not part-time."

If he'd Googled her, he'd know what that business was. She pulled her suitcase over the front door step.

"I can get you the part of Samantha Drake's cousin," Hank said point-blank. "It's a very small part. Maybe ten lines in all, and they're not very significant. You'd only have to film in Charleston. But you'd work with her, at least. Remember, Ella? How we always wanted to work with Samantha? You'd be in a couple of scenes with her. You'd exchange lines."

"*Hank*. This is crazy."

"Just listen," he said. "They still haven't cast the part. The person taking it fell through at the last minute. I heard the director talking about it this morning. You'd hardly have to be on set. You could keep your day job."

"Do you know what that day job is?"

"Of course I do. You're a matchmaker at a very successful agency. I keep up with you."

"Oh," she said, a little embarrassed she'd asked—as if she cared whether or not he kept up with her. She didn't!

"You might have to do some juggling with your colleagues, but I'm guessing it won't be any worse than taking a few vacation days here and there."

"I don't know." She really didn't.

"This gig with Samantha could be yours," Hank said. "We both know full-time matchmakers in Charleston don't often win roles with Oscar-winning actors. When will this chance come again?"

They had a little staring contest.

Ella let go of her suitcase. "I'm interested," she said. "I know it's a ridiculous notion, but I am. If you can make the thing with Samantha happen, I'll stay here. But I have to know something else."

"What?"

"Why'd you take this movie in Charleston? For your career? Or to keep an eye on Pammy? Or both?"

He looked at her for a long time. What was he thinking? Ella's heart was in her throat. It had taken a lot out of her to ask that question.

"No," he finally said. "I didn't need the movie. And I was perfectly happy to help Pammy from afar. It's about you."

Ella felt lightheaded, hearing that. It was a huge shock. Yet she deserved this crazy scenario to be about her too. Not just Pammy and the movie.

But the unexpected truth was, it was *all* about her.

Well, then.

At one time in her life, she'd given this man her entire heart and soul. She'd always thought that gift had better have had an effect on him. Apparently, it had. It was a sweet acknowledgment.

But it had come far too late. She was almost positive about that. Yet a tiny, very stupid part of her was dancing.

"Why ten years later?" she asked him.

"Because we never resolved anything, that's why."

"According to you, maybe. So you're here to . . . what?"

"I don't know. Say hi?"

"*Hi*," she said.

He laughed, damn him. "Maybe we can get to know each other again. Be friends."

Be friends? Was he kidding?

And accomplish that in a week, no less?

She had plenty of friends, and yes, friendships mattered. Her friendships had made her life rich. But she'd had only one true love—*him*!

He was asking too much.

One of his eyebrows shot up. "Are you up for it?"

"No, I'm *not*." She gripped the handle on her suitcase. "My life is great, and I don't need you screwing around with it. I'll stay here at Pammy's, and you'll get me that part because yes, bucket lists should be attended to. You'll be on your best behavior around me and take good care of your cousin. And you and I will get along fine, for Pammy's sake. But I'm absolutely not interested in re-solving anything with you. In my opinion, that was done when you left. And I still don't blame you for it. We both vowed to put our careers first. You did that. Kaboom. End of story. We've moved on."

He came closer to her, close enough that his frame in the doorjamb cast a shadow over her. "I hear you," he said quietly. "Consider the deal made. I'll get the movie people to call you later today."

"Fine," she said.

He bent down, picked up her suitcase. Gave her a good long look in the eye. "I got this," he said.

"Fine," she said again, her nose in the air. "Now I'm going to the office. And after five, if you're available—"

"I'm available."

"—I'll run to the Harris Teeter and pick up some wine and pimento cheese. We'll have a little get-together tonight, the three of us. Lay down some house rules."

"House rules, check. But what the heck's pimento cheese?"

"You'll see. I'll take the bottom shelf of the fridge."

"Okay," he said.

She turned around one more time. "And I'm serious, Hank. You'd better take me at my word."

"I always have."

"Hmmph," she said, and could feel his eyes boring into her back.

She kinda liked it.

# CHAPTER SEVEN

Hank did the deal over the phone in the privacy of his tiny room upstairs at the carriage house right after he talked to Ella. She was in. She was going to play Samantha Drake's cousin. He spoke to Isabel, who immediately agreed without even seeing an audition tape. Hank vouched for his "old friend," as he described Ella to the director. He also said he wasn't going to see anyone from the movie until the following day.

"My first day here is about family," he told Isabel.

"Samantha wants drinks and dinner with you tonight," she said.

"I'm flattered, but sorry. We'll have to talk tomorrow."

"You sure about that? I mean, she's *Samantha Drake*."

"Positive."

"All right then. We'll see you and Ms. Ella Mancini tomorrow."

Isabel was great. Hank was excited to be working with a female director. He saw big things in her future, and he wanted to be a part of making that happen for her.

"Stop thinking about Ella," he said out loud to the oil painting of three boys in Little Lord Fauntleroy outfits in a portrait over the tiny fireplace. The frame was carved and gold-leafed, very old. A horse and carriage was painted in the background. So was the carriage house.

It had been ten years, but did people change that much? He thought he still knew Ella well. And the best thing he could do was go along with what she said—not try to resolve anything.

So be it. He wouldn't try to resolve anything. He'd coast.

He had a card up his sleeve. He knew from their time together that Ella didn't like when he immediately challenged her about any sort of proclamation she made. Her proverbial dukes went up. That woman could stand her ground and fight for what she wanted better than anyone he knew.

At the same time, she also hated when he went along with her a hundred percent. Pushovers bored her. Eventually, if he could maintain his patience, she would start poking at him in hopes that he'd fight back. Which, of course, he would. All in his own time. It was a fun game. A power play.

"Waiting her out," he said out loud again to the three little boys in the portrait. "That's the strategy."

And when that day came—when Ella got bored by calling all the shots—then all bets were off. He wasn't sure which way she'd want to go, but he knew that he wanted a second chance, an opportunity to say, "Let's see what we have here. Let's just see."

But he didn't have time to be patient. A week was nothing.

"Crap," he said as he peered frustrated and panicked out his bedroom window at the little backyard garden. He tried to concentrate on something else for a minute. He loved the modesty of the whole set-up of this little house. It was a relief not to enter a plush but sterile hotel suite. Neither did he have to worry about living in some luxurious home the movie people would rent out for him, where he was always afraid of knocking over the owner's priceless figurines or spilling wine on the fine French sofa.

This old place belonged to Beau and Lacey, dear friends, and it was elegant—but in a faded, friendly way. He could see himself putting his feet up on the coffee table downstairs, and he had no worries about spilling coffee or wine on the sofa. Not that he'd ever done that, but if it happened here, he just knew it wouldn't be the end of the world to the Wilders. The sofa downstairs was over-stuffed, pink-and-brown plaid, with a million pillows on it, all mismatched with slogans like, "QUEEN OF EFFING EVERYTHING," and "LET'S SAIL AWAY." You wouldn't lose too much sleep if you lost some cracker crumbs in the cushions or accidentally splashed some wine on it. You'd just stick a pillow over the stain, and if you had a dog, you'd invite it to jump up there and snarf up the stray cracker crumbs.

When he was done putting his clothes away in a mahogany wardrobe and small bureau, he peeked into Ella's room next door. It was very girly.

He noted that he had a double bed, and she had a queen. He'd live—he guessed. It had been years since he'd slept on a double. Last time had been with Ella. It was perfect for spooning but hell if one of the sleepers tossed and turned all night, which Ella tended to do. But he hadn't cared. He'd slept like a baby. And it was because he'd been so in love.

Now he slept terribly and alone in a king-sized bed in Brooklyn.

How would he sleep here? With Ella in the room next door?

He suspected it would be very difficult.

He called his father. "I'm here," he said.

"In Charleston?" There was the sound of New York City traffic in the background.

"Yes. I'm going for it."

"Good," his father said. "I'm proud of you."

"Thanks, Dad. I'll do my best."

"It's all you can do."

The call was short and sweet. Hank wasn't doing this to make his father proud. Not by a long shot. But it helped knowing his dad was rooting for him.

He went back to hanging up his shirts. Which one of them would he be wearing when he put it all on the line with Ella? When he showed her his heart and offered it to her, knowing full well she could toss it aside—and justifiably so?

He didn't know. And he needed to be thinking about the movie script. Time to dig in there. He had to justify why he was in Charleston, after all. Like his father, he hid behind his job. He wasn't sure he had the courage to live a life apart from his work. But he was in Charleston to try. He was there to find balance.

He hung up his last shirt. "Eff the script," he murmured to the portrait of the three boys. At least for now, he'd ignore the movie.

He was in Charleston on a sunny day, and he was going for a walk.

The cobblestones on Love Lane weren't exactly easy on four-inch-high heels. But Ella had developed a way of negotiating them: she walked like a fairy, staying on her toes. Ten minutes after she'd left Hank at Pammy's carriage house, she reached the historic wrought-iron gate with the two hearts and the hidden, intertwined initials that they'd discovered when Macy was falling in love with Deacon.

Now Ella could relax.

Not that she could *really* relax. She didn't think she'd relax again until Hank left for good that coming weekend. She'd be on pins and needles the whole time he was in town. But she tried to soothe herself by taking in the glory that was Two Love Lane, the most charming address in Charleston. The house shone with the kind of welcoming beauty you could look at all day and never tire of. Right now a cloud shadow hung above the left turret, and a gentle breeze blew over the magnolia and oaks in the front yard and back garden.

For over two hundred years, Two Love Lane had been a respite for weary souls searching for love, and one of the latest candidates for romance was inside: Roberta Ruttle.

Ella loved her job. But on rare occasions she had challenges that gave her pause, that made her question herself: Did I do the right thing? Am I really meant to be a matchmaker?

Roberta, a fifty-three-year-old woman who'd never married, was one such challenge. Ella had been trying to find her a soul mate for two years, and literally every man Roberta went on a date with through Two Love Lane came back to Ella with the report that the very savvy entrepreneur wouldn't speak to them beyond giving yes and no replies and short answers to basic ice-breaker questions, such as, "What do you do for a living?" It made for a really difficult date.

Roberta wasn't shy. She ran a high-end real estate

company in Charleston, and if you caught her at a cocktail party, she'd talk your head off about business or her latest golf game. She had a real flair for fashion. There was a definite sparkle in her eye, and she knew everyone in town. She got along with everyone too, which was unusual in a city fueled by juicy gossip, a staple of the competitive, somewhat unruly crowd that populated the Lowcountry. At business or charity events, or even cozy dinner parties, everyone was always angling for power positions. It was a sport, and woe unto anyone who took a wrong step. A sense of humor was helpful because inevitably, your day would come: you'd be the subject of whispered conversations.

Lucky for Roberta, so far she'd missed being the butt of gossip. None of her dates had kissed and told . . . probably because they never got to the kiss phase.

Whenever Ella tried to get the sophisticated maven to explain why she wouldn't speak up on dates, Roberta would get huffy and hang up on her. But she wouldn't leave Two Love Lane either. She kept forking over cash for Ella to fix her up with a soul mate, and Ella was desperate to find her one.

Just last week Ella had spoken to Roberta on the phone about her most recent date. "So," Ella had said, "this latest date said you wouldn't speak to him beyond answering yes and no, and you saying in very vague terms that you have property on the beach when he asked where you live. So he doesn't really want to move forward. He doesn't think you're at all interested in him."

Ella had been referring to a great guy, a widower about Roberta's age, who had just taken her out on a moonlight sail and provided her a catered dinner aboard his yacht. He'd even brought out his guitar and played her a few romantic tunes.

"Fine," the usually loquacious Roberta had said.

Ella had wracked her brain. "Maybe we could have a sit-down about our approach again. Playing hard to get or mysterious can only get you so far, and we both know you're a great conversationalist, so—"

Roberta had hung up.

The mere thought of Roberta hanging up on Ella made her stiffen: How on earth would she ever be able to help the woman if she refused to cooperate? Not only that, how could Ella even think of solutions to Roberta's problem when Hank was always on her mind? How could she do her job properly when she was already mooning about him?

Yes. She was mooning, which was such a dumb word, but there you had it! And it was so humiliating.

She'd have to come up with a way to stop thinking of him. She'd ask the girls for advice once Roberta was gone. In the meantime, her chin went up and she strode through the front door, determined that the Roberta problem would not defeat her. In fact, it was a very good sign that Roberta was there at all. Maybe she wasn't going to complain, and she certainly couldn't hang up. Maybe she was ready to work harder.

"Yoo-hoo," called Miss Thing. "Ella?"

"It is I," Ella called back. Miss Thing liked to keep things elegant at the front of the house.

"We're in the kitchen," Miss Thing said. "Come on back, sugar!"

Ella walked across several gorgeous rugs and gleaming hardwood floors, the same ones ladies in their kid slippers and gents in their riding boots had walked across in the olden days. She was glad to get to the cheery yellow kitchen with the AGA stove. There she saw three of her favorite ladies—Macy, Greer, and Miss

Thing—gathered around the table with Roberta, whose hands were wrapped around a steaming mug of coffee.

Their guest looked so at ease. What could possibly be the problem when she was on a date?

"Roberta, ladies," Ella greeted them all, and slung her purse onto the back of a chair. "How is everyone?"

"We're doing great," said Macy. She looked gorgeous and summery in a tailored white-and-navy-blue-striped suit and navy heels.

"Fine, fine," said Miss Thing, effervescent in an emerald green sheath with a large peacock brooch on the lapel. Very Queen of England, her favorite fashion muse.

Greer puckered her brow at her phone. She was in one of her usual chic pantsuits. This one was ivory linen. "Doing well, Ella."

"What's on your phone?" Ella couldn't help wondering. Greer was concentrating so hard.

Her recently married friend looked up. "Oh, Ford just texted. Said that he's been commissioned to do some sketches of Samantha Drake while she's here." She grinned. "It's good news, actually. But Samantha, he's heard, is a bear to work with on every level."

"But if she were a man, everyone would call her ambitious," said Ella. "In command."

"True," said Roberta. "I get that all the time in my line of work. Some of the boys 'round here don't call me a go-getter behind my back. They use more choice words." She gave a wry shake of her head.

"It's not right," said Ella. "But speaking of the boys 'round here—" She cast a meaningful glance at Roberta. Did she have to say it out loud? "I presume you're here to chat with me about a few of them."

Roberta tossed her a saucy grin. "You presume *wrong*. I just came by to sell y'all some tickets to the Aquarium gala and silent auction. Surely Two Love Lane wants an entire table." She held out a thick cream-colored invitation to Ella and named an exorbitant price.

Ella plucked it from her fingers. "Yes, we'll take a whole table." She tucked the invitation in her purse. "But the deal is you have to sit with us. You and a date."

"Honey, I'm running this thing. I have my *own* table."

"With a date?" Ella persisted.

"Harvey, my brother in Boston." Roberta put a hand on her hip. "He a darling. If a bit dull."

"Come on," said Miss Thing. "You want to bring a real date, don't you? This is your night to shine!"

Roberta finally looked discomfited. "It would be nice," she said, "but I'll be so busy I won't have time to talk to a date anyway."

"A good man won't care," Macy said. "He'll be proud to be there to support you."

"Right," said Greer. "Go with someone you've already hit it off with on an earlier date. When is this gala?"

"A month from this past Saturday," said Roberta. "And there is no way I'll find someone in time." She patted her hair. "Ella hasn't had the best of luck finding me men who appreciate me."

She looked around the room with a gimlet gaze, almost daring them to challenge her.

Ella took the invitation back out of her purse and held it out to Roberta. "It's a little more complicated than that."

Roberta's brow furrowed. "Why are you giving this back?"

"We can't get a table unless you promise me to try to get a real date," Ella said, "which means you're going to have to admit it's not just my guy choices keeping you from true love. We're going to have to work on some things. That is, if you really want your own happily ever after."

"Which believe me," Greer said, "is worth all the hard work you're going to probably have to go through to get it."

"Amen, sister," said Macy.

She and Greer high-fived.

Greer was now an indulgent aunt to twin baby girls in England. Her artist-husband Ford had taken on the role of uncle because the twins' real father wasn't in their lives. Their mother was an English socialite and Ford's old girl-friend who'd once left him at the altar.

Ford and Greer had decided to spend every summer in England to be with the girls, and when they were older, the girls would come to them in Charleston. Greer wasn't cut out for motherhood, she'd decided. And Ford enjoyed their adult-only lifestyle too. So the "occasional kids" situation suited them both well.

"Oh, yeah, these two ladies went through hell to get to their happily ever afters," Miss Thing said airily. She was examining her nails with great pride. She'd just had a manicure, and each nail had a tiny heart in the middle. "And now they're leaving at lunch time for quickies with their hubbies."

"We are *not*," said Macy, but her cheeks reddened. "At least, not *every* day."

Greer laughed her big, honking laugh, which didn't match her otherwise sleek vibe. "I plead the fifth."

Roberta stared at the proffered invitation. "Put it back in your purse, Ella," she said dryly. "I'll cooperate. I'd love to have quickies with my future husband too, if he's out there. The sooner we get started, the better."

Ella grinned. "Let's go then," she said, "to my office."

"Fine." Roberta rolled her eyes, but she followed Ella

as docilely as Oscar, Macy's cat, was doing. Oscar loved when visitors came to Two Love Lane and always insisted on checking them out. He trotted alongside Roberta.

"Oscar is Two Love Lane's love mascot," Roberta said when she sat in Ella's office and Oscar brushed up against her leg.

Ella laughed. "He's everyone's good luck charm." She took a deep breath. "Now let's talk more bluntly about why you clam up on dates. Up until now, I've sort of beat around the bush. But the fact is, a gentle strategy isn't working. Would you rather discuss this with a licensed counselor and get back to me? Or should I dive right in with some blunt questions?"

"Dive in," said Roberta.

"Are you shy?"

"No."

"I didn't think so. You've never acted shy." Ella smiled. "Are you a snob?"

"Absolutely not." Roberta laughed.

Ella did too. "I've never thought so." She thought for a second. "Do you have some kind of phobia?"

"Hmm," said Roberta. "I don't know that I do. Except a pretty strong fear of spiders."

"As do I." Ella sighed. "And that has nothing to do with your dating life." She tapped her fingers on her desk. "When you're on your dates, are you aware that you're not speaking much? Or is it always a surprise to you when I tell you afterward?"

"I'm very aware," said Roberta.

"I've asked you to explain it before," said Ella, "and you always fob me off. Would you be willing to explain it to me now? Why don't you talk on dates? Everywhere else, you do."

"I know," said Roberta. She folded her hands in her lap. "It's quite easy to explain. And I haven't up until this point because I thought I could wait it out. But nothing's changed."

"What?"

Roberta leaned forward. "I got put under a spell. When I was twenty-five."

"Huh?"

"I met this guy in a bar, a lawyer from an old family in Mobile, Alabama, who does tarot card readings at a really high-end restaurant when he's not in court."

"That's sort of incongruous," Ella said. "I don't usually think of an attorney doing tarot readings on the side."

"Me either," Roberta said. "It was *intriguing*."

"I'll say."

"So anyway, I met him at the restaurant. I was required to pay for his meal, and let me tell you, he ordered an expensive bottle of wine and the most expensive entrée on the menu."

"It sounds like he was using you."

"I wondered that too, but he came so highly recommended."

"You met him at a *bar*," Ella reminded her.

"Yes, but I went to his tarot card website, and he had five stars."

"From how many people?"

"Oh, about four or five."

"*Roberta*."

Ella's most baffling client waved a hand. "I know. Maybe I went to see him because he was incredibly good-looking, okay? And he was an attorney who drove a very nice Beemer."

"Now I get it," Ella said.

"So anyway, I accidentally spilled wine on his tarot

cards and ruined the set. At least ten cards shriveled before our eyes. I felt terrible. He was very upset, understandably so, because he'd inherited them from his grandmother. He said to me, 'May your tongue disappear whenever you seek true love,' which I took with a grain of salt. But sure enough, ever since, on dates, I just can't speak much. It's super hard."

"Now *that's* a weird story."

"Tell me about it," said Roberta.

"You don't really believe it, though, do you?" Ella leaned forward. "I mean, it's psychosomatic. Not a real spell. You've simply convinced yourself."

Roberta shrugged. "I was sure it was too. But a month after I met the tarot card reader, I met a guy I really liked, and right away, I started having trouble with him. I just couldn't *talk*. We didn't get past the first date, and it all went downhill from there."

"Did you ever go back to the lawyer?"

"I did," Roberta said, "two months later. He told me he was really sorry he lost his temper about the ruined tarot cards. And he wished he could take the curse back, but it was out of his hands. He consulted with some friend in Alabama on his phone—I have no idea who it was, but I could swear he called her *Mama*—and when he hung up, he said that maybe this will help: 'A penny for your thoughts, the ten thousandth for your tongue.' I had no idea what it meant. He didn't seem to know either. Ten thousand pennies equals a thousand dollars. So I scraped up a thousand dollars and gave it to him. He refused it. He said he didn't want my money, that he knew for sure the advice wasn't about him scamming me out of a thousand dollars. And I never saw him again. He moved out of town."

"At least you didn't lose a thousand dollars."

"I suppose." She paused. "But I'm so desperate, I still try to break the curse. Every once in a while, I donate a thousand dollars to a charitable cause hoping it'll do the trick. So far, no dice. Lucky for me, I can afford the price of foolishness."

Ella smiled. "You're not being foolish. This must be a very bothersome thing. You're just trying to fix it. And the charities must love your donations." She bit her thumb. "I'll say it again: I think the curse is bogus, and your poor subconscious mind just can't get past it."

"I can't tell you how many times I've said the same thing to myself in the mirror," said Roberta. "I went to several hypnotists. I've also been seeing a psychologist off and on the past three years. Nobody's been able to help me, which makes me think it might really be a curse. Except I don't believe in them—even the ones that are working, like this one."

"So drinking wine or martinis doesn't loosen your tongue?"

"No. I've been prescribed anti-anxiety meds too. Nothing works."

"Wow." Ella swiveled her chair and looked out her window, past the long gold velvet curtains to a beautiful view of the right side of the front garden. She saw an oak, the cherub fountain spouting water, and part of the wrought-iron gate. "There's got to be away around this."

"I wish I knew," said Roberta. "I never told you because it's embarrassing. I sound like a kook telling you the reason. All these years, I've been hoping to out-run this curse. I wake up on date mornings and think, 'This time, tonight's date will be different. I'll have a wonderful time. I'll be able to speak.' But it never is."

"How awful for you," Ella said, turning back to face her.

Roberta's eyes grew shiny. "I know."

Ella reached across her desk and took her hand. "We'll figure this out. I promise. I'm so glad you confided in me."

Roberta sniffed and nodded. "I'm glad I did too," she whispered.

"Don't you worry," said Ella.

But inside, she *was* worried. What was she going to do?

# CHAPTER EIGHT

After Roberta left, Ella checked her phone. *You're in*, came a text from Ancient History. Ella chuckled at the name she'd given Hank. *They're sending the script over tonight to the carriage house.*

She closed her eyes. Acting in a movie starring Samantha Drake! Ella never would have believed this could happen to her. All right, a long time ago, she could have believed it, when she was actively pursuing acting as a profession in New York City and she'd honestly thought it was the only thing she ever wanted to do. But not for years and years and years . . .

She opened her eyes and texted Hank: *I can't believe it.*

*Believe it*, he wrote back. *Samantha Drake better watch out!*

She laughed. *What the heck. I'll have fun with it.*

*I hope so*, he wrote. *We can trade notes. Meanwhile, we have a read-through tomorrow at 8 a.m.*

*Okay*, she texted.

And then told herself, *No more texting Hank!* Although that little exchange had been necessary, right?

Maybe she shouldn't have said she'd have fun with it. But it had been something she'd have said to anyone.

How about the "trading notes" part?

Well, they were going to be professionals on the same movie set. There was nothing particularly personal about saying they could exchange helpful information about how to deal with Samantha Drake.

She had to report back to the girls. Starting tomorrow, her schedule at Two Love Lane would need tweaking the rest of the week.

"You're *what*?" Greer's gorgeous eyes flew wide.

"Going to be in a movie with Samantha Drake," Ella said. "It's a small speaking role, but who cares? It's on my bucket list. I'll exchange lines with a Hollywood icon. So for this week, could you guys help me out here? I'm sorry I didn't give you any notice."

"We don't need notice," said Macy, clapping her hands. "Of course we'll help you. Maybe this will be your big break."

Ella's eyes almost—*almost*—filled with tears. Papa had always used that phrase: her *big break*. He'd so wanted it to happen. Every time she thought of Papa and her acting dreams, she thought about their annual trips to Serendipity 3, which were some of the happiest memories of her childhood and youth.

She missed him so much.

"Maybe this *will* be my big break." She never wanted to give up being a matchmaker, but now . . .

Now maybe she could become a ginormous star and Papa would look down from Heaven and see she'd finally done it. She could become Samantha Drake's best friend, and Samantha would see her talent, and—

And—

Ella could become as big a star as Hank, and then she'd show him!

And make Papa happy. The *nonnas* too. They'd love to see her become a big star.

Ambition filled her, ambition she'd forgotten so long ago.

It came roaring back.

*But you love being a matchmaker*, an inner voice reminded her.

Yes, she did. In fact, she could do both! She could be a big star *and* be a matchmaker. Maybe part-time. From Hollywood. With occasional trips to Charleston, maybe once a month. Although that might be kind of hard to do if she was making movies.

None of which she'd star in opposite Hank. She would turn down all *those* scripts.

She had it all figured out within seconds in her head.

*This movie was her second chance.*

And then she remembered she was only in three scenes and had only a few lines, and she'd be with the cast and crew four days—hardly long enough for Samantha to catch on to her star quality.

But a girl could dream, couldn't she? A girl could hope that a few days shy of a week could change everything!

"When did you audition?" Greer asked.

Here was the hard part. "I didn't." At everyone's baffled look, she blinked—and then told herself to simply spit it out. "Hank got me the part, sight unseen. He's replacing Frampton Cooke."

"He *is*?" all three women said at the same time.

Ella nodded. "Frampton's wife is pregnant and having some complications—triplets, as a matter of fact—so he's leaving immediately."

"My land!" exclaimed Miss Thing.

"So Hank is on board now," Ella said, "starring opposite Samantha."

"He's here in Charleston?" asked Greer. "Right now?"

"Yes. He told me he'd be glad to get me a minor speaking role, one where I trade a few lines with Samantha. Apparently, the actor they'd already hired for this part also left the movie. I'm happy to fill in."

"I should say *so*," said Greer.

"Wow, just wow!" Macy added. "I can't believe Hank is here and that this movie stuff is really happening."

Miss Thing waved a hand in front of her face, her standard move when she was overcome with emotion. "Honey, it all sounds wonderful, but back up. What's this about Hank Rogers being *glad* to get you a role? Did he offer you this in the note he left with the flowers in your dressing room Saturday night?"

"Your dressing room?" Greer exclaimed. "He was here? He went to the play?"

"No," Ella said, "he was in New York at the time."

"Have y'all been in touch?" asked Macy.

"No." Ella explained how Hank had wanted a favor—for her to meet Pammy. "But there's been a development. He's here now."

Greer and Macy exchanged glances. And then they both looked at Miss Thing.

"I can see you!" Ella exclaimed. "Don't make those secret faces in front of me! Nothing has happened. And nothing *will* happen." She crossed her arms over her chest. "He's only here until Saturday."

"Whatever," said Macy, sounding bemused.

Miss Thing giggled.

Greer shot Ella a sympathetic look.

Ella let out a gusty sigh. "You have to understand.

There is no going back. None. Nada. The night I thought he was going to propose—"

"He forgot it was your birthday and came home with two hoagies in a white paper bag from his favorite deli," said Miss Thing.

"Exactly," said Ella.

"And then he told you he was getting a movie in Hawaii. A big one," said Macy.

Ella made a flourish with her hand. "*And?*"

"And you had just secretly turned down a major acting opportunity," said Greer, "because he was so depressed about how his career was going nowhere, and you thought it might crush him for you to accept the role and go away for five months' filming in Australia."

Ella sank into a chair. "And then what?" she whispered.

Miss Thing knelt next to her and took her hand. "And you two broke up. On your birthday, of all days. It was the practical thing, you told him, considering he was going to be gone the next three months. But then you confessed you thought you'd be getting engaged that night, and breaking up was about more than being practical. You'd been ready to commit to him, heart and soul. You told him about the role in Australia that you had turned down. For *him*. Because he needed you."

"And *he* said you never should have done that," Greer continued. "He felt terrible about it, but he also reminded you that you'd both vowed you wouldn't commit to each other, that you'd focus instead on creating trajectories toward successful careers. He said you were both well on your way, that your movie offers proved it."

Ella laughed. "He hadn't been so confident in his prospects the night *before* my birthday. All it took was getting that Hawaii movie, and he bounced back."

"Isn't that always the way?" Miss Thing tut-tutted. "We let our fears rule us."

"Remind me what else happened," Ella said, and tried to forget that even when Hank was at his lowest about his own acting future, he'd never wavered about hers. He's always told her he knew it would be bright.

"That movie role you turned down," Macy said, "the actress who took the supporting role you were offered now has a huge career. The movie won four Oscars."

"Yeah," Ella whispered. "It was a really great script." She looked around at all of them, feeling like she was coming out of her little trance of self-pity. "Hank was smart to take the role he did. It led to other great supporting roles, and then he broke out two years later and became a megastar on his own."

"Right," said Greer. "That movie in Hawaii started it all, his path to fame and fortune."

"So I'm glad he did it," said Ella. "Even though at the time, it was weird and painful. He forgot my birthday. He'd never even contemplated getting me a ring. And the next day, he was gone."

No one said anything.

All these years later, Ella cried softly, just a few tears rolling down her cheeks. It was sad, that was why. It was plain sad. And it had been years since she'd thought about it in any sort of detail. Those details made a heck of a story, and they still caused her pain.

Her three best friends rubbed her shoulders, murmured words of comfort.

"I'm okay," she said after a few seconds of TLC, and stood. "But I'm glad we talked about it. It's good to be reminded."

"We have your back, always," said Macy.

She knew they did. "So now I have to tell you what

else is going on." And she told them about Hank living with Pammy—and that she was too.

This time her best friends didn't exchange any half-amused, half-worried looks with one another. They nodded seriously and kept their eyes on Ella.

"You sure you can handle that?" asked Greer. "Living with him for the rest of the week?"

Ella shook her head. "I know I'm taking chances here. But Samantha Drake!"

They all agreed—working with Samantha Drake would be awesome.

"Let's get really real," Macy said. "Surely some of this is about Hank, not just the movie role. Or helping Pammy."

"It might be," Ella admitted. "Maybe I need more resolution, you know? I never got it, although it sure felt final to me at the time. It would feel great to be able to walk away after this week with no more regrets about my past."

"Peace would be nice," said Greer.

"It would," said Ella. "Hank said something similar, that he wants resolution too. In fact, he said that's the main reason he came here. Not for the movie. Not for Pammy. But for me."

All three friends got in a tizzy about *that*. The tizzy lasted at least five minutes.

Miss Thing even cried. "Happy tears," she said, and pulled out a lace handkerchief.

"No, no, no," said Ella sternly. "No crying. He said that, but he didn't mean he wants to get back together. It only means he feels the same way, that it was such an abrupt way to end our relationship, and it would mean a lot to him to be able to tie up some loose ends. If that's even possible in a week."

"Got it," said Greer.

"It's still gratifying, isn't it?" asked Macy. "That he's not done. He came to work things out with you."

"It's about time," said Ella. "Well past time."

Macy, Greer, and Miss Thing agreed, although Miss Thing could not stop saying that sometimes resolving things involved *sex*. "Hanky-panky," she explained further because she never got tired of talking about sex. "With Hank." She waggled her finely plucked eyebrows.

"Not this time," said Ella, refusing to smile.

Miss Thing's disappointment was palpable. "Are you *sure*?"

"Very sure," said Ella, and immediately regretted it. Her papa used to warn her to never say never about anything—because it would come back to haunt you. "Helping Pammy adjust to Charleston and acting in the movie are my main focus. Resolution with Hank is just gravy, if it happens at all. I'm putting no expectations on anything."

"All right, sweetie," Miss Thing said, but Ella knew she had her secret hopes.

Still, Ella was thrilled everyone at Two Love Lane was in the know. She'd made it clear to them that she and Hank would have a professional, courteous relationship and might perhaps, if they were lucky, find some level of accord about their shared past.

Later, she'd call Mama and the *nonnas* and tell them about the movie. Better yet, she'd stop in to say hi and see their reactions in person. The *nonnas* and Mama all loved Samantha Drake.

It was so awesome working with your best friends. She exchanged hugs with them, and then each of them went on with their day at the office. Ella had two lengthy appointments with new clients and lots of online work, especially research. She was always trying to find good dates for the patrons of Two Love Lane.

At four-thirty, she cut out to pay a visit to Harris Teeter. *Wine and pimento cheese*, she kept telling herself to block out the memory of Miss Thing saying that sex was sometimes involved when old lovers came to a resolution.

That was an outrageous notion, and so typical of Miss Thing to say! She loved shocking "her girls," as she called them.

But Ella couldn't get the words out of her head. All the way back to the carriage house, they kept coming, keeping time with her steps: *hanky-panky with Hank, hanky-panky with Hank . . .*

# CHAPTER NINE

On their first day as roommates, Hank and Pammy played English rummy at a beat-up mahogany table with the initials *BW+LC* scratched into the surface: Beau Wilder and Lacey Clark, two lovebirds with Hollywood roots whose marriage was working beautifully. The table was in the corner of the cozy living room of the carriage house. Pammy was winning. Hank never had luck with cards. He was just picking up the ace of clubs he desperately needed, astounded that the tide was turning in his favor, when Ella yelled from the front door, "Yoo-hoo! I'm home!" like Lucy calling to Desi.

Hank's heart leaped. He was embarrassed about that, but yeah, Ella had always been like a rainbow appearing in his sky, which was filled with too many squawking birds, gathering storm clouds, some occasional rain, which switched off to a glaring sun, and loud jets. And maybe some mild pollution from a nearby factory. Only one person had ever been the rainbow.

He saw her through the door panes carrying a paper sack bursting with stuff, including a French baguette sticking out of the top, just like in the movies. No plastic grocery bags in sight. He had no doubt it was because she was still worried about the seagulls. She'd always been worried about the seagulls when they were together.

He stood up and threw the door open, maybe a little too forcefully. "Let me get that for you," he said about the bag, but she maneuvered around him, bumping him with her purse, never once looking him in the eye.

"Oh, no," she said, "I've got it."

"Food!" Pammy cried, as if she'd been on a desert island for the past ten years, living solely on coconuts.

Ella hurried into the tiny kitchen.

Hank strode after her, slowly, willing himself to stay chill and not come across as heavy-handed in any way. He let her pull things out of the bag and start putting them away before he said, "I hope you had a nice day at work."

Her head was in the fridge. "Oh, yeah!" she called out to him, and was busy opening veggie bins and putting yogurt, cheese, milk, and oranges on her shelf. *Her* shelf. She'd made it clear they'd have boundaries, some of which might be trivial, but she was making her point. As always. More power to her.

He waited for her to reappear.

Meanwhile, Pammy showed up. "You have a very nice rear end," she said to Ella.

Ella stilled.

Hank had noticed Ella's spectacular posterior too, but was trying hard to focus on more cerebral things, like how to get her to speak to him.

"You must work out," Pammy went on.

"No, not lately," Ella said from the depths of the fridge.

"Not that I'm into girls," said Pammy. "But I appreciate the human body. Whoever's body it is, you know?"

"Thanks," Ella said, her voice muffled by refrigerator insulation and the giant, unbound head of lettuce she was trying to stuff into the veggie bin. Maybe it was kale. Hank wouldn't know. It was so fresh and nutritious-looking, it scared him.

Finally, Ella reappeared, and he made eye contact with her. It warmed him all over. Then she turned to Pammy, and he felt cold and left out.

"You can have any of my stuff," she said, looking back and forth between them, which he appreciated. "I mean, I put it on my shelf, the bottom one, but I'm okay with sharing. Please. Take whatever you want. I only put it there so I can remember what I bought. Otherwise, things get lost behind pickle and mayo jars, and then it goes bad. I hate wasting food."

"I get it," said Pammy. "But you won't be here that long. Only a week."

"I know." Ella looked at Hank. "And you're here only a week too."

"Right." The thought depressed him.

"I never have food-wasting problems since I pretty much just eat Taco Bell and cereal," Pammy said. "How about you, Hank?"

"Whatever you decide works for me," he said.

Ella knew damn well he didn't have a food-wasting problem either, because she would guess—correctly—that he had a full-time chef who did all the shopping and kept an eye on the fridge contents. When he and Ella had been poor and living together, she'd handled all the food. He'd barely even known what they had in the cupboards. She would often whip up a delicious, simple pasta dish, usually with sautéed veggies and a bit of ham, chicken, or sausage—they could never afford steak—and often substituted beans.

He'd been in charge of wine and beer and liquor. They were always having parties back then.

"Who bought the hazelnut creamer?" Ella asked.

"I did." Hank wouldn't tell her he'd bought it for her. She *loved* hazelnut creamer. If he told her, she'd get all flighty, maybe, and think he was coming on too strong.

Her cheeks turned slightly pink. "You went to the store?"

"That Harris Teeter you mentioned," he said. "It has all kinds of great free stuff at the deli. I had a chunk of cantaloupe and a piece of prosciutto . . . together. It was delicious. And then I had a free cookie. Oh, and a chicken nugget."

He hadn't had fried food in years. That greasy, fried chicken nugget dipped in mustard sauce had tasted like heaven. So much so, he tried to sample another one in the teriyaki sauce, but the lady told him no, only one nugget per person, and he'd slunk away feeling greedy, but still glad he'd had that nugget, like a real person who didn't have to always watch his weight, thanks to camera angles and PR people breathing down your neck all day.

"No one bothered you?" Pammy bumped into him on purpose. She loved knocking into him, punching him, and generally getting in his face. She could probably take him down if she wanted to.

"No," he said. "I wore a cowboy hat I found in the front closet. Must be Beau's. And some sunglasses."

"Did you buy anything else besides the creamer?" Ella stood straight now. She sounded breezy. *Too* breezy. She was onto him. She knew he'd bought it for her.

"I was going to," he lied. "And then I got a business call and had to leave. You shouldn't talk on the phone in a store. I hate when people do that."

"You could have gone outside and come back in," said Pammy.

"It was a long call," he kept lying.

He wished he could tell them that damn creamer had been hard to find. He hadn't been to a grocery store in years. There were so many choices in everything, especially in creamers. It was ridiculous. He'd almost given up, and then suddenly he saw three different brands of hazelnut-flavored stuff and had to figure out which one Ella would like best. He chose the carton with the pretty pink font and the flower in the corner.

"Hank!" Pammy cried. "We could have used some cereal and bread. And milk. And maybe some steaks and potatoes. Sour cream. Butter. Bacon bits. Beer. Cheetos. Geez. All the good stuff."

Ella looked at Pammy, and they both laughed. Well, Pammy snorted. Which was her way of laughing.

"I'm sorry I'm such a busy man." How could Hank explain what an adventure it had been merely walking into Harris Teeter? How free he'd felt? How purposeful, too? Finding that creamer had been everything because he'd wanted to please Ella. Actual food had been the last thing on his mind.

And now he looked like an idiot. Buying only creamer.

"Thanks for the creamer," Ella said primly.

See? She knew it was for her. He couldn't have that. What had he been thinking?

"Oh, sorry, but I . . . *like* hazelnut creamer now," he said, scratching his jaw. It made a loud, manly sandpaper noise that he liked to hear when he was feeling not quite sure of himself. "I use it every day."

Sure he did! He despised flavored creamers. He took his coffee black. Ella knew that.

She merely stared into the distance. He was such a bad liar.

"My doctor told me I need more calcium," he added for effect.

"But this is *non-dairy*, cuz," Pammy said. She was at the fridge now, peering into it to see what Ella had gotten. She held up the hazelnut creamer.

"Whatever," Hank said, silently wishing his cousin to perdition. "It's still good for you. I'm going to make some coffee before our meeting. Anyone else want some?"

"No, thanks," Pammy said. "Especially with hazelnut creamer. Ugh! Let's break out the wine and that weird-looking orange cheese in a tub." She grabbed some crackers from the pantry.

"I'm going to have wine and pimento cheese with Pammy," Ella said. "But feel free to have coffee." She still wouldn't look at him.

She and Pammy put the cheese and crackers on a plate, and Pammy took the bounty into the living room.

"Meet me out here, guys!" she yelled. "I could watch the tourists walking on the Battery all night from this bay window."

"We'll be there in a minute!" Hank put a K-Cup into the receptacle in the automatic coffee machine. As the brown liquid sputtered and flowed into his newly claimed Star Wars mug—no one else had better touch it!—he cursed a blue streak inside his head. "Feel free to use that creamer whenever you want," he said to Ella. He hoped she'd drain the carton fast so he wouldn't have to.

"No, thanks," she said, "I drink my coffee black now. Unflavored. Just coffee."

He picked up his mug. Took a sip. Forgot he had to add creamer. Added the hazelnut poison, cringing inside while he did so. "So when did the big change happen?"

She finally looked at him. "The day after we broke up.

I started drinking my coffee black, got both my ears pierced"—that was shocking! She'd been scared to do that!—"and started listening to jazz, the kind that makes you feel you're in an existential, black-and-white movie with no ending."

"Oh," he said.

"I also got a ride on a motorcycle with a guy I didn't even know. I saw him drive by and called him over. He took me around the block."

No way. Ella was terrified of stranger danger.

She flashed him a quick smile, and he could tell it wasn't a friendly one. She was like a shark saying, *Don't mess with me.*

"Wow," he said.

"And I've never looked back."

Unlike him. He'd looked back a million times. "Taken any more motorcycle rides?"

"One was enough." She pulled a bottle of red wine out of the paper bag and went looking for a corkscrew.

They couldn't find one. But they knocked elbows looking through the meager kitchen drawers and cupboards. She actually got him right on the funny bone. An uncomfortable zing went up his arm. But he'd never tell. It was something, some kind of contact. Much better than nothing at all. Hell, he'd take her breath fanning against his cheek the way it used to when he'd pick her up and carry her—his woman—to their bed.

"Shoot," she said. "Pammy? Can you go look in the big house for a corkscrew, please?"

"Sure!" Pammy called back. She thumped across the living room floor and slammed the front door behind her.

Hank locked eyes with Ella. They were alone. But he could *not* focus on that. "You're really nice to live with her this week," he said, deflecting to Pammy. "And me," he added. "Thanks again."

Ella's shoulders drooped a little. "No, it's okay," she said. But she seemed troubled. She fingered the two wine glasses, pushing them around a little.

"If it's too stressful—" he began.

"I'll be fine," she interrupted him, and abruptly left the counter to sink into a kitchen chair. She put her fist on her right ear and leaned into it. "I'm tired, is all. The show is over. You know what that's like. And one of my clients is having issues I'm not sure how to handle."

He sat down next to her. "Is there anything I can do?"

How familiar this all seemed. Talks around the kitchen table, hearing about her day, her woes, her triumphs.

"No," she said. "It's a conundrum for the ages." She paused. "And Pammy's great. She's just a little lacking in confidence sometimes. She whips out her level when she's not sure what to say. Have you noticed that?"

"Yeah. She goes into construction-girl mode."

Ella chuckled. "She's a sweetheart, though. Already I love her. I think what I'll do this week is simply remind her that she rocks."

"Me too." Hank decided he could be so much kinder, wiser, and more tuned in than he was. Ella reminded him of that, not by nagging but by her good example.

The truth was, she made him a better person.

They listened to the sounds outside. Somewhere a truck was backing up, making that *beep, beep* noise. Cars swept by. A gull cried.

Hank hoped Pammy wouldn't find a corkscrew and they'd have to send her to Harris Teeter for one.

He looked at Ella. She looked at him. Her eyes always

drew him in, now more than ever because he had no claim upon her whatsoever. He wished he'd never mentioned her at the Plaza to his parents. See what tea did to him? Made him a maudlin fool. With other guys, it was bourbon.

With him—tea.

And look where it got him. Here in Charleston, sitting next to the person who made him vulnerable, the only person in the world who could effectively break down the identity he had worked so hard to build up.

She laid a hand on his arm, and the feeling of her fingers pressing into his flesh made him happy in the most inexplicable way.

"I think you're a good cousin," she said. "Pammy's lucky."

He looked down at her with a fondness she probably didn't like but he couldn't disguise. "You were always one to see the good in me."

"Because there *is* some, Hank. Give yourself some credit."

He was acutely aware of their two very human bodies. Warm flesh close to warm flesh. And she seemed to be just as conscious of the tension between them. They were mere inches from each other.

*Noooo*, his brain said, even as her beautiful eyes hypnotized him.

*Noooo*, his brain said again when he moved half an inch closer. She stared right back at him, her mouth slightly parted. He felt a lust that was more than lust. Because it was Ella, who was like a fine work of art to be appreciated, protected, adored.

"But I will not, *cannot*, forget how things ended between us," Ella added. "On my birthday, no less. I know it was a mutual decision, but the timing was terrible.

Luckily, ten years have gone by, and I can sit in a room with you and hold a civil conversation." She gave a little laugh.

Ouch. That comment was like ice water thrown over Hank's entire body. He leaned back in his chair. "Thank God for that," he said, and tried not to be anything but cheerful.

But he wished he could defend himself. At least a little. She'd admitted they'd both agreed to end it. Yes, forgetting her birthday had been a terrible misstep on his part, but hell. That was ten years ago! He'd been a kid—a kid so afraid of failure, his relationships had not been his top priority. His career had been.

"I've learned since then," he said. "I've learned about balance." Sort of. He was still struggling with that.

But they never got to finish the conversation because the front door whined on its hinges. "Hank Rogers?" It was a feminine voice, as finely timbered as a Bach cello suite performed by Yo-Yo Ma. Until it wasn't. "Are you in here, you bloody man?"

Hank's eyes narrowed. It was Samantha. Ella recognized her voice too, obviously. Her eyes widened.

"I'm in the kitchen," Hank called, and stood up. Walked around the corner to the entryway. Joined his co-star on the front porch. Pulled the door halfway shut behind him to keep the gnats from flying in the house, supposedly, but really because he was embarrassed she'd tracked him down like a hunting dog on the scent, and he didn't want Ella to witness his capture.

"Look at you," he said, "coming to see me. What a nice welcome."

"Welcome, my arse," Samantha said. "I'm hosting a dinner across the street at the Carolina Yacht Club. You *must* come. And bring your family with you."

# CHAPTER TEN

"Samantha Drake, three-time Oscar winner, was in this house," Ella whispered aloud to herself for posterity. Why not?

Thank God one of Hollywood's biggest female stars had shown up to chase down Hank. Even when Ella made clear how Hell would freeze over before she'd forget their past, his gaze had been like a fair attraction—the booth with the huge teddy bear you could win if you shot three rubber duckies. She was such a sucker for that booth! He was no teddy bear, that was for sure, but he was big and warm, and if Samantha hadn't appeared, maybe something totally wrong and stupid would have happened. Something that would have been from sheer muscle memory: Ella gliding into Hank's arms and them making out like two twenty-one-year-olds who'd seen enough of the world to know they still knew very little about it. Clinging to each other, basking in pure, hot sensory experience, was a way to forget their confusion.

Ella could still remember exactly what that felt like.

When he'd looked toward the sound of Samantha's voice, the cords of his throat had been taut, and the stubble on his jaw made her yearn to kiss him on his neck, right below his jaw. He'd always loved that when they were together.

Ella was horrified and more determined than ever to steer clear of him.

But then he came back inside alone. "Want to go to the yacht club for dinner?" he whispered, sounding harried. "She's waiting out there. She said she didn't want to come all the way in. She wants to get back to the yacht club."

Ella's brow furrowed. "I think I'll pass," she whispered back. "I'm not dressed for it, and honestly, you're the star. And"—she raised her right pointer finger—"I'm not family."

She could have been. She *should* have been.

She was gratified by how disappointed he looked. "All right," he said low. "*This* time I'll let you off the hook."

"Have fun," she said in her softest whisper yet—it felt way too intimate between them—and watched him walk reluctantly out of the kitchen. It was so clear that he wanted to stay with her right there. That was bad. Very bad.

It was only their first night together.

*Get it together, Mancini.*

She peeked around the corner and couldn't help admiring the way he visibly changed, though, when he left her. He squared his shoulders and walked purposefully toward the front door, like he was a king or the President of the United States or something. Of course, he could do that. He'd played a young version of a president once. And damned if he hadn't played a king too.

Ella kept her arms crossed over her pounding heart.

And then she heard a thumping come from the front

porch steps. "Yo!" It was Pammy. "I got the corkscrew! I also found a weird piece of hardware in the kitchen I might be able to use in my carpentry class. I think I can make really narrow strands of wood putty with it. Or caulk."

"*Pammy*," Hank said, sounding almost jolly, but Ella knew that voice. He was totally stressed. "Give me that."

Ella listened from the kitchen, her ears wide open. She didn't want to miss a thing. *Samantha Drake, world-famous actor, was outside!* And Pammy found a weird kitchen tool? Ella put her hand over her mouth to stifle a giggle.

"That's a garlic press," she heard Hank say. "Geez."

"Ohhh." Pammy chuckled. "How was I supposed to know? I don't cook."

"I can see why," Hank said. "Samantha, this is my cousin Pammy. Pammy, this is Samantha Drake."

"Nice to meet you, Miss Drake," said Pammy. "You're lovelier in person than you are on-screen, and that's saying something."

"What a delight you are," Samantha said. "Please call me Samantha."

"Pammy can join us for dinner." Hank sounded somewhat less stressed.

"So you'll come, Hank," Samantha said. It was a statement. Not a question. Almost a reprimand for his declining earlier.

"Who could turn down a personally delivered invitation from Dame Samantha?" he shot back with the charm audiences around the world loved him for.

Samantha laughed. It was low and velvety. Ella suspected Hank had just raised her hand and kissed the back of it.

"My apologies, guys," said Pammy. "But I'm not coming. I'm having wine and that weird orange cheese with Ella."

Ella giggled again.

"Pammy, come on now," Hank said. Ella could hear how embarrassed he was. "Samantha just invited us to a nice meal across the street at the yacht club."

"Sorry," Pammy said. "I'm not that interested in sitting around a table and yakking about stocks and bonds or whatever it is people talk about at yacht clubs. You go do your thing, though."

"In that case, I'm ready to go," Samantha said.

Ella bit her thumbnail.

Pammy must have found a way around them because she stopped in the kitchen and tossed her the corkscrew. "Be right back," she said, and raced down the hall to her bedroom. Her door slammed shut behind her.

"Sorry about that," Ella heard Hank tell Samantha. "She means well."

"It's neither here nor there," said Samantha. "Let's go, shall we? Unless you want to wait for Ella. Who is she? Another cousin?"

"No, she's actually an old friend from my early acting days."

Ella wasn't sure she approved of how Hank described their history, but she also understood that revealing intimate details about his life wasn't something he liked to do or should feel forced to do. And it could possibly kill Ella's chances of keeping her role in the movie—that is, if Samantha was into Hank.

"She's playing the part of Wendy in the movie," he said.

Samantha must have forgotten. Ella reminded herself it was good to stay grounded.

"Oh, yes," said Samantha. "You wrangled that role for

her this morning. She must be a very *good* friend." She was fishing for insider information, big-time.

"She is," Hank said, not taking the bait.

Ella felt vaguely annoyed because *no*, they were not very good friends, but she appreciated that Hank hadn't thrown her under the bus either.

"Ella! Can you come outside?" He sounded mellow— yet stressed again. It was the voice he used to use in po- lite company that promised later commentary when they sat around the kitchen table at midnight and had cheese toast done under the broiler—or maybe popcorn with ex- tra butter—or went to bed and had pillow talk, her head on his chest, his hand curled around her waist.

This time, he'd have to handle his angst alone. Well, maybe they could still do the cheese toast or popcorn, but no hugging. No sharing a bed.

"In a second!" Ella called to him. It hit her hard that she was about to meet someone she really, *really* ad- mired. She promised herself she'd keep it together in front of Samantha Drake. She would be calm, cool, and collected, yet also somehow show the world-famous ac- tor that she could never have a better fan, friend, or pro- fessional colleague than Ella.

Pammy's bedroom door opened. "Ell-aaaaa!" she called. "Can you get the wine open?"

"J-Just a second!" Her mind started spinning a crazy, ridiculous fantasy: What if Samantha loved her so much, she'd want her in her next movie too, but in a bigger part?

*Oh my God*, she thought as she grabbed a bottle of wine from the counter, *maybe it's not so crazy-ridiculous. Maybe I'm actually poised on the precipice of a very big opportunity.*

Like Hank had said, when would she get this chance

SECOND CHANCE AT TWO LOVE LANE    111

again? Why shouldn't she try to make her fantasy become a reality?

Maybe she was supposed to. Her *nonnas* always said, "Play the cards you're dealt." Mama said, "Don't ignore the opportunities Fate puts in front of you." And Papa used to say, "You're a born star."

Papa was Papa. Of course, he'd thought his daughter was a star. But somewhere, deep inside, Ella believed it too. And she didn't even feel like she was that deluded. After all, she'd proven herself time and time again on a very reputable local stage. How many stars went undiscovered in community theater?

A lot. She knew that for a fact.

She'd do this for every community theater actor who would never get the chance she was getting.

But first, she called her girlfriends at Two Love Lane. Very quickly, she rattled off to them what was happening. Very quickly, she told them what her family had always said about opportunities, Fate, et cetera.

"Your family has a lot of sayings," Greer said with a chuckle.

They had her on speaker.

"They do," said Macy, "but I agree with all of them."

"Me too," said Miss Thing. "Here's mine: *Jump on it!*"

Ella grinned. "I could still be a matchmaker with Two Love Lane," she whispered.

"Of course, you could," all three of them said at once.

"While you're on set, not just this one but future ones, you can pick up some high-flying clients for us," Greer said.

"And when you're not making a movie, you'll be back here, and you can pick up where you left off," added Macy.

"You'd be our traveling matchmaker," said Miss Thing. "Love on wheels. Love in the air. Love—"

"Okay, I get it." Ella whispered. "Thanks for the support. You're sure I'm not crazy?"

"Just a little," said Macy. "But so are all of us. That's why we're successful, right? We think out of the box. We go after what we want."

"You're right," said Ella.

"Dang tootin'," said Miss Thing.

"Break a leg," Greer added, right before they all hung up.

Ella stuffed her phone back into her pocket and picked up on the stream of conversation again between Samantha and Hank.

"So this friend of yours playing Wendy, did you ever do shows together?" Samantha asked him.

Ella froze to hear Hank's answer.

"No," he said. "But we cheered each other on."

"She and Pammy are friends?" Samantha asked.

"No, we're not!" Pammy called from down the hallway. She was clomping toward the kitchen. "Not yet! But I bet we will be. Especially if she lets me fix her mother's mantel. It's crooked."

She walked in right as Ella was uncorking the wine. Ella handed it off to her. "Here you go," she said. "Pour me a glass too. I'll be right back."

"Where's the orange cheese?"

"In the fridge," Ella said, and left Pammy in the kitchen to get it out.

It was time to meet Samantha Drake and tell her there was no way she, Ella Mancini, amateur actress and professional matchmaker, was going to dinner with Hank Rogers. Ever. Not outside of this carriage house, that is.

She'd remind him that he was missing their house rules meeting too. And she'd do it with her head held high.

She pulled the front door wide open. Hank and Samantha swiveled their heads to look at her. Ella had just made what anyone with a dramatic bone in her body would call an entrance. She clung to the doorknob. Did they feel it too? Her presence? As in, *stage presence*? No one could outdo Samantha, but Ella could open a door with aplomb.

"Hello," she said, and left her special "stage" spot. "I'm Ella." She extended her hand to Samantha. Inside, she was starstruck. And terrified.

And then she wasn't.

*You are everyone's equal.* Papa's voice came to her. Samantha was only human, like everyone else, and when she made a moue of concern at Ella's proffered palm, that sealed the deal. Damned if Ella was going to withdraw her hand. She kept it stuck out. She was going to keep it stuck out as long as it took for Samantha to acknowledge it.

After a half-beat's pause, Samantha extended her own. "Hello."

So she wasn't a big talker. Maybe the Brits, too, weren't into shaking hands. Ella would have to ask Ford. Whatever the reason, she supposed Samantha was too famous to have to bother with the social niceties. Her handshake was weak at best. Ella only got the tips of her slender fingers with their long, tapered nails.

"Will you be joining us?" Samantha was standing awfully close to Hank, who was looking at Ella in a way she used to find so gratifying, as if hanging on her every word. "We have several other people waiting. The director and her wife. And our executive producer."

Big shots, all. Ella would be dining with people who could make or break an actor's career.

*Come*, Hank was clearly saying with his eyes. *Please, please come.*

But Ella had already told him she wouldn't go. And Samantha's tone wasn't impolite, but it wasn't encouraging either.

Why wouldn't Hank want to go alone with Samantha and those other VIPs to dinner? *Her* presence shouldn't matter to him in the least.

"No," Ella began, "we have a house-rules meeting tonight, and I promised Pammy—"

"Fine," Samantha cut her off. "See you on the set in the morning, I suppose." She started to walk down the porch steps.

"I guess our house-rules meeting can wait," Ella said. Some imp in her prompted her to. It was so obvious Samantha didn't care about her being there at the yacht club. But Ella would go and talk to her, whether Samantha wanted her to or not. And while she was there she could angle for some notice from an up-and-coming director and producer.

But then she had to consider whether this was a way for her to please Hank. And to be near him.

No way. She certainly didn't need to be *near* him for any reason other than professional ones.

But then Hank lit up in the subtle way only Ella and his favored friends and family could recognize and appreciate. It involved a lopsided grin that was scarcely there—just a tilt of one side of his mouth upward—and the barest heightening of his eyebrows, a warmth in his eyes that was like a banked fire come to life.

A strong crush feeling swept through Ella, which she tried to ignore by focusing on Samantha. She felt grateful to be living such a weird fantasy come to life: hanging out with an iconic movie star. And if she had to be with Hank again, troublesome as the idea was, at least he was also helping her get out of her comfort zone in general.

She didn't get back anything warm and fuzzy from Samantha when she made her pronouncement about going with them to the yacht club after all, but she wasn't surprised. Disappointed, maybe, but not surprised.

"*Ella!*" No one said her name with quite the determination Pammy did when she came out carrying an opened bottle of wine and two glasses. "You can't leave me here alone with the orange cheese and the wine."

"I'll be back soon," Ella assured her, "although why don't you accept Samantha's invitation, too, and come with us?"

"Yes," said Hank. "Come on, Pammy."

"Indeed," Samantha said faintly.

Pammy stood still. "Uhhhhh . . . okay."

"We'll wait while you change into something a little more yacht-club friendly," Samantha said. "Can you make it quick?"

Pammy looked down at her sneakers, her ripped and faded cargo pants, and the T-shirt with a picture of a goat and the words DON'T WORRY, I GOAT THIS. "I'll be back in a jiffy," she said.

"The shirt," Hank called after her. "And the shoes. *And* the pants!"

"*Everything?*" Pammy yelled from inside.

"Yes," Hank told her.

"This town ain't Bend, Oregon, that's for sure," Pammy called back.

Hank smiled grimly at Samantha, who, thank God, thought to scroll through her phone while waiting for

Pammy. It gave Ella a little breathing room. Things were moving too fast. Just a few days ago, none of this was happening. She was living her normal life. And now . . .

Her world was upside down.

In the sixty excruciating seconds Pammy was gone—during which she let one F-bomb fly from her bedroom—Ella exchanged a look with Hank that said, *This is going to be an interesting dinner.*

He silently concurred with his own look.

Ten seconds later, Pammy came out in a cute sundress. "It's my emergency dress," she said, out of breath to Hank. "You can pack it and it doesn't wrinkle."

"Shall we?" Samantha asked Hank, and stuck her hand through his elbow.

"Let's go," he said to all of them.

Ella could tell it was his apology for paying more attention to Samantha than to them.

Why had she said yes to this crazy idea of working on the movie again? She was torturing herself.

Ella discovered that Pammy was a fast walker. She was too. But they stayed behind Hank and Samantha all the way across the street to the yacht club.

Who would dare get in front of Samantha Drake, unless it was to put a trench coat over a puddle for her so she could avoid getting her fine kid slippers wet, or her Jimmy Choos, or whatever it was she wore? The woman commanded attention.

Even Pammy felt it. She leaned over to Ella and said, "If we walk in front of her, I'll bet she'll freak."

"Well, maybe not freak," she whispered back. "But I think she likes to be in charge."

"Tell me about it," Pammy said. "She's obviously crushing on Hank already. As per usual." She huffed.

"You're the only woman I know who doesn't fall for him right away."

"Pammy, we used to *live* together." Not long, only four months, and they'd started out saying it was all about saving money, and Ella's family had had no idea because her mother never would have approved. They thought she was living with a girlfriend from high school (who covered for her).

Dear God, Ella had been so young. Practically a baby. But their love had felt so big, so real. It had felt like a forever love. "I did fall for him at one time, remember?" she said to Pammy. "And it was pretty immediate."

"Yeah, light years ago that happened," said Pammy. "Someday Hank'll meet someone who doesn't think he's the cat's meow right away, and maybe she'll be the woman for him. If love even exists."

Hank and Samantha reached the door of the yacht club. He opened it for her, and she walked in with a toss of her head.

"Guys!" Hank held the door open.

"Go in," said Ella. "I have to fix my shoe first."

"Okay," he said, looking vaguely worried.

"We're fine," Ella said, and winked at him. "Give us just a second."

He got her drift—she was going to prep Pammy. "See you in a sec," he said, and followed Samantha inside.

Ella pulled a lipstick out of her purse and applied some to her lips. "You want some?" She held it up. It was a nice neutral shade.

"So this is the part where I go glam," Pammy said.

"Not if you don't want to," Ella said.

Pammy rolled her eyes.

"If you don't believe in makeup, I respect that," Ella said. "Or if you just don't like it."

Pammy rolled her eyes again.

"Okay, sorry I asked." Ella put the lipstick away.

"I'm not offended," Pammy said. "I'll take some so the rich yachtees and the fancy matrons inside won't talk about me that much. They'll talk anyway, but maybe not as much if I make an effort."

"Who cares about them?" Ella shrugged. "Do it for you."

"Whatever." Pammy suffered through the application.

"Smack your lips."

Pammy smacked.

Ella leaned back. "There. You're naturally gorgeous, but this gives you a little polish. And that might give you more confidence." A car rolled past them, and someone inside waved at Ella. She couldn't see who it was. "Before we go in, I just wanted to say you're awesome, and don't let anyone inside make you feel otherwise."

"I'm a world-class woodworker," Pammy said. "I never forget that I totally rock. It's a hassle trying to blend in sometimes, is all. I don't want to bother, but there are moments when I need to try. Like when I'm with Hank and all his VIP friends."

"I get your frustration," Ella said. "But back to what you were saying about Hank. He isn't so superficial that he'll fall in love with someone just because she's a challenge. Oh, and love exists." Ella knew. She knew from experience. She'd just watched the (Former) Love of Her Life opening the door for another woman.

"I don't know if I'll ever experience it," Pammy said.

"If you remember only one thing I ever tell you, Pammy, it's this: Let go and let love."

"Okay, Miss Love Doctor," Pammy said. "I'll let go

and let love. As if that'll ever happen. Shall we go inside? I'm starved."

Ella was too. But not for love at any cost. She had her pride, and whatever Hank said about wanting to catch up with her, to be friends, she was going to keep him at arm's length.

# CHAPTER ELEVEN

Three o'clock in the morning, and Hank was still awake. How could he sleep with Ella next door? He never slept well the night before he first joined a movie set anyway.

There was a knock on the wall behind his headboard.

*Ella.*

All kinds of ideas swirled through his head, every one of them totally inappropriate. *Get real, Rogers. She's not going to jump in the sack with you.*

Nevertheless, he felt some hope that maybe, just maybe, Ella was at least thinking about him too. Even if she just wanted to chat, he took that as a good sign. He reached up and knocked back. "Hey," he said in a daytime voice, "you're up too?"

But there was no answer. That was weird.

Maybe he should check on her.

He got out of bed, threw on a robe—because he was in the habit of sleeping in the buff now that he could afford luxury Egyptian cotton bedsheets—and opened his door. Good. No squeaky hinges. He padded ten feet to his left to her door, which was closed, like his.

He thought back to just a few hours before, how she'd gone upstairs after she'd sat at the kitchen table with him and Pammy. They'd talked about Samantha and how she and Pammy had stood outside the yacht club after dinner and waited for Samantha's assistant to come pick her up. Samantha had told Pammy all about her ex-husbands. But when the assistant drove up and Pammy offered to take Samantha out to play pool at the Blind Tiger, Samantha had clammed up and ignored her. Didn't even say goodbye after Pammy opened the car door for her.

They all decided that Samantha was insecure. Bada-boom. Instant analysis. And then they'd gone out for one round of pool at the Blind Tiger themselves, and had a couple of drinks when they should not have, but it had been a lot of fun. Especially with Ella, even though she was doing her best not to talk directly to him. Pammy was her buffer.

Even so, she beat both him and Pammy at pool, and according to the bet they'd made, that meant she didn't have to do the dishes the next two days back at the house, a heady prize to win.

Now Hank wondered, should he open her bedroom door? Or just knock?

He'd better knock. Of course. What was he thinking? He needed to consider her a virtual *stranger*. That night, at the dinner table, he'd been mesmerized by how much she didn't need him. In his head, in between bursts of conversation with his tablemates, he'd cursed the worst curse words he could think of and downed more Scotch.

The truth was, he kept finding out over and over in the two days since he'd come to Charleston, Ella was great without him.

Really great.

Her door remained closed. He stared at the panel

probably thirty seconds more, imagining her in a silky negligee, and then headed back to his room.

But right before he crossed the threshold, her door opened, and she poked her head out. She looked very sleepy. Her hair was every which way. He saw the edge of a floral nightgown, the strap sliding down her shoulder.

He stopped. Tensed.

"What's going on?" she said in the throaty midnight voice he remembered so well. "Is everything all right?"

"Oh, sure." He tried his best to sound like a good guy who didn't have errant sex thoughts. "I heard you knock on the wall. So I thought maybe you needed something. You know, like a glass of water."

She drew in her chin. "A glass of water?" She gifted him with a small grin. "I can get that myself. But thanks."

"No problem," he said.

"Besides, I never knocked." She sounded perfectly serious.

"You didn't?"

"No."

"Isn't your bed on the other side of our connecting wall?"

She shook her head. "No. Between the two windows."

"Oh," he said. "I forgot. So . . . you didn't get out of bed?"

"No."

"Did you hear the knock on the wall?"

She shook her head. "I was in a deep sleep until I heard you knock on my door."

That was right. She always used to sleep like a log.

He scratched his head. "Maybe I was dreaming."

"That was probably it." She paused. "You did that a couple of times when we were . . . together."

"Oh, yeah." It seemed like an intimate memory to talk about.

"Good night." She lingered a second longer than he expected she would, which meant his mind went back to its very debauched thoughts.

"Good night," he said back.

She smiled a little shyly and pulled her door shut.

That was that.

When he got back to bed, Hank pulled the sheets up very carefully and lay on his back, staring at the ceiling. He was thinking about Ella, about the old days, when she'd had the occasional nightmare and would wake him and tell him about it. Most of the times she'd snuggle up next to him and go back to sleep. And other times, she'd want him to make love to her, when the city was quiet, save for the occasional siren and muffled laughter or talking coming from the street four stories below. Either way, he'd made sure she was happy again. And then he'd always wait until he heard her even breathing before he fell back asleep too. He'd felt it was his duty as her boyfriend to ensure her a sweet, untroubled slumber.

Now he thought back on those nights and realized he'd never been happier. He'd loved feeling needed by her. He'd mattered.

*They'd* mattered.

The ceiling was boring. Hank's eyelids started feeling heavy. He lifted his head off the pillow and took one last glance at the portrait of the three little boys on the wall, in deep shadow now. They must have been brothers. Or cousins. He thought about how the canvas had looked in daylight, how the boys had stood so plainly, their faces holding nothing back, that staid black carriage and the house in the background.

Every day was a new adventure, their expressions said.

Had they been going somewhere in that carriage? Or had it been bringing a visitor to them? Either way, they'd have been able to create a make-believe quest around whatever was being commemorated in the painting, Hank was sure.

He yawned and remembered feeling like every day was an adventure. He remembered being a boy who had brothers. He was lucky to still have them. He needed to call them more.

The final words he thought before he fell asleep were *I need to pay attention to the people in my life*. The last vision he had before he nodded off was Ella's face at her bedroom door.

Tuesday morning, Hank's alarm went off at seven. He and Ella had to be on the set at eight, and it was a ten-minute drive. They were playing it close. Luckily, Hank could get in and out of a shower fast. And there was no need to get too worried. Today was only a read-through. A half day at most. He sat up, grabbed the robe at the foot of the bed, and heard a distant, steady pelleting of water against tile coming from the downstairs shower. Must be Ella. Pammy had told them last night she didn't have to be at Beau and Lacey's big house until nine and that she'd wait for the bathroom until they were done.

So Ella was totally naked and in the same house, and Hank never thought that scenario would happen again. But here they were. He hadn't even heard her wake up and walk past his bedroom door.

He stood at the top of the stairs and smelled coffee percolating. Ella again, no doubt. He'd seen a Mr. Coffee in the pantry. Sometimes it was nice to skip the coffee pods and drink the freshly brewed stuff from the pot.

He'd have to grab a cup before she got out so he could have some *without* hazelnut creamer in it.

What an idiot he'd been to concoct that story.

He was standing there gulping it down when she whizzed by the kitchen in a short towel, her hair dripping wet, and took off up the stairs without a word. Maybe she thought he was still in bed.

Seeing her like that was enough to torture him for the rest of the day.

And then he heard the hair dryer start up, and she was humming a song from the musical she'd just finished. The song about her rotten ex-lover whom she'd gotten completely over.

"That's me," he said aloud as he rinsed out his cup and put it on the side of the sink. He usually had two, but he'd get the second one at the set. There'd be food there too. All he had to do was jump in the shower and get dressed in half an hour.

Entirely doable.

Unless you have three ladies show up at your door, unannounced, with a box of Krispy Kreme original glazed doughnuts and chocolate-covered ones. With sprinkles.

Man oh man.

"Well, hey there, Hank Rogers, you handsome thing," said the oldest one in a thick Southern drawl. She was very attractive, probably mid-forties or so. "Don't mind us. We're here to tell Ella to break a leg on her first day on the set. You too." She beamed in her yellow suit. "I'm Miss Thing."

So this was Miss Thing!

She fluttered her fingers at him in a little wave and grinned.

He was glad he'd just had his first cup of coffee. "Come on in," he said, and grinned back.

The other two were Ella's age, beauties both. One wore a flowery skirt and white blouse, her hair in a ponytail. The look was very romantic and feminine.

"Hello, Mr. Rogers," she said with a warm smile in a lighter Southern accent than Miss Thing's. She was carrying the boxes of doughnuts. "I'm Macy."

"And I'm Greer," the third woman cut in with a twinkle in her eye. She wore a sleek pantsuit and her hair loose in a sexy wave. "We're Ella's colleagues and BFFs."

"Nice to meet you all," he said. "And please call me Hank."

"*Hank*," they all said at once.

It made him happy, somehow, that they said his name all together. *Like three sweet angels*, he couldn't help thinking. Or enforcers. He couldn't decide. These were Ella's colleagues and best friends . . . he'd better be on his best behavior. He wanted them on his side.

"I hate to leave you, but I need to shower," he said.

Miss Thing started fanning herself. "Lawd, it's hot in here."

"Do you want a glass of water?" he asked. Her two friends didn't seem too worried.

"I'm fine." Miss Thing walked to the sofa and perched on the edge, her feet turned demurely to the side, her hands folded in her lap. "I'll just sit here a minute."

"Good," he said. "Make yourself at home. Ella and I have to leave here in"—he looked at the old clock on the mantel—"twenty-five minutes."

"We understand," said Macy. "We'll head upstairs to see her, if that's where she is."

"Yes, she just ran by in a towel," he said.

"Oho!" Miss Thing chuckled.

Greer made a face at her that Hank caught, then redirected her gaze to him. "You go shower, Hank. We will see you again, I'm sure."

He grinned again. "I'm sure too. See you soon. In about five minutes, actually. I gotta move fast."

"Ta-ta 'til then!" Miss Thing called after him. "We'll save you a couple of doughnuts."

"Thanks," he said.

"Bye, Hank!" Macy said too. "Have a good shower!"

It wasn't as if he had to go far. Just down the hall. But they were sending him off like he was going to war or something.

He waved awkwardly. "Yeah. See ya."

The whole time in the shower, he thought about how Ella had just been in it before him. And now she must be upstairs laughing and chatting with her friends. Was she still in that towel? Why didn't she have a robe? Maybe she'd left it at home by accident. He hoped she'd never go back and get it.

The door swung open a second with a small whine, and he felt a slight draft.

"Hello?" he called from behind the vinyl curtain. He was in the middle of washing his hair.

Then it swung shut again.

He could swear he'd locked that door! But it was old. Maybe the latch mechanism didn't work right. He scrubbed under his left arm. And then his right. Maybe it was Pammy getting up. All that noise out front had probably woken her and she stumbled half asleep into the bathroom, forgetting he was in there.

It was time to get out anyway.

He rubbed down with a small white cotton towel, more like a washcloth. It was too small, but it was also nice and rough, the way he liked towels. None of that fabric softener stuff for him. He'd buy a good set of towels for the house today online—a small gift to Beau and Lacey—and get them sent overnight. He'd wash them himself in the big house tomorrow. That was one thing he still knew how to do: use a washer and dryer. Too many of his assistants ruined his clothes, at least the ones he didn't send to the dry cleaner.

He looked around for his robe. Damn. He'd left it upstairs.

"Wait a sec—" he murmured. He hadn't forgotten his robe. He'd been naked underneath it. He'd met the women at the front door in it. He'd walked to the bathroom in it!

Whatever had happened to it, he had no choice now. He'd have to do the towel thing too.

# CHAPTER TWELVE

Ella was so nervous about going to the movie set Tuesday morning. Would she trip over some wires when she got there? Would anyone look at her and talk about her behind their hand to someone else? Would they say, "That's the woman who came on board because of Hank? Maybe she can't even act?"

Or did only Isabel and Samantha know how she got the part?

She had no idea. She simply had to hold her head up high.

"You'll be amazing," her mother said that morning as she held Ella's cheeks between her hands. She had tears in her eyes. "Your papa would be so proud. He *is* proud." She looked up to the ceiling and blew a kiss. Luckily, they were in the living room, not the kitchen, where Jupiter would have been the recipient of Mama's affection. No, her kiss went all the way up to Heaven.

"Thanks, Mama." Ella had tears in her eyes too. "It's not a big part, but yes, Papa would be excited for me."

"Don't forget your *nonnas*!" said Nonna Boo. "We're proud too."

She and Nonna Sofia were snug in the new recliners Cosmo had sent down from New York. They were ergonomically designed, he said, especially for beautiful ladies from Sicily who didn't feel like pushing themselves out of their chairs. These chairs pushed them out without their help. The seat cushions rose up and gently placed the *nonnas* right onto the carpet.

"That's right," said Nonna Sofia. "Samantha Drake better watch out."

Ella heard that over and over that morning. She'd stopped by her mother's, leaving Hank on his own with that big box of doughnuts her friends had left them. At a nerve-wracking time like this, she needed her family too.

But now she was on the movie set. She'd been preparing for it in her head, and it was nothing—absolutely nothing—like what she'd imagined. Nobody was lounging around with clipboards, staring at the morning arrivals, ready to size them up. In fact, when Ella got to the portion of a block of King Street that had been cordoned off and was surrounded by trucks, including the "Desi" and "Lucy" restroom truck, which was found on most movie sets, she couldn't find anyone, and that was because they weren't there, according to a police officer watching all the equipment. She'd been supposed to meet the cast and crew in a nearby music hall, a sort of glorified bar with a massive floor and a stage at one end, a popular watering hole and music venue for regional and even national acts. They were going to do a read-through on chairs on the stage, and on the floor was going to be another big breakfast spread.

Ella was legitimately hungry now. She hadn't had time to eat at her mother's, and that had concerned both Mama and the *nonnas*. They'd tried to get her to have a little grappa to soothe her, but she reminded them that nine o'clock in the morning wasn't anywhere close to happy hour. She needed to be sharp on set.

She hoped Hank wouldn't be watching her, to make sure she was living up to the description of her he'd given the producer and director. On the other hand, she hoped Samantha would be more interactive today. After all, they were doing several scenes together.

Her nerves came back when she walked through the doors of the music hall. Lots of people milled about, plates in hand, filling up at the breakfast buffet. She caught the back of Hank's head and her heart leaped. She didn't want to be happy to see him, but she was. Samantha was next to him, her hair done up in a gorgeous chignon. They were talking animatedly as they strolled over to a picnic table and sat down. No one joined them, Ella saw.

"Hi, I'm Ella Mancini," she said to a person with Bluetooth earbuds and an iPad, not a clipboard.

"Great," the girl said, and tapped on her iPad. "Gotcha signed in. Why don't you get some breakfast? The read-through starts in twenty."

"Okay," said Ella, and then was left alone. People walked right by her and didn't even notice she was there. In this crowd, she was a big nobody. But that didn't mean she had to be ashamed of her small role. No, it meant that she was a genuine actor who took parts for the love of the dramatic arts. She did this because it was like breathing to her. She couldn't imagine never being able to act in a play. Or in this case, a movie. She had to be around a stage or a set. Not that she had a whole lot of experience on a set, but she had a little. She'd been in several commercials in New York.

"Fine," she said under her breath. And then realized, with utter shock, that she hadn't read the script they'd sent over for her to peruse the night before—

*And she'd never even noticed.*

Because she'd been out with Pammy and Hank at dinner, with his professional cohorts. And when they got home several hours later, Ella did her best to avoid Hank by making Pammy cheese toast under the oven broiler, which fascinated Pammy, who had only used toaster ovens and pop-up toasters before that night. But then Hank wanted some cheese toast because Ella had bought really good Jarlsberg and Irish cheddar, and while she was cutting it, she realized she did too, especially because she'd bought a loaf of brioche, her favorite kind of bread.

So they sat around the kitchen table eating gooey cheese toast and drinking Prosecco, and they never discussed the movie for even one second. Ella tried not to directly address Hank, focusing instead on how Samantha had behaved to Pammy outside the yacht club and what it was like for Pammy to grow up in Oregon. And then right as they'd decided to call it quits for the night, they went to play pool at the Blind Tiger. And there Pammy asked Hank how he'd met Ella, and he went through the whole Serendipity 3 story very quickly. He'd been a busboy. He'd met Ella there and vowed to meet her again, four years later, after she graduated.

And they had. Neither one had forgotten their date.

"And that was that," he said, and then had lousy luck sinking all the solid balls on the green baize top of the pool table.

*At least for a while, that was that*, Ella had thought, and went on to beat both Hank and Pammy at pool. And while she appreciated that Hank didn't linger over the details of their relationship with a bunch of sappy, romantic comments, she also felt sad that their love story didn't matter anymore.

And now here she was the next morning standing in a music hall, picking up a paper plate to fill it with eggs and grits and bacon. The brave Mancini in her decided she was going to be social and sit at a table with people she didn't know and leave Hank and Samantha to themselves. She wasn't going to run after either one of them.

Of course, she wasn't supposed to anyway. They were the stars.

So she sat with two camera grips and a makeup artist. They'd all been to school in North Carolina to learn their trade, and over the course of their training, they'd become NASCAR fans, which she knew nothing about. But she managed, somehow, to engage with each of them and have a good time. *And* finish off her plate. *That* would make Mama happy.

However, Ella wasn't happy. She watched Hank and Samantha ignore everyone and stay chitchatting at their own private picnic table. Samantha was beautiful when she was engaged. It was why the world and the camera loved her. The expressions she could conjure!

She was using them to full effect on Hank.

"Look at the lovebirds," one of the camera grips said, and laughed. He sounded a little bitter.

"Isn't it too early for that kind of talk?" asked the makeup artist, with a wry lift to one of her brows. "I mean, come on. It's his first day. Give him a break."

"Those kind of people don't work on the world's usual timelines," the grip said. "And ten years' difference in age is nothing. Especially with the miracles plastic surgeons work these days."

"That kind of flirting is everywhere," the other grip said. "They're no different from us. If I were straight, I'd want to hook up with Samantha the first day I met her if I had the chance, wouldn't you?"

The first grip shrugged. "Sure. But gossiping is fun. It makes the day go faster."

Ella didn't know what to say. She focused on finishing up her coffee. Inside, she felt stupid for caring that Hank and Samantha were already being talked about as a couple.

"Have you ever met either one of them?" the second grip, the one without a chip on his shoulder, asked her.

"Yes," said Ella. She wasn't going to lie and be caught out about it. "I had dinner with them last night."

"Whoa," said the makeup girl. "That's a big deal."

Ella balled up her napkin, picked up her plate and plastic utensils, and stood. "I'd never met Samantha before. But Hank and I are friends from back in our audition days in New York."

"Ohhh," said the grouchy grip. His neck got slightly red.

"Just friends," Ella said. "And we lost touch ten years ago. But I have to be honest because you'll probably hear this from another source: Without Hank, I wouldn't have this part."

"Really," the second grip said, sounding fascinated.

"I know I can handle it," Ella said. "But when the other actor withdrew, Hank got me in. I live here and do a lot of community theater. I gave up my professional acting ambitions long ago. I'm a full-time matchmaker. My colleagues are filling in for me at work, and my part is very small. But it'll be fun."

"I love your attitude," said the makeup girl. "It's refreshing to see someone not so ruthlessly ambitious, who's here for fun. God, I've almost forgotten what that feels like, doing this gig for fun."

Ella felt a twinge of guilt. She'd been daydreaming about making a comeback. About getting a second chance. That was ruthlessly ambitious, wasn't it? And she was agreeing to live with her ex just so she could get a part in *Forever Road*!

"But you have a lot to prove too," the first grip said. "I feel that in you."

"I guess I do," said Ella. "How many actors get to be in a scene with Samantha Drake? I'm in three, and I'm really grateful."

The makeup girl smiled. "Thanks for letting us know how you fit in. There's nothing worse than finding stuff out that you wish you'd already known before you spout off at the mouth. Which we just did." She angled her head toward Samantha and Hank's table.

"No big deal." Ella chuckled. "But I've made it a practice not to gossip on set." Looking back on her short couple of years working as an actor in New York, she saw that that was true. She'd been a professional. She'd been the same way in community theater—refused to become involved in the various soap operas that developed over the course of a show. "It's tough, considering how juicy the stories can get, but I got more jobs the less I was involved in the drama."

"You're speaking in past tense," said the second grip. "Girlfriend, you're here. *Now.* You're back."

Ella felt a thrill at those words. "Wow," she said, "thanks for helping me feel I belong."

"I want to hear about your matchmaking job," the makeup girl said.

"Me too," said the grouchy grip. "I have no luck in love."

But the read-through was upon them. The girl with the Bluetooth earbuds stood up in front of everyone at a mic and told them to find their places. A rush of nerves shot through Ella. She couldn't believe she was doing a read-through without ever having seen the script.

She was living dangerously, she supposed. And why not? What did she really have to lose here? It wasn't like she had a lot of lines to say, anyway. Not to mention that she had Two Love Lane and a very rich life in Charleston. She glanced over and saw Hank, still talking to Samantha. He caught her eye—she saw him light up, which made her heart beat faster—and he gestured for her to come over.

She gestured back that it was time to go to the stage: she pointed at an invisible watch on her wrist, then pointed at the circle of chairs. But she smiled too. They could be friends. That wouldn't hurt anything, as long as they were friends from across the room, like now.

*Don't believe it*, a warning voice inside reminded her. *Even from across the room is too close.*

Samantha caught her smile right before it disappeared and looked pointedly away, moving toward the stage like a swan. Ella had to wonder whatever happened to girl power when it came to Samantha. Or was she all about it, and Ella simply didn't know her well enough to understand how she worked? If Ella were a big star, she would never look away from another woman in a smaller role who was only trying to be friendly—

And had secret, nefarious plans to make Samantha her best friend.

Oh, well. Maybe that was what kept Samantha so removed, at least from her. She might sense Ella wanted to ride her coattails to some great acting role. Even famous people wanted to be valued for themselves, right? Surely, they didn't want to be seen as nothing more than a rung on a ladder to someone else's dream.

Hank had told Ella just last night walking home from playing pool at the Blind Tiger that it had been great to be there. No one had bothered him. Usually, he had people cozying up to him all the time, wanting something from him. It got old, he'd said.

Pammy had retorted, "Save your famous-people problems for people who care."

And Hank had challenged her to an arm wrestle for that remark once they got back to the house. Apparently, they used to do that growing up, and they were fairly evenly matched. A few minutes later, they were sitting at the kitchen table again, and he won, but Pammy said it was because she was laughing so hard and that she'd beat him next time. Hank then challenged Ella to a thumb wrestle, and she said no, her thumb needed working out, and she only played games she could win, like Scrabble.

They vowed to play Scrabble soon. And next thing they knew, Pammy left the kitchen. She'd drunk too much at the Blind Tiger. Ella and Hank had to awkwardly head to their rooms at the same time, so Hank stayed downstairs to wait while Ella was in the bathroom upstairs getting ready for bed. She hustled and jumped into bed and forgot to shut her door. So he shut it, and before he did, said, "Good night. Tonight was fun," and she said, "Yes, it was. I'm glad I beat you at pool." He chuckled and said, "What a gracious winner you are," and she laughed, and said, "Thanks for including me in the dinner." And he replied, "My pleasure."

And then they both sort of froze in silence at the word "pleasure" and he shut the door, but too slowly, and she lay in bed a whole hour thinking of how cute he was, especially his butt and his shoulders when he'd leaned over the pool table. And then she tried to forget by remembering her birthday that long-ago night, when he'd forgotten it, and she'd gotten no ring or surprise party but just that news about him getting the movie, and how the next morning, they'd split up.

And she cried again before she fell asleep.

Why was she crying all these years later?

# CHAPTER THIRTEEN

Now in the music hall Ella was glad when her new friends on the crew agreed they'd have to have breakfast again with her soon, and she headed to the stage, her knees wobbly.

The chair backs all had nametags taped to them. Ella sat down on hers. Then Hank went over to his chair, on the opposite side of the circle.

Good. The farther away, the better.

But then he pulled off his tag and came straight over to her. She felt her face flush. *Calm down*, she chided herself. *It's just Hank trying to be friends.*

She really wished he wouldn't. She needed to focus on her part. And she didn't need that old crush feeling to rear its ugly head and send her right back into the tailspin she'd experienced a decade ago.

She deserved better. She'd *earned* better. And anyone who wanted to be in her trusted inner circle needed to merit that space.

But Hank removed the tag on the chair next to hers on the right anyway. It belonged to someone named Ida. He brought Ida's tag to his old chair. Then he came and sat down next to Ella. He crumpled his nametag and tossed it into a nearby trash can.

Slam dunk.

Did anything go wrong for him?

"Hi," he said, his eyes warm, his whole body exuding positivity.

All around them, people were finding their seats, laughing, talking loudly.

"Hey," she said lightly back.

"You'll do great." His gaze was a little too perceptive, as if he could sense all her rattled feelings. About the movie. About *him*.

She prayed he couldn't sense any of the latter. That would be too humiliating. Let him think she never gave him a moment's thought. "Thanks," she said. "You'll do great too."

There was an awkward pause.

"Tonight—" he began.

"After this is over—" she started to say.

And they both clammed up.

"Go ahead," he said.

She shifted in her seat. "I was just going to say that after the read-through, I'm going to my office for lunch then coming back for a costume fitting this afternoon. If you want to come and see where I work."

She instantly regretted the offer. But it was too late, and the truth was, she'd spoken impulsively because she wanted him to see how successful she was, how her own heartbreak hadn't held her back from becoming who she wanted to be.

"I'd love to," he said, "but I probably won't be able to. We'll see. For the next week, I'll be booked from seven a.m. to somewhere around eleven p.m., probably."

"Wow." She had to admit to herself—she was disappointed.

"Pammy knows she won't see much of me," he said. "But a little is better than nothing."

Against her best judgment, Ella was thinking the same thing. Catching a glimpse of Hank was better than not seeing him at all. But then she struggled to remember—and succeeded!—that she'd be so much better off when he flew back to New York. She could go back to her normal life. Her *safe* life.

"Thanks for asking, though," he said. "I'd love to see your office."

"Maybe someday. What were you going to say about tonight?" She shoved aside the very reckless hope that they could hang out again and tried to focus on how she should find something to do that night apart from him, so he'd see she had a whirlwind social life. Not that she did lately, apart from her theater activities.

"I was wondering if—" He had to stop again.

Isabel had started to yell at someone on the phone. She was standing in the middle of the circle. "I've had it, Saul. Get your grandmother on the line. *Now.*"

"Her teenage son acts out a lot," said Hank under his breath.

Ella looked back over her shoulder toward the agitated director and saw Samantha behind her, looking at Ella and Hank, her mouth grim. Ella worked up a smile and waved at her. *Insecure*, that was all Samantha was. She wasn't a mean girl. Mean girls were getting their comeuppance these days, thank God, and most women were hyperaware of that fact and doing their best not to be part of the problem.

*Most* women. Hopefully, Samantha had gotten the

PSA message that kindness was in and girl power was, well . . . empowering!

Samantha gave her a limp wave back, and Ella's heart lifted. See? She wasn't so bad. The woman named Ida sat to Samantha's left—Hank's original chair. She had really cute corkscrew curls. She waved at Ella too. So Ella waved at her.

Everyone was making nice. And it was a huge relief.

"Okay, people!" Isabel said above the chatter. "Let's get going."

And the reading took off. Ella was enthralled. It was a great script, and she kept getting goose bumps. This movie was going to be good, really good, maybe worthy of awards if the script was anything to go by.

She felt so lucky to be a part of it!

As compelling as the lines were, she couldn't help being very aware of Hank's thigh so close to hers. And once their knees even bumped. She flinched and moved away. He didn't seem to notice because it happened right in the middle of one of his best lines, when he was telling Samantha's character he'd stolen half a million dollars from her closet—money she'd stolen from her dying sister—and used it all up gambling in Vegas.

The tension between the two stars, both of them playing people who'd made very bad choices, was riveting, Ella thought. And she could tell everyone else did, too, by the way they followed the dialogue between Samantha and Hank, swiveling their heads as if they were at a tennis match.

And now . . . now Ella realized why Hank had moved his seat. It wasn't because of *her*. It was because he wanted to be able to look directly across the circle at Samantha. And she looked directly at him. When they spoke their lines, it was like an invisible electric current snapped and sparked between them. If they had sat next to each other, it would have been awkward, almost impossible, to maintain eye contact without bumping legs and shoulders. And the full dramatic effect of owning the entire stage between them would have been lost.

With each passing minute, Ella felt smaller and smaller. She wished she could move to another chair. She'd been stupid to think Hank wanted to sit next to her for any reasons other than professional ones. She was acting like a freshman in high school, really. What was she expecting next, for him to pass her a note asking her to meet him behind the bleachers?

She should be relieved he was all about his professional concerns and not about her.

And then, inexplicably, she started thinking about a very strong memory she had of them at their apartment in New York. . . .

"Ella!" Isabel's voice came to her, sharp, almost annoyed.

Ella looked down at the script and nearly jumped out of her skin. She'd missed her line! Hank's character had left the scene—which was in Samantha's character's apartment, and now Ella's character had shown up to give Samantha's character her undivided cousinly attention.

Ella didn't have time to berate herself. Instantly, she became an ex-con from Texas. "It's been too long," she told Samantha, "way too long. Got any wine?"

And the scene proceeded. Ella had three more lines. She and Samantha read them well together, so that was encouraging.

Even so, Ella's face was burning. What would Hank, the director, Samantha, and all the cast think of her daydreaming during the read-through and missing her line?

She'd nearly forgotten her screwup by the end of the

reading because the script was that good. So she didn't even remember that she should probably slink offstage. She was too exhilarated. The final page, which was totally owned by Hank and Samantha, had made her tear up and laugh, all at the same time.

"So," she said to Hank with a grin, "wow."

He grinned back. "I know. Pretty incredible, huh?"

"I'd say. I'm glad the other guy . . ." She intentionally didn't say Frampton's name and lowered her voice. "What I mean to say is, I'm surprised they didn't call you first."

He leaned in a little closer. "They did, and I said I wasn't interested."

"Really? But it's such a great script!"

"Think about it, Ella." He picked up his folding chair and hers, put them in a nearby stack, then turned to look at her. His expression said it all. He hadn't been interested in taking the part because he knew it was filming in Charleston, and she was here.

"Oh," she said, her stomach dropping.

He walked back toward her.

"But you shouldn't have—" she began. What else could she say? It was *his* business.

"It's a moot point, isn't it?" he said. "I'm here. I got a second chance. And this time, I said yes."

"I can see why you'd take it. This script is incredible."

"It wasn't the script," he said. "As I told you when I arrived."

"*Hank.*"

"I gotta go." And he did. He was pulled away by the costume designer and the producer. And then Isabel joined the group. They were walking with great purpose to the exit to the lobby, probably to head outside, down the street, and to Hank's trailer on the set, where they could chat in private about whatever it was they needed to talk about. And then Hank stopped. Pulled out his phone.

Ella's phone purred. *Please let it be Hank*, she thought. No matter how wrong it was to feel that way, she did. Sure enough, Ancient History was on the line. "Yes?" she asked, striving to sound cool.

He looked over at her. "I meant to ask you earlier if tonight you can hang out with Pammy. I got the impression from her last night that you two are already bonding. She really likes you. And I feel like this is a great opportunity to, you know, have her listen to someone smart she respects."

"Sure. We'll talk. Maybe we'll do something very Charleston-y together." Ella couldn't help feeling disappointed he wasn't going to be there.

"Aw, that's nice," he said. "I have something I need to go to tonight, or I'd try to tag along."

Oh, she'd have liked that! The mere idea left her a little short of breath. "Won't you have movie stuff to do every night?" It was silly that they were speaking on the phone while they were looking at each other from across the music hall floor.

But it was romantic, too. She couldn't deny it. And at that moment, she didn't want to.

Hank didn't seem to care that he was holding up Isabel, the producer, and the costume designer. "My schedule is tight," he admitted. "And you're going to have some late nights on the set too. You can't be with Pammy all the time."

"It wouldn't be good for her, anyway," Ella said. "She needs to make her own friends."

"True. But anyway, thanks. At least for tonight "

"My pleasure," she said, using the same words he had last night.

He shot her a long look.

She stared back, fluttered her fingers at him the way Miss Thing waved. Had she wanted to tease him with *My pleasure*? Sure she did. But maybe she was also mocking him since he'd told her the exact same thing the evening before and had left her alone in the dark to have illicit thoughts about him.

Let him think whatever he wanted.

He and his cohorts disappeared through the swinging doors that led to the lobby.

Samantha appeared at her elbow. "What were you thinking, Ella?"

Ella, flushed still from chatting with Hank, turned to her. "I'm sorry?"

Samantha lofted a brow. "Your line. The one you forgot to say. What were you thinking?"

"Oh." It all came back to her. The cringey moment. So Samantha was going to go there. Ella didn't deserve a break, but still, it wasn't easy to be called out by the female lead. "I'm really sorry."

Samantha laughed. "Darling, I don't care that you forgot your line."

"You *don't*?" Ella regrouped. She'd had hopes Samantha was going to be, if not a friend, someone she could really admire and look up to. Maybe she still could.

"It was only a read-through. Everyone misses a line now and then. I only want to know what was going through your head. You had a look on your face. . . ."

"Oh, what was I *thinking* . . . literally." Ella laughed. And then a low-level hum of embarrassment ran from her head to her toes. She'd been thinking about making love with Hank, the last time they had. She remembered it in great detail, the dress she'd worn (red, with lace-up strings down the back), and the night (they'd attended a concert given by her favorite male solo performer at Madison Square Garden). When they'd returned to the house, Hank had shut the front door behind them and immediately grabbed the strings at the back of her dress and started unlacing. She'd laughed.

He'd said, "When you think about other guys the way I know you were tonight, it's sexy as hell. And I get very jealous."

She'd said, "You don't need to be. Silly." She'd turned to him then, filled with such love for him, and that wonderful longing to be one with him, to show him with her body what she couldn't say in words because sometimes words weren't enough.

They'd had the bawdiest coupling they'd ever had right there by the front door, against the wall. But it had been so much more than great sex. Way more. It had been about love too, *real* love, the kind she never knew existed until she'd met Hank.

Now, with Samantha, she gave a little laugh. "I was thinking about a concert I went to once." She smiled and shrugged. "I know that sounds weird. I mean, why in the middle of a read-through? I think I heard one of the guy's songs right before I got here this morning."

Samantha narrowed her eyes, but she was smiling too. "It must have been an amazing concert," she murmured.

"It was," Ella said, and felt like an idiot.

"Who was it?"

"Justin Bieber."

Samantha clapped her hand over her mouth and stifled a very girlish giggle. "*No.*"

Ella laughed. "Yes. I'm a big fan. Still."

"Who did you go with?" Samantha asked, her tone bright.

Ella's face fell. She was a good actor but a rotten liar.

"I-I can't remember." She swallowed. "No, I do. A couple of girlfriends from high school."

"Ah." Samantha gave her a lingering look. "Perhaps I should start listening to Justin Bieber."

"He's awesome," Ella said, and laughed. Nervously. Like she'd been caught in a big lie, which she had. Not about Justin, who would always hold a special place in her heart, something Hank had been amused by but had never made fun of. He'd bought her those tickets, after all. But she'd lied about whom she'd gone with.

She suspected that somehow, Samantha was on to her.

But how could she be?

And why would Samantha want to know what she was thinking, anyway?

Samantha laughed too. "Do you have plans for lunch? Want to join me in my trailer?"

Oh, God. *Samantha was reaching out to her.* Ella was astounded. But she had to go to Two Love Lane at lunchtime. Miss Thing had said she'd had to talk to Ella about something very, very important, but she wanted to tell Ella in person because it was so mind-blowing. She hinted that it involved baking, which seemed the opposite of mind-blowing to Ella. So she was more intrigued than ever.

"I wish I could," Ella said. "But today I can't. I have to get back to the office for a quick meeting."

"Oh, that's right," said Samantha. "You have a regular job as a matchmaker."

"It's Monday through Friday—and sometimes weekends—but I wouldn't call it regular," Ella said with a wry grin. "No day is ever the same. And talk about drama."

"I can imagine," said Samantha. "Another time, then. I wanted to ask you a few questions about Hank. You two are friends, and I thought perhaps . . ." She trailed off, but she had a rather wistful smile on her face, which Ella instantly recognized.

Samantha liked Hank. *Like*-liked Hank. As in she was already crushing on him. And she was confiding in Ella. The matchmaker. Duh.

"Oh," Ella said, having put two and two together. None of this attention had been about Samantha wanting to take her down a notch—thank God—but neither had it been about them forging a friendship. Samantha, it seemed, was looking for an alliance of a different kind. "You want to talk about Hank? In terms of . . . ?"

Samantha gave a little shuddering sigh. "You don't know how much I campaigned for him to be in this film. And when Frampton had to leave, I was thrilled Hank finally said yes."

She had it bad.

Ella scratched the side of her nose. She couldn't very well ask Samantha to uphold the principles of girl power and not practice them herself. She wished she didn't have to, because she was violating Hank's privacy—he hadn't disclosed the true nature of their relationship to anyone on the set—but shouldn't she tell Samantha about their romantic past? Wouldn't it be weird not to? Samantha might feel foolish if she found out later, especially since she was confiding in Ella about her crush on Hank.

Ella was a matchmaker, so that was like wearing a big sign on her chest saying, *Tell me your deepest secrets.*

But did professional matchmakers have to divulge their past to their clients?

Ella didn't think so . . . *unless the client wanted to date your old boyfriend.* Not that Samantha was an actual client. But still, Ella never thought she'd run into a problem like this.

There was no way around it. She had to tell Samantha. Hank's privacy would be compromised. But there
was girl power. And Hank would survive. She didn't owe
Hank anything anymore, and she—*and* he—needed to
remember that.

"Samantha," Ella said. "I have to tell you something."

"Yes?"

Ella took a mental breath. "I used to date Hank. I lived
with him, in fact, ten years ago. Not long, and we were
pretty much still kids, now that I look back on it—"

"I know all that," Samantha said, chuckling.

"You *do*?"

"Sure." Samantha lifted a shoulder and dropped it.
"Hank might think he lived in a vacuum before he got
famous, but he didn't."

"You mean—"

"I Googled him," Samantha said. "I mean, my private
detective did. Doesn't everyone do that?"

Ella nodded slowly, remembering how Pammy had
Googled her. "I guess so. Maybe not with the private
detective . . ."

"I make no apologies about my snooping," Samantha
said. "I do it to all my costars. I prefer to call it practic-
ing good security measures."

"I understand you're in a unique situation," Ella said.

"Unique, no," replied Samantha. "I'm not the only
famous person—"

"I meant, unique in that you're part of the point zero
zero zero one percent of the population that is an A-list
movie star," said Ella.

"Right." Samantha folded her arms over her chest.
"There are a few of us around. Mainly in L.A. and New
York, and London, and Paris, and the French Riviera, and

Monte Carlo. Occasionally, we're found in Nashville. We do exist."

Ella knew that. And now the rare species was roaming in Charleston, and quite frankly, they were wreaking havoc in her life. "Okay," she said, "so you don't care that I dated Hank."

"Yes, I *do* care. I lobbied to bring him here because he's an amazing actor I've always wanted to work with, but little did I know I was playing Cupid, too, by insisting he come." Samantha waggled her brows.

Ella laughed out loud. That was one expression she'd never seen on Samantha on the big screen. "You're playing Cupid? How?"

"You and Hank," Samantha said with a soft smile. "He obviously still adores you. In fact, I'm sure you're the reason he's here. He's putting on a good front about the movie, and he's a professional, so he'll do an outstanding job. But he and I have been in the business long enough to have figured out that taking home an Oscar isn't as fulfilling as having a happy personal life."

"Samantha," Ella actually chided her. "Please don't try to get involved. I'm not interested. Hank and I have too much history."

Samantha sighed. "Darling, let's have a little slumber party. Divulge all your secrets to me. I'll sort out your issues with Hank, I promise. What have you got to lose?"

"A lot," said Ella. "My peace."

"Overrated," said Samantha. "You're young. Go wreak havoc."

Ella chuckled. "You're very sweet, but even with the friends I have now, I don't tell them intimate details about my past relationships."

Which was a white lie. Greer, Macy, and Miss Thing knew an awful lot about Hank, things that would make him blush, but they were her very closest friends, and Hank would never know.

"All right," said Samantha, clearly disappointed. "But I can't forget that photo."

"What photo?"

"The one of you two at an ice cream shop in Manhattan. You *were* young, as you said. The Facebook caption read, 'Ella and I on our first date.'"

Ella blinked to hold back the sting of tears. That picture had been taken by a food server at Serendipity 3 the day they'd met up for their first date, four years after Hank had asked her out. She'd put it on social media a few times—so had he. She loved that picture. But it also reminded her that her father had died her senior year at the College of Charleston, and when she'd returned to New York after graduation, things weren't the same. She went out on auditions, knowing Papa was looking down with approval from wherever he was. But she really struggled with the decision to go or not to go to Serendipity 3 to meet Hank. She'd been afraid to return to a place filled with so many memories she'd shared with her father. And she'd remembered what he'd said the last time they'd been there together: Don't let any man get in the way of your dreams.

But she'd wanted to see Hank.

So she'd done it.

And look what had happened as a result. Her whole life since Hank flashed before her eyes. She was alone, she had a job she adored—

And she wasn't an actor on Broadway, television, or in the movies.

*Papa*, she thought now, and turned away from Samantha for a second.

"Are you all right?" Samantha asked.

She nodded and turned back. "I'm fine. I was about to sneeze, is all."

"Very well," said Samantha. She sighed again. "At least we got everything out on the table. And I'm here to help, if you need me."

"Thanks."

"Goodbye, Ella. Until our next scene."

"Goodbye, Samantha. See you then."

Samantha walked away, then turned around. "You're sure I can't meddle?"

"Yes."

Samantha seemed surprised. "You don't care that he's gorgeous and rich and an international celebrity?"

"No."

Samantha shot her a soft smile again. "That's nice. He's more than that, isn't he?"

Ella nodded. "Much more."

"You don't mind that we're going to have two sex scenes? And lots of kissing in between?"

Ella shook her head. It killed her, in a way, as it had when she'd seen his previous movies with love scenes, but what could she do?

"I hoped you'd be jealous," Samantha said.

"Oh, I am."

"Don't be." Samantha waved again dismissively—she had a tendency to do that. "We'll be surrounded by camera people and hot lights. It's torture."

Ella laughed.

Samantha left, and Ella realized they'd been the only two people still in the music hall. Everyone else had gone back to the set.

She needed to get to Two Love Lane and find out Miss Thing's idea. She hoped it was good. Usually, Miss Thing's ideas were outlandish. She lived to be outlandish.

It was her whole vibe. Ella was nervous the idea would be too far out. As she walked to her office, she decided to remain calm and pessimistic.

She also thought about how Samantha was going to kiss Hank. And have fake sex with him.

"It's not your business," she told herself, and walked through the front door of Two Love Lane. When she approached Miss Thing's desk, the office manager threw down her pink feather duster—she'd been dusting her keyboard—and started applying lipstick, which she always did before she was going to make a big pronouncement.

"What's so important?" Ella asked her.

Miss Thing tossed her lipstick into her top drawer. "I know what to do," she said, "about Roberta Ruttle."

# CHAPTER FOURTEEN

Hank had no idea he was being set up when he walked into his trailer after leaving Ella at the music hall. One minute he was talking to Isabel, the producer, and the costume designer, and the next minute, all three of them got phone calls and had to leave.

*Supposedly* had to leave. He had his doubts. Because that was when Samantha walked in, looking gorgeous, smelling like lavender and grass baking in the sun. It was a good, nature-infused smell. And her dress was spot-on, as the English would say, feminine and chic. She'd changed clothes since the read-through.

It was immediately apparent she was up to no good. Which was a complication he had not expected.

"Hello, there," she said. There was something in her eyes, something speculative. It wasn't awful, but he sensed an agenda that involved going beyond talking about the script or venting about the director or someone else working on the film.

"Great to see you," Hank said, and stood. "I gotta go."

"Oh?"

"I have an appointment." That very moment, he decided to go visit Ella, after all. He texted her: *On my way to Two Love Lane.*

"What kind of appointment?" Samantha was awfully nosy. And she'd probably figured out he'd made it up on the spot.

"I'm going to see my friend Ella at her matchmaking agency," he told her.

"Your ex-lover, you mean."

Wow. That was blunt. He opened the door to the trailer and stepped out. "How did you know?"

"She told me." She stepped out too.

He shut the door behind her. He had no idea why Ella would have told Samantha that. It didn't seem like her. He looked down at his phone and saw that Ella had texted back: *Oh, good! See you in a few.*

"It was a long time ago," he told Samantha.

"Why are you so private about it then?"

"Because people on sets talk. Which is why you and I shouldn't be alone in my trailer. You know better. It's a new day in Hollywood."

"But we're in Charleston."

"You know what I mean, and you should be on board with it."

"Oh, I am," she said. "I have a stellar, no-nonsense reputation on all my sets."

"I know that. I have the same, and I guard it well."

"If every once in a while you can't rely on a reputation you've worked hard to earn, what's the point?"

"You can't rely on it," Hank said. "Those days are gone. Isabel, Chad, and Todd just exited my trailer at the same time. I suspect you texted them. And while it goes against their best interests to participate in the gossip mill, maybe someone else saw them leave and you walk in. And there goes your hard-earned reputation. And mine."

"I didn't text them."

He refused to buy that. So he said nothing.

"Okay, I did," she finally admitted. "But I only wanted to get to know you a bit better. We hardly spoke last night at the yacht club. That's all."

He'd take her at her word. But he hadn't gotten his great reputation by being naive either. "We can fix that," he said agreeably. "We can chat over coffee, in public. Or have breakfast together again, with the crew. I'd love to hear more about you too."

"Fine," she said. "How about I go with you now? To the agency?"

"Why?"

"Because I don't have any friends to hang out with, as you Americans say."

"Fair enough. How would you phrase that in England?"

"I don't have any friends with whom to hang."

"That doesn't sound right."

"It isn't." She gave a low chuckle.

"Okay," he said. "Walk with me. But in those heels?"

She nodded. "I wouldn't know what to do in flat shoes."

"Then you didn't grow up on the moors. You must be a city girl."

"That's true. I grew up in a suburb of London."

They talked about their childhoods, mainly hers, all the way to Two Love Lane, which was about three blocks away, close to the harbor. They stopped to sign a few autographs for a carriage full of tourists and eventually traversed the cobblestones on Love Lane without mishap.

"I've walked on far older cobblestones," said Samantha.

"Show-off," he said back.

She stopped suddenly. "Thank you for making a genuine effort with me."

"What do you mean?"

"To be my friend."

Hank was touched. "Samantha, you say it like—" He didn't want to finish.

"As if I don't have any friends," she finished for him. "Tell me something. Do you have any? Real ones? People who see *you*, and not the celebrity?"

He had to think a few seconds. "Apart from some high school friends and a few people I met during my audition days"—he was thinking of Ella, of course, and some of their mutual friends who used to hang out at their apartment: two cooks from her diner, several other kids their age making the audition rounds, and a couple of British guys who lived in the apartment below theirs, all of whom he'd stayed in touch with, except Ella—"not really. Everyone since then is tied in somehow to my job." He paused. "I love my agent."

"Agents don't count, no matter how much you love them."

"I have my brothers—"

"Family doesn't count either."

They both stared at each other a moment. "Well, this is pretty sad, isn't it?" he said.

She laughed. "No one would ever believe us. We're lucky, you and I. That's what they'd say."

"We are," he replied.

"But there's a price to be paid," Samantha reminded him.

"Maybe we're not trying hard enough," he told her. "To make real friends."

"Socially, I'm not around many people not in the business," Samantha said. "I'm never quite certain, too, when I meet them, how to behave."

Hank thought about Samantha's chatting with Pammy about her ex-husbands outside the yacht club the night before, and then abruptly leaving in the limo without a farewell.

"I'm a little out of practice too," he said. "But we can get more today. Look what we're doing right now."

"True." She brightened a little, which again made him feel for her.

It also made him step back and wonder if he was heading down the same path toward loneliness and isolation. And he was. He definitely was. It was a wake-up call he really didn't want at that moment.

But there it was.

"Let's live it up," he said. "I mean it, Samantha. Let's *be normal*. Let's forget about the movie when we're off the set together. We'll call it Operation Friendship. We'll start with you and me. Friends." He held out his hand.

"Friends." She shook it.

"We're in the business together," he reminded her, "but it's a start. Our next step is to move outward. I challenge you to make at least one friend not in show business."

"Very well." She smiled. "Challenge accepted." She hesitated. "Did you think I was coming onto you in the trailer? I mean, you obviously did, right? You gave me that speech about our reputations."

Whoa. How should he reply? "I kind of did." He winced, sensing it was the wrong answer. "Okay, I *really* did."

She laughed. "I have no designs on you, Hank. I wanted to talk to you about Ella, is all."

"Ella? Isn't she working out as your cousin?"

She nodded. "Not a single worry on set. No, it's about something else. But we can chat later. Look at this place!"

They both stood at the wrought-iron gate, enchanted. At least Hank was sure Samantha was as captivated as he was. She gazed at the turret, her mouth slightly agape, and then at the front garden with its cherub fountain spouting water. She ran her hand over the top of the gate, which was a work of art itself, two hearts intertwined in the middle of it.

"Gorgeous," is all she said about the entire tableau.

"It is." He felt a sense of pride that Ella was part owner of the house, that she and her best friends had created a thriving business headquartered here.

And then he realized he hadn't warned Ella that Samantha was coming too. He hoped she'd be okay with that.

They heard some mild gasping and a curse word behind them and turned to see a woman in her late forties or early fifties navigating the cobblestones. She wore a purple suit and big sunglasses and a little snakeskin purse that flapped against her side. Her platinum blonde hair and sophisticated blunt cut shouted well-to-do.

She'd fit in well on the Upper East Side in Hank's mother's crowd. Ella had told him that when she'd lived in Charleston in college, she'd seen a lot of women like the one approaching. Many of them lived South of Broad Street in the historic district. The locals called the residents there SOBs for short. Hank had never forgotten that. It was a funny designation.

But the truth was, according to Ella, most people in Charleston were pretty damn nice. And if you weren't in the upper-crust crowd, you could probably count your blessings. When they'd first started dating, Ella had told him about Macy. She'd only just been a debutante at the oldest debutante ball in the United States, which took place right here in Charleston. The fuss around that event had stressed Ella—and Macy too. Macy had gotten into big fights with her mother about what her gown would look like and who was going to sign her dance card.

Ella thought all the focus on maintaining tradition and social standing—which seemed to go hand in hand in Charleston—seemed more trouble than it was worth. In college, she'd told Hank, she'd had fun the way most people around town did, by going to the beach—which was accessible to the public—having porch parties, shucking oysters, and riding bikes along the sea wall, where a bunch of big mansions faced Fort Sumter in the harbor. One of those mansions, of course, was Beau and Lacey's, and Hank, Ella, and Pammy were living behind it in the carriage house right now.

The irony wasn't lost on Hank. Here he was in Ella's Charleston, the one she'd told him stories about when they were younger. He never thought he'd wind up in the Lowcountry doing a movie. But so far, he liked it. The flowers smelled good. The salt air off the harbor was invigorating. The people were friendly. The walk alone from the set to Two Love Lane had lifted his spirits. It was made even more satisfying knowing he was heading toward Ella.

"Hey there!" the woman in purple called cheerily to them both. Her Southern accent was as pronounced as Miss Thing's.

"Hi," Hank said with a grin.

"Good afternoon," Samantha chimed in.

Hank noticed she sounded friendlier than she usually did. Good for her.

The woman caught up with them. "Y'all are headin' to the same place. I'm Roberta Ruttle."

Introductions were made.

"You're both so charming," Roberta said. "Welcome to Charleston."

And that was it. Didn't acknowledge their movie-star status directly. Didn't ask for an autograph. Hank could get used to this kind of treatment. He opened the gate. "After you, ladies."

Samantha trailed behind Roberta. "Lovely St. John suit," she called up to her.

"Thanks," said Roberta. "Junior League Thrift Shop. It used to belong to my good friend Mimi, and when she saw it on me, she said, 'Honey, that looks way better on you.' She was wearing one of my missing special-collection Hermes scarves at the time. I couldn't figure out *how*. I knew she didn't have one from that particular collection. She said she'd bought it at the thrift shop too. I realized I must have left it in a set of suitcases I'd donated. I couldn't very well snatch it back from her, could I?"

Samantha laughed. "I suppose not. But she didn't offer to give it back?"

"She did," Roberta said. "But I wouldn't take it. How could I deny her the pleasure of finding an Hermes scarf at the thrift shop? It's a great story. And I got her St. John suit, didn't I? Friends don't split up over scarves, bottom line."

"I suppose," Samantha said. "I must go to this thrift shop."

"I'll take you," Roberta said.

Samantha looked over her shoulder at Hank, her eyes twinkling. He gave her a thumbs-up. *Way to go*, he mouthed to her.

She winked.

At the front door, Roberta rang the bell.

It was flung open almost immediately by Miss Thing. She wore a white suit with aqua buttons and aqua shoes dyed to match. Hank knew all about dyed shoes, thanks to his costume-designer friends. But while Roberta Ruttle looked up-to-date in her suit, Miss Thing looked like she was from an old *Life* magazine, circa 1965. Her hairdo added to the effect. It was rolled tightly like the Queen of England's.

"Come in, one and all!" she cried.

When she saw Samantha, her cry turned to a strangled gasp. She twisted an invisible key in her mouth. "Not a word," she said. "I won't say a *word*!"

"Thank you," Samantha said, her smile a tad weary but authentic all the same.

Miss Thing clasped her hands in front of her underwhelming bosom. "Roberta, I'll take you to Ella's office. And as for you two stars of the big screen, one of whom is an outright *legend*, although Hank, you're on your way too—"

He chuckled. She was a real performer.

"Please head that way, if you would be so kind"—she pointed a manicured finger down the hall—"and I'll meet you in the kitchen. I'll get the tea kettle going, and by then, Ella will probably be available." She blinked her fake eyelashes at him. "She told me you were on your way."

"Yes." Hank took no offense at Miss Thing's leaving him off her list of stars who'd achieved legendary status in Hollywood. It was refreshing to be reminded that he still had mountains to climb.

"I'll start the kettle," said Samantha.

"You *will*?" Miss Thing practically quivered with delight.

"Of course," said Samantha.

The office manager put her hand on her heart. "The Brita pitcher's in the fridge, and the kettle's on the AGA."

Samantha smiled. "So glad you have an AGA stove."

"We'd have nothing less," said Miss Thing, and then in a stage whisper, added, "I told the girls I can't work here unless I get an AGA in the kitchen! I have home-made cookies too. We'll have a tea party!"

"Lovely," said Samantha. She seemed genuinely pleased.

Miss Thing whirled to face Hank. "If you prefer coffee, we have a machine there for that. But don't tell Pete. He runs Roastbusters at the top of the lane. He's one of our dearest friends."

"No, tea's good," Hank said, to be polite and to please her and Samantha. He wasn't a fan, but if he could handle hazelnut coffee creamer, he could do tea.

"Why don't I grab Ella, and we'll all have tea?" asked Roberta. "I could use some, honestly. I love your mint juleps, Miss Thing, but we are nowhere near five o'clock. And I had an Arnold Palmer right before I got here, so iced tea or lemonade doesn't suit my fancy right now."

"Why didn't I think of that?" Miss Thing exclaimed. "Tea for all! But I believe Ella wanted to talk to you in private. She has an update for you."

"On my dating situation?" Roberta asked without blinking an eye.

Miss Thing fingered her pearl necklace. "Yes. I think that's it." She stole a sideways glance at Hank and Samantha.

"I don't mind if they listen in," Roberta told her.

"Well, in that case, I *know* that's it!" cried Miss Thing. "Wait until you hear. It's so exciting!"

"Oh, so you know what's going on?" Roberta asked her.

"Not usually. Ella respects your privacy." Miss Thing gave a tiny hop. "But honey, sometimes she consults us if she needs extra inspiration, and it was *my idea* she loved. Or didn't love. But is willing to try." She clamped her mouth shut. "But it's Ella's place to tell you," she couldn't resist adding.

"I'm right here," Ella said, raising her hand. Hank looked over and saw her grinning outside her office door. "Miss Thing, I wish you'd buzzed me."

"I was going to, but then it got very exciting, and now you're in the middle of it," Miss Thing said. "See?" She looked around, lifted her hands, and let them drop.

"Dear God, Ella, what is going on?" Roberta asked. "I left a big meeting to come over."

"I promise I'll tell you," Ella replied. Then she saw Samantha. "Oh, hi, Samantha! It's good to see you."

Hank thought she sounded genuinely glad to see his costar, which he appreciated, especially considering that Samantha hadn't been particularly warm to Ella at the yacht club last night and earlier today at the read-through.

"I tagged along with Hank," Samantha said.

"I meant to text you," Hank said.

"It's fine," Ella assured him.

Hank couldn't help feeling relieved. He didn't like to displease Ella. Sometimes he disappointed her because he had to, like when he broke up with her—*idiot!*—and that one time he'd accidentally washed her favorite white blouse with his red shorts, and it turned pink. He also re-membered favoring a cuss word she hated, and it took him about twenty mild reminders and then a few tongue-lashings from her to cut it out of his life for good. To this day he didn't say it.

All in all, he much preferred to see her happy. It warmed his heart. A happy Ella was a gift to the world.

"Tell me *right now* what's going on," said Roberta. "I don't care who hears."

"I'll go get the tea party started," said Miss Thing.

"Let's all head that way, then," said Ella. "You sure, Roberta, about not wanting to meet in private?"

"I'm sure."

Hank was now walking between Ella and Samantha. This was an exciting day. Not because of the movie but because he was here with Ella, and everything was so crazy. Was her life like this all the time? He suspected it was if Miss Thing was always in it, as apparently, she was, and breezy characters like Roberta Ruttle, who didn't care who heard her private business.

Charleston was *fun*.

"All righty," Ella said when they were all finally in the kitchen.

"Everyone, take a seat," said Miss Thing, "while I get the tea going and the cookies out. I wish Greer and Macy were here to say hello. They're both out on scouting visits."

"What's a scouting visit in your world?" Samantha asked.

Everyone knew what it was in the movies—when you looked for places you could use in your film as backdrops or scene settings.

"It's when we look at possible romantic date sites," said Ella. "Sometimes our clients don't know where to go or what to do. We stay on top of the latest goings-on, as well as the tried and true. And Miss Thing writes most of them up on our blog."

"I sure do." She did her thing at the stove, prepping the tea.

"But a few we keep to ourselves," Ella said. "We pull

them out for our clients when they want to go the extra mile."

"Those sound intriguing," said Samantha.

"Believe me, they are," Miss Thing said, her eyes wide. "I especially like the scenario we call Operation Shrimp Trawler."

"Operation Shrimp Trawler?" Roberta laughed.

"Oh, honey," said Miss Thing. "You have no idea how romantic a shrimp trawler can be."

"No, I don't," Roberta said.

Hank was scratching his head at that one too.

"All right, don't give away all our secrets, Miss Thing," Ella said fondly. "Y'all, take a seat. We really have to get moving. Everyone's on a schedule."

Hank pulled out a chair for Roberta at the small farm table. Ella and Samantha sat on a bench on the other side. Miss Thing was still bustling around the stove. He'd save the other chair for her. He took a seat on the bench between Ella and Samantha. Roberta put her two elbows on the table and said, "Shoot," to Ella.

Ella sat up a little straighter. "Miss Thing thinks she might understand the tarot card reader's riddle, if that's what we want to call it."

"Excuse me," Hank said. "Tarot cards? A riddle? Am I in the middle of a scripted mystery series?"

Samantha chuckled.

"Just hold your celebrity horses, you two," said Roberta with a mischievous grin. "This is something very important to me. So you need to sit tight and listen."

Hank and Samantha looked at each other. The mild surprise in her eyes reflected his own. When was the last time anyone had spoken to them like that?

He couldn't remember.

And he knew she couldn't either.

"I'm sorry," he said at the same time Samantha did.

"*Really* sorry," Samantha added.

He saw Ella trying not to laugh. Miss Thing giggled.

"It's okay, it's *okay*," Roberta said, grinning. "My land, it's obvious you two haven't had anyone talk back to you in a long time. If you listen to what happened to me a long time ago, all is forgiven."

So Hank and Samantha listened. He found the whole story weird but fascinating. Apparently, Samantha did too. "I don't know what to say," she said when it was over. "What an interesting problem to have."

"Thank you," said Roberta. "I don't want it. But it's nice to be able to share it with you."

"So is everyone ready to hear what Miss Thing thinks the tarot card reader meant?" Ella asked them.

"I'm certainly ready, more than anyone here," said Roberta. She tapped her fingers on the table.

"Tell them, Miss Thing," said Ella.

By this time, Miss Thing had set out the tea things, along with a platter of cookies that Hank thought resembled Frisbees with pink and white sprinkles. Miss Thing poured everyone a cuppa and they all grabbed cookies, except for Samantha, who said the costume shop would kill her.

Hank smiled over the rim of his cup at Ella. He liked having her so close by. The corner of her mouth tipped up, but then she looked away. He'd say she was playing hard to get, but he knew better. She wasn't playing. She meant it.

*Patience*, he told himself, although he didn't have time for patience, did he? He needed hope. Because that woman was stubborn. And she had excellent reasons for putting up a wall between them. He took it very seriously.

Neither was he sure what would happen if she decided to let him in.

Maybe nothing. That would suck. A *lot*.

But he wanted to try. He had to at least try. He thought back to his dad saying how he'd liked Ella and how Hank should go down to Charleston, which was so out of character for his dad to say. That gave Hank a little boost. He wasn't crazy to try. Ella was special.

Ella was—if he dared to admit it—the love of his life. When he was younger and told her he'd loved her, he really had.

And he'd never stopped.

He loved her *right now*. What would she do if she knew? He had less than a week to figure out how to tell her without her running away.

To hell with the costume shop. He ate a whole cookie. Ella did too.

He was surprised that somehow they'd made it this far—eight minutes, judging by the Kit-Cat Klock on the wall with the swinging tail—without Ella yet revealing the news Roberta was waiting for.

And then the front door opened and slammed.

"Hey, Ella! Ya here?" It was Pammy. "I'm done for the day. I have a date tonight! Where are you? Hellooooo? What am I supposed to say on this date? *Ella*?"

# CHAPTER FIFTEEN

"Back here, Pammy!" Ella yelled. "The kitchen! In the rear of the house!"

Loud footsteps clomped down the hall, and Pammy burst into the room. "My date's with the mayor of Charleston, and he's hot. Hotter than Hank. Not that I think Hank is hot. He's my cousin. Gross." She flipped the bird at him.

"Nice," Hank murmured.

"The mayor?" Miss Thing's voice went up an octave. "Reginald?"

"Yeah, he's so cute," said Pammy. "I love that gap in his teeth that makes him whistle his *S*'s. And he's got hair like a monk. I call him Reggie. I think he wants to jump my bones too. But I'm not ready. I mean, I don't have the right underwear."

"Stop talking, Pammy," Hank said. "I don't want to hear this."

"Get over it, Hank," Pammy said. "I have to see your naked butt on a large screen at the movies. Right? You owe me, cuz. Samantha, scoot over. I want a cookie."

Samantha scooted over, almost onto Hank's lap. So he

scooted over, almost onto Ella's. She liked it. She couldn't lie. Their thighs were squeezed so tightly together, she could barely breathe from the delicious tingling feeling that overwhelmed her. And then it got worse when her side touched his. Not just touching, smashed up against.

Hank was hot. Hank was *next to her.* Dear God, why? Why was she being tortured? What had she ever done so wrong that she had to endure having such tempting, wicked thoughts about the only single guy in the world who was off-limits to her?

Miss Thing poured Pammy a cup of tea, and Pammy grabbed the now-vacant spot on the bench and then a cookie.

"This is really exciting news, Pammy," Ella said, "and I want to talk about it, but first—"

"He's forty-one, practically an old man." Pammy paused. "Sorry, Samantha. I mean, you're not forty-one *yet*. At least according to the tabloids."

"No apology needed," Samantha said with spirit. Okay, it was with a somewhat dampened spirit, but still. She was being pretty nice about Pammy's stark observation about her age and the sly implication that maybe the tabloids didn't have the real facts—maybe Samantha was even older, in other words.

Hank glared at Pammy over Samantha's head, but she ignored him.

"Uh, this all sounds fascinating," said Ella, "but we really need to move on to Roberta and an idea we have for her. Pammy, you want to stay?"

"No can do," Pammy said, reaching over Samantha for another cookie. "I'm off to Victoria's Secret."

"Try Bits of Lace," Roberta told her. "That's everyone's favorite lingerie shop around here."

"Great advice," Pammy said. "I'll be a local for real, prancing around in my sexy new underwear from a Charleston boutique."

Samantha, Ella noticed, sat completely still as Pammy clambered off the bench. At one point a lock of Samantha's beautiful chignon flew up in the air where Pammy's watchband accidentally caught it. But then she lifted her teacup to her mouth, seemingly recovered.

Ella breathed a sigh of relief.

Hank blew his cousin a kiss. He was wedged, still, between Ella and Samantha, but not as much, which was too bad because Ella had loved being squished next to him.

"See ya later," Pammy said, and slapped the side of the kitchen entryway with her palm when she left.

"She's a force of nature," Hank explained into the silence.

It was true the room felt a little empty without Pammy there, but Ella was sure they could liven things up. "Okay, Roberta," she said. "Thanks for your patience. I'm going to let Miss Thing explain, since it's her idea."

Miss Thing put her teacup down. "All righty, so the tarot card reader said, 'A penny for your thoughts, the ten thousandth for your tongue,' right?"

"Right," said Roberta. "And I thought maybe he wanted me to give him a thousand bucks. Because ten thousand pennies equals a thousand dollars. But he said it wasn't about money and wouldn't take it. I still donate a thousand dollars to different charities, hoping that'll do the trick. But to this day, I still clam up on dates."

Miss Thing smiled grimly. "Honey, he knew what he was talking about. Giving him a thousand bucks would be too easy. When you've been cursed, you need to put some real effort into getting out of it, not just pull some money out of a bank account, especially one that can afford to lose it."

"So what did he mean then?" Roberta asked.

"He was from Mobile, Alabama?" Miss Thing asked.

"Yes. From an old family there."

"It all fits," Miss Thing said.

"What?" Roberta's eyes widened.

Ella was on the edge of her seat too, even though she already knew what Miss Thing was going to say.

"He meant *cheddar* pennies." Miss Thing smiled triumphantly. "Not real ones."

There was another brief, underwhelmed silence. Ella knew this would happen. She'd been that way, too, when Miss Thing had first told her. It was an idea that needed time to build.

"What are cheddar pennies?" Samantha finally asked.

"I know what they are, but this is weird," said Roberta. "As weird as Operation Shrimp Trawler. I had no idea you people at Two Love Lane were so off the wall."

"It's what makes us so very successful," said Miss Thing, bragging only just a little.

"Be patient," Ella told Roberta. "I promise it will start making sense."

Hank leaned over and whispered, "What's in those cookies of Miss Thing's?"

"Sugar and butter," Ella said, trying not to enjoy the feel of his warm breath on her ear. "And lots of love."

Miss Thing looked sympathetically at Samantha. "Cheddar pennies are a big tradition down here, the Southern version of cheese straws."

"Cheese straws?" Samantha asked Hank.

He shrugged. "You got me."

"They're a savory snack," said Ella. "Cheez-Its are the closest I can come to describing their taste."

"I love Cheez-Its," Hank said.

"Never heard of them," Samantha said.

"We'll get some on the way back to the set," Hank said. "Now I have a craving."

"You won't after you've had my cheddar pennies," Miss Thing said. "They come out at happy hour. I always keep some in the freezer for when guests come over after five o'clock. I've got a wonderful recipe for them passed down from my grandmother."

"I have a family recipe for them too." Roberta drew in her chin. "But this makes no sense."

"What was that curse again?" Hank asked.

"'A penny for your thoughts, the ten thousandth for your tongue,'" Ella and Miss Thing said together.

"I think"—here Miss Thing put both her hands on the table and stared at Roberta—"I think that lawyer wants you to bake ten thousand cheddar pennies and eat the ten thousandth one. And that'll break the curse. Plus"—she raised her index finger—"the silver lining is that you can freeze thousands of them for your next ten years' worth of happy hours."

"That's insane," said Samantha.

"I agree it's outlandish," Ella said, "but honestly, if you look at what the tarot card lawyer said, and where he's from, there's a slight possibility Miss Thing is right. And I believe we should try it. We should bake ten thousand cheddar pennies to help Roberta find her voice."

Roberta sat there, saying nothing. Ella couldn't tell what she was thinking.

"That's a helluva lot of cheddar pennies," Hank said.

"It is," said Miss Thing. "But we could split up the baking duties."

"Roberta?" Ella asked. "Are you okay?"

"I'm just thinking," said Roberta. "I have a lot of

friends who keep cheddar pennies in their freezers. Maybe I could get them to give them to me. That would be a good start. You think those would count?"

Miss Thing brightened. "Why didn't I think of that?"

Roberta grinned. "I'm sending out a group text right now."

Ella put up a hand. "Wait. Miss Thing, you said getting past this curse would take real effort. If Roberta simply asks for cheddar pennies from her friends and we bake some for her, how is that any harder than her pulling money out of her bank account?"

Miss Thing's arched eyebrows dropped. "It's not, really."

"Whether you believe the curse is real," Ella told Roberta, "or it's simply a mind game, your putting in effort is what is going to get you past it."

"Are you saying I have to make all the cheddar pennies myself?" Roberta cringed slightly. "I'm not a baker, honey. I buy all my cakes and cookies at Saffron. I get my bread from the Tiller Baking Company. When I have a hankering for cheddar pennies, these days I hand off my family recipe to my chef who comes in once a week and preps all my dinners."

"You might just have to try to bake them yourself," Ella said. "The more I think about it, the more I'm sure this is the way to go. But I don't see why we couldn't at least help you shop for the supplies and help you count the pennies after they're baked."

Roberta blinked. "My momma's recipe usually makes eighty a batch, but my chef makes them small and can get double that. That's a hundred and sixty from one log."

"You roll the dough into a log, chill it, and then slice it," Miss Thing explained to Hank and Samantha, which was a good thing because they both appeared clueless.

Ella took out her phone and opened the calculator. "That means you'd have to make around sixty-three batches to reach ten thousand."

"That's impossible," said Roberta.

Hank's expression was cute—he was trying so hard not to pity Roberta. Ella could tell he wanted to help, but in this case, there wasn't much anyone could do but encourage her.

Roberta released a huge sigh. "It takes my chef about forty-five minutes, including the thirty minutes putting the dough in the freezer, to make one batch."

Ella tapped her phone again. "That's about forty-seven hours in the kitchen," she said. "If you worked eight hours a day for six days, you could do it."

Roberta brightened at that. "So if I took a week off work. . . ."

"You could do it," said Ella.

"But I can't take a week off work," said Roberta. "I simply can't. Y'all, I have to make a living. That comes first, before romance."

"Amen," said Miss Thing.

"A hundred percent agreement here," said Samantha.

A slightly bleak silence hovered.

But Ella forced herself to rally. "Okay, then," she said, "let's regroup. You need a date for the Aquarium fundraiser in less than four weeks, Roberta. It's got to be a good date too. Someone who will not only be happy to see you shine, but someone you'll be proud to have at your side."

"True," said Roberta.

"But before you can get a date for the fundraiser," Ella said, "you need to go out with several men over the next several weeks. I've got a list of them ready to have dinner with you. Hopefully, one of them will be the right guy."

"That would be nice." Roberta smiled wistfully.

"But going on dates where you don't speak is unlikely to net you the right man to take to the fundraiser," Ella said. "You really need your voice."

"Yeah, I do." Roberta sighed.

"So we need to try this theory of Miss Thing's," Ella continued, praying that Roberta wouldn't give up, "and have you bake ten thousand cheddar pennies in the hopes that the curse will be behind you for good, whether because it's a real curse or it's a psychological block that you'll break down by going to extreme lengths to dissolve its power over you."

"Exactly." Roberta nodded vigorously. "'A penny for your thoughts, the ten thousandth for your tongue,'" she murmured. "My, oh, my."

"So many hurdles," said Samantha, sounding sympathetic.

There was another small silence at the table.

"It's too much right now," said Roberta, then bestowed a grateful smile upon Miss Thing. "Next time I get time off, which probably won't happen for a few months, I'll bake those ten thousand cheddar pennies. I just can't do it before the Aquarium fundraiser."

"I understand." Miss Thing patted Roberta's hand. "I'm glad you're going to work on it later. Meanwhile, Ella can try to find you a decent date for the Aquarium shindig."

Their friend in purple shook her head. "No, that event is too important. What if I can't speak to him? It will ruin my whole night, and I need to be on fire. I'll play it safe by taking my brother. But thanks."

Ella wished she knew what to do. "Maybe we could all chip in and bake with you, after all."

Roberta shrugged. "But then I wouldn't be making the whole effort myself. And I'd hate to have y'all go to all that trouble, only for it to fail. I'm going to do this right. I don't want to bake ten thousand cheddar pennies for nothing."

"Or maybe—" Hank began.

Everyone turned to look at him.

"What?" asked Roberta.

"Maybe you rent out a block of time in a commercial kitchen," Hank said, "on your own, make a couple of huge batches of dough, roll 'em out into logs"—he said *logs* as if he couldn't believe they used that word in baking circles—"freeze 'em for a little while, then slice them up and bake them—all in a day. Or two days, at most."

No one said a word.

"That's brilliant," Miss Thing finally said.

And it was. Ella was so proud of Hank. She had no right to be, but she was.

# CHAPTER SIXTEEN

Hank looked around the table. Samantha and Roberta had little grins on their faces, but it was Ella's face he wanted to see. Her mouth was slightly open. Her eyes were sparkling.

He'd hit a home run!

"I *love* that idea," she said.

Hank couldn't help feeling sort of shy. "Good." He grinned. "But you do all the research," he said to Roberta, "so this curse doesn't have a leg to stand on."

"I don't even need to," she said. "I know exactly where to go. There are a couple of commercial kitchens in Charleston. I have a friend with a food truck who's used them. Both have giant mixing bowls. That's what I need. And ovens with a lot of racks."

"Time to get baking," Samantha said.

Roberta stood up. "If I can rent one out in the next couple of days, I will. And I'll check back with y'all to let you know how it goes."

Everyone else stood too. Ella gave Roberta a hug. "Best of luck. I'll be on pins and needles waiting to hear what happens."

"You're crazy, you do know that," said Samantha. "But I admire you for thinking outside the box."

Roberta chuckled. "At least I'm trying something new."

Miss Thing hugged her too. "I hope this does the trick."

Hank stood back, not sure what to say. He'd made his contribution. He caught Roberta's eye as she was stuffing her cell phone back into her purse. He lifted his hand in goodbye. "Hey," he said, "I'd go out with you even if you never spoke a word."

Roberta paused. Smiled. "That was a very nice thing to say, Mr. Rogers."

"Please call me Hank."

"Hank, then." Her eyes got shiny. "You're a sweetie."

"I wasn't kidding," he said. "You've got presence. You walk into a room and don't have to say anything, but people are aware of you. In a good way. That's highly valued in the acting community."

"I have presence?" Roberta sucked in a little breath. She was too dignified to gasp outright.

"Yes, you do," Hank insisted.

"I agree," said Samantha. "A very warm presence. You're delightful, in fact."

Roberta's mouth dropped open. "Thank you both so much." She paused. "Can you come? To the fundraiser?"

"I wish," said Hank. He loved dolphins and other sea creatures—who didn't?—and it was always a good thing to help local charities when he was on location. "But we'll be finished shooting here in a week."

"Yes, I'll be in England," Samantha said. "And then we take up filming in Montreal."

Roberta's shoulders dropped. "What a shame."

It struck Hank then, how temporary his life felt in gen-

SECOND CHANCE AT TWO LOVE LANE    181

eral. He was always going from place to place, following the work, and then heading back to Brooklyn to regroup. But staying home never lasted longer than eight or nine months, tops. Often, he was only there a few months. On rare occasions, he'd get two weeks' break between jobs.

So why was he here to try to get Ella's notice? Had he assumed if things worked out between them that *she'd* drop her life and hang out in New York or L.A. with him? He hadn't thought about that. And he was embarrassed.

But Ella looked happy. Maybe he had something to do with it. He managed to get close to her a few seconds later, while everyone else was chatting in front of them as they walked toward the front door. "Did that just really happen?" he murmured. "You told your client to bake ten thousand Southern, savory happy-hour treats? We call it nosh in New York."

"I remember," she said. "Once a New Yorker, always a New Yorker."

"Well said," he answered. "But I like it down here. It's kind of exciting. You guys—*y'all*—are a little impulsive, in a good way."

"You will be too. It only takes about a week. It's all that sun we get. It keeps us happy. We can afford to joke and take chances. And you're already starting to. Look at you, thinking out of the box. Giving Roberta such a good idea about the commercial kitchen. I owe you."

"No, you don't."

They stood and looked at each other a second too long.

*I did it for you*, he wanted to say. But instead he said, "I'm proud to know you. You have a really amazing calling in life."

She swallowed, then said, "Wow, that means a lot. Thanks, Hank. I'll do whatever it takes to make love happen."

"Really?" Hank didn't want to be obnoxious, but he didn't quite believe her.

"Well, for other people," she amended, sounding sheepish.

"Why not for you?" He knew he was pushing his luck.

"Because I'm too busy. And—"

"And what?"

"I've been lucky." Her brow furrowed as she considered something. "At least," she said carefully, "I've experienced it before."

Her confession felt fragile, like a beautiful china cup, offered to him. Now it was his turn not knowing what to say.

"I could ask you the same thing," she said, sounding her usual lively self again. "What's kept you from falling in love? You've had ten years to make it happen."

He stared at her a second. "I plead the fifth."

"You can dish it out, but you can't take it." She tossed him a mock-triumphant look, which was very sexy.

"You can get information out of me," he said, "but it'll require the right touch. I don't cooperate easily."

"Huh," is all she said. But she didn't sound angry. She sounded almost intrigued.

He'd poked the bear. She hadn't ignored him or roared at him to get lost. It had been a gamble, and he hoped it would pay off. *Soon.*

Hank and Samantha left Ella at her office with Roberta and Miss Thing, the three of them making up a shopping list for the cheddar pennies. When he shut the front door of Two Love Lane behind him, he could swear he heard Roberta say she'd need twenty pounds of butter.

Twenty pounds of butter! He couldn't even imagine that.

He'd had a good afternoon, he thought, as he walked back to the set with Samantha.

"Dinner tonight," she reminded him. "With some studio people."

"Right," he said.

"Hank—"

"Yes?"

"We're peers," she said.

"Not really. You've got a lot more clout in this industry than I do."

"Well, we make about the same amount of money."

"Which really isn't fair to you," said Hank, "considering how much more experience you have."

"Agreed," she said. "But that's how it is right now."

"Things are changing," he said. "Which is good."

"I know. And I appreciate your professionalism. But I wanted to talk to you about something personal—about Ella."

"Okay," he said, feeling a little leery.

"She's your ex-lover. We all have them. But I sense some unresolved feelings between you two."

"You're right." He didn't mind admitting it. He was ready to stop running from all his regrets. "We were together ten years ago. And I blew it."

"You were very young."

"Yes, I was. But I can't really use that as an excuse."

"Sure you can. You were confused. You didn't have what you needed yet. You had growing up to do."

"You make it sound . . . okay."

"It's *life*," she said.

They walked together in silence.

Samantha stopped a moment to peek into a garden through another magnificent wrought-iron gate. "So do you think she'll give you another opportunity?"

"No," he said, admiring the blooms and the carefully trimmed hedges over her shoulder. "I have to create my opportunities."

"I see." Samantha turned back to him. "Do you need some help?"

"You'd *help*?"

She shrugged. "Why not? But if it doesn't work out between you two, after we stop filming, I'll be calling. And you'll say yes to at least one whirlwind weekend on a tropical island with me—as *friends*—because I worked my ass off trying to help you win Ella's attention. Agreed?"

He stuck out his hand. "Agreed."

She shook it, and he pulled her close. "You're a good egg, Samantha."

"I know," she mumbled into his chest. "I'm far more than a pretty face that's been Botoxed more often than I'd like to admit."

He pulled back. "I'd never guess. Seriously, I wouldn't." He explored her face, not looking for wrinkles but for a sign that she really meant what she'd said. "But tell me this. How can you help me with Ella? I don't have a lot of time. Less than a week."

"I'm not going to do anything shady, like pretending I'm after you so she'll get jealous."

"Hmmm. Maybe that would work, though."

"No. It would give me a great deal of pleasure, flirting with you off camera, but we don't want it to backfire and scare her off. It will be difficult enough for her to see us staging sex scenes together. And kissing on film. I already rubbed that in."

"You did?"

"Yes, earlier today. I'll take on the role of burr under her saddle. If she likes you, she won't cut me off completely when I try to throw you together. I'll take some pressure off you to get her attention. I'll talk you up on the set. I'll invite you both to a dinner party. Let her do some comparisons of you with other men by getting a few of my out-of-town friends to stay, the ones who seem like they have potential at first but the more they talk, the more she'll realize they're self-absorbed." She paused. "You're not self-absorbed, are you?"

"For a while I was. I thought I was only being smart, putting my career first. But I sacrificed too much, and it got lonely."

"Self-absorbed people don't get lonely. You couldn't have been self-absorbed. You were just young and ambitious. And you were probably too scared to let someone down to pay attention to your heart. Most likely your parents."

"How did you know?"

"It's a common story. Anyone else you were afraid of disappointing?"

"Not really. It was mainly my father. He wanted me to go to law school."

"Ah. My mother wanted me to marry the boy next door, now an excellent butcher in Devon."

"If I could do it all over again . . ."

"This is your chance."

"Ella's a matchmaker. Won't she recognize everything you're doing as a matchmaking strategy?"

"Of course she will. I won't be hiding anything. She might not like that I'm taking on that role, but how can she stop me from trying? I didn't get to where I am by *obeying* other people."

"I like you, Samantha."

"Thank you. Have you told her you've come to Charleston for her?"

"Yes. I told her."

"So you're really not here for the film."

"I hate to admit it, but no."

She was quiet. "That's all right. As long as you do a good job in your role, who cares?"

"Would you have told Isabel and Chad not to hire me if you'd known why I really came?"

"No."

They were back at the set. It was going to be a long night. An hour and a half went by, and in that time, Hank rehearsed one scene eight times with Samantha, their third one. Then filmed it once, to test the lighting.

So much of movie making was repetition, and rehearsing scenes out of order. It was chaotic. Of course, then the editor and director smoothed out the story.

Maybe Hank's crazy life could fall into place and become meaningful too. Eventually.

Samantha pulled out her phone during a break. "I have an idea. Let me text Ella and tell her to come visit after her costume fitting. You disappear somewhere. I'll ask her to go to dinner with us and the studio heads."

But a business dinner sounded boring. Hank couldn't make Ella sit through one of those. "I won't be able to talk to her much with the studio heads around. So why bother?"

"It's the best I can come up with at the moment," Samantha said, "considering your parameters. You have to be at that dinner."

There seemed to be no perfect solution.

The truth was, other people meant well. But no one comprehended the delicacy of Hank's situation the way he did. No one understood Ella the way he did. And no one cared as much about *them* as he did.

What should he do?

*What should he do?*

He raked a hand through his hair. "Pammy is out on a date. An early one. God knows, she might be back by eight."

"And?" Samantha waited expectantly.

"I'm skipping the dinner tonight," Hank said. It was a risk, but he was willing to go through with it.

Samantha raised a brow. "How do you propose to explain your absence to the studio heads?"

He shrugged. "I'll tell them I'm sick. It's not as if tonight is crucial. I've met them before." Then he got an idea. "Maybe you can tell them you saw me puke. In a trash can. Something gross so they'll want to change the subject fast."

"No, I won't lie for you."

"Fine. *I'll* tell them I puked in a trash can. I'll even text that little green face emoji to them to prove my point."

A little dimple appeared in Samantha's cheek. "Have fun with Ella. I hope Pammy's date goes well, too, and that she's out long enough for you to make some romantic strides."

He grinned. "Thanks."

"I shouldn't say this, but I like that you're slacking off on the job. At least it's just on the schmoozing end. Not the acting end."

"I won't let you down there."

Three hours later, at seven o'clock, Hank walked out the set door and onto the street. He called Isabel, told her he couldn't make dinner. He was free—

And he'd put Ella first.

# CHAPTER SEVENTEEN

Ella stood in the kitchen at the carriage house, wearing an apron with dancing cupcakes on it. She held a big wooden spoon and was stirring a pot of something that smelled delicious. "Hank!" It made him happy to see her eyes light up. "What are you doing here? Did you . . . do one of the sex scenes today?"

He laughed. "Nope. Not today. Tomorrow we're doing both. Why?"

"Because it's, uh, weird," she said, with an apologetic shrug. "I mean, you and Samantha. I don't know *why*. I mean, it's not the age gap. You're both beautiful people. Maybe it's your personalities. I don't know if they mesh."

Was that a little bit of personal jealousy he heard? Or was she in acting mode, speaking of the craft and of film essentials, like believable chemistry between characters?

"As long as our characters are willing to jump in the sack, we go along, right?" He'd assume she was speaking from a purely academic standpoint. "I can get you on the set if you want. So you can see how technical it actually is."

"No, thanks." She flashed him an embarrassed smile.

"Anyway, I thought you wouldn't be home until really late."

"I got out early." He loved how she said "home." It sure felt like home. He peeked into the pot. It was filled with tomato sauce and some kind of meat. "You made enough for an army."

"Italian sausage and red pepper sauce, with some portabella mushrooms and a generous splash of vino," she said. "The *nonnas*' favorite recipe."

"The *nonnas*?"

She chuckled. "My two grandmothers. They've both moved to the States since I last saw you. From Sicily. And I'm so glad they're here. They make a lot of trouble for Mama. But she loves the challenge and the company."

"When you say 'here,' are they visiting Charleston with your mother? Or are they all in New York?"

She shook her head. "*Here.* Everyone in New York moved to Charleston within a year of my setting up shop with Two Love Lane."

"*Everyone?*" He was shocked.

She chuckled. "Twenty-three Mancinis. Mama's house is the headquarters of all our get-togethers. Unless we're at Uncle Sal's pizza parlor on Wentworth Street. Sometimes he shuts it down just for us, but it's so popular, he rarely does."

"What's it called?"

"Mancini's, of course. It's already become a Charleston institution. The college crowd loves it. But so does the older crowd. Uncle Sal makes the best specialty pizzas in Charleston, and he delivers. If he can keep up with the downtown rents, he should be there quite a while."

"Wow." Hank was flabbergasted. "I had no idea. Your entire family came south."

He was happy for her. But on a deeper level, he was

panicked. She didn't need him. She had the entire Mancini family to love her, to support her, and always would, even if by some freak chance, they moved back to New York and she had to fly up to see them all the time.

She would never actually *need* him.

Ella shrugged. "After Papa died, things changed. He was the patriarch, really, of the American branch of the family. I think everyone wanted a change. They saw me leave the big city and the snowy winters, and they decided to try it too."

He wondered if she'd left because of what had happened between them.

She looked up at him. "I know you're wondering if I left New York because of our breakup."

She read minds very well. "I did wonder," he said. "And if I had anything to do with it, I feel terrible. And I'm sorry."

Her mouth quirked up in a semblance of a smile. He saw the sadness still there, after all these years. "When we broke up," she said, stirring slowly, "I was shattered for a while. I quit auditioning, and I moved home with Mama to figure out my life. I decided, for me, the best thing was to leave New York. I love Charleston, and Macy was here, so I came and taught at a children's theater. It took me a while to get situated, but when Greer moved back and Two Love Lane happened, everything clicked." She put the spoon down on a bread plate and looked up at him, her expression brighter. "It was the smartest decision I ever made, to move to Charleston. And now everyone in my family lives here, and honestly, I can't regret what happened. It was for the best, in the end. I feel very lucky."

*For the best.* Those were hard words to hear.

He didn't know what to say, so he just went with whatever came. "After we broke up," he said, playing with the spoon on the bread plate, "things clicked for me in acting, as you say they did for you with Two Love Lane." He decided to leave the spoon alone and instead leaned back on the counter, his arms over his chest. He looked at the cupboards opposite him, their dull gray faces, the worn corners. "I got famous. And rich. I was offered great roles—fulfilling ones." He paused. "But I'm still waiting."

"For what?"

He flicked a glance at her. "To feel lucky."

Their gazes held. Did she understand? He was the luckiest actor on the planet. But he wasn't the luckiest man. Not by far. He couldn't be. Not without her.

That was it. That was *really* it.

But he couldn't say that. He'd come across as narcissistic. Cocky. Maybe a crybaby, even. She didn't deserve to have him dump his regret on her.

"Oh, Hank." Ella shook her head and stirred her sauce. She looked briefly up at him. "I'm so sorry."

"Thanks," he said, "although I don't deserve any sympathy from you."

She lifted and dropped a shoulder. "Sympathy doesn't need to be earned."

He wanted to ask her, *Did love?* Did love need to be earned? What could he do to win *her* love? He so wanted to reach out and touch her hair. To kiss the top of her head. To pull her away from that stove and into his arms.

"You're right that I'm feeding an army tonight," she said. "The whole Mancini clan is heading to Mama's so we can all hang out with the Sicilian relatives. They're here on a visit. It's one reason I'm staying here. I gave four of them my apartment for the next week."

"That was nice of you."

"And Pammy was nice to let me stay here."

"I'm glad you decided to."

She gave the contents of the pot another stir. "I'm in charge of the sauce tonight, and it's got to be good. Mama wants me to be a better cook. And you know what? It's kind of fun." She looked up at him with the sweetest smile he'd ever seen.

"How many people will that feed?" he asked.

"About thirty," she said. "We'll have close to that number. You're welcome to come, you know."

She said it with genuine warmth and enthusiasm, which Hank appreciated. It was a step in the right direction, was it not?

Even so, his heart sank a little because tonight he definitely wouldn't have her all to himself. And then he got a brilliant idea . . . he remembered Mama Mancini. She'd been a lovely, warmhearted woman. He'd never met the *nonnas*. Maybe, just maybe, if he could get some people in the family on his side, he'd have better luck getting a second chance with Ella.

"I'd love to," he said. "Thanks."

And instantly got nervous. He'd played a Mafia guy in an Oscar-nominated movie (along with the film's nomination for Best Screenplay and Best Director, he'd been nominated for Best Supporting Actor). The character had been a real loser. Italian stereotypes in Hollywood abounded. He'd never really noticed until he'd read a few articles and letters in the last couple of years in *Variety* and the *Hollywood Reporter*. They'd been written by Italian Americans who were fed up with Italians being portrayed as gangsters and lowlifes in cinema and on television. They'd had enough of *The Godfather* and *The Sopranos* and movies like the one Hank had been in. They wanted something fresh, something that didn't smack of old prejudices against the Italian immigrants who'd flooded New York in the early twentieth century at the same time movies were taking off.

Would the Mancinis hold that Mafia role against him? Even more important, would they despise him for breaking Ella's heart?

Of course they would. He remembered how protective Ella's sisters had been when he'd met them the first time. Ella had taken him home to meet her family. On that visit, he'd seen a picture of her father, too, in a frame on the wall in their living room in the Bronx. Mama Mancini had said to Hank, "You're lucky he's not here to grill you." She'd chuckled fondly. "He was very protective of his girls."

Hank remembered telling her she had nothing to worry about. And Ella had come up to him then and wrapped her arm around his waist and said, "Papa would have loved Hank, Mama. He's looking down right now with approval. I can feel it."

Ten years later, Hank realized none of the Mancinis would care that he was a movie star. Usually, that would make him happy. Except they were the one group he longed to impress—to deflect, actually, with his celebrity. Instead, the only Hank Rogers they cared about was the one who'd hurt Ella a long time ago. She was their beloved sister, niece, daughter, and granddaughter, a professional actor who'd left her dreams behind in large part because of him.

But he had to do it. He'd hang out with the Mancinis tonight, and gladly. He'd show Ella he wasn't a coward. He'd face the music, and if they threw him out, then he'd simply have to take it.

"Don't worry," she told him, reading his mind again. "They won't be mean to you."

"Hey," he said, "if anyone is, I can't say I don't deserve it."

She chuckled. "You're actually going to have to put up with a lot of speculation, hints being dropped, people wondering if we're getting back together, speeches about fate and love and how it never dies."

"I can handle that."

"And don't be surprised if someone asks you for your autograph."

"Really? After our history, someone might do that?"

"Oh, yeah. You're still Hank Rogers. I mean, come on! Sometimes I forget, but other times I look at you and think, 'It's that guy from *Shadowsfall*, or *Kelly's Gang*,' and I can't believe you're standing in my kitchen."

"Pammy's kitchen." He felt embarrassed and pushed off the counter. "I don't want you to think of me that way."

"It's a compliment," Ella said. "It means you were really good playing those roles."

"So you saw them? On the big screen?" Somehow her answer felt important to him.

"Of course I did," she said. "I'm still your biggest fan, no matter what happened between us. I want you to be happy. And successful."

She was too good for him. She was a treasure.

He loved her.

Hank took a deep breath. "I was never sure if you saw them. But I always wanted to call you and ask. I wanted to know if you followed my career—"

She quit stirring and turned to him. "Stop beating yourself up. Of course, I follow your career. We were in love, Hank. We lived together. We shared our hopes and dreams. I can't just lop you off like a bad limb from a tree, especially when your dreams came true. I needed to celebrate with you, from afar. Without contacting you, because that wouldn't have worked. But I was there on opening day for all your films. And I always will be."

His heart ached—with love. With regret. With pride and gratitude. And of course, with sadness. He'd had no idea she followed his career at all. He'd hoped that she'd seen every single movie. He'd wanted her opinions on them. None of them had ever felt like true successes to him because he hadn't been able to share them with Ella.

He wanted to tell her. But how to explain that even feeling her absence keenly, he hadn't wondered if he should try to win her back? It had never occurred to him as an option, not until this movie came up in Charleston. He might have gone on for the rest of his life *not* pursuing a second chance with her.

What had held him back, and what was different *now*? Why had he finally said yes to this movie and come here and told her he wanted another chance? He needed to know himself better before he felt able to move forward.

But time was short. *Too* short.

He realized he hadn't even asked her about her afternoon on the set. He wasn't the only one in the movie. "How'd it go today in the costume shop?"

Her face brightened. "Really well. It took way longer than I thought. About three hours. But I have four costume changes, and in each one, my hair is going to be different."

Because the timeline in the movie spanned a decade. "In one scene, you're supposed to be pregnant. What was that like?"

"Fun. Strapping on the belly of a woman eight months along is a bit awkward. But I loved strutting around in it. Someone who walked in thought I was really pregnant and asked me when I was due."

They both laughed.

"Isabel wanted to speak with me about a change on one of my lines," Ella went on, "something I totally cheered for because it makes my character slightly more complicated."

"More stuff to latch onto."

"Exactly. I want to play someone three-dimensional. Anything I can do to make her feel real, I'll do. I'm flattered Isabel even asked my opinion about it."

"I'm glad to see she's so invested in the actors," Hank said.

"Me too." Ella glanced at the clock on the kitchen wall. "I have to be at Mama's in about an hour. Is that too soon for you?"

"No, that's fine. I need to bring something to her as a hostess gift."

Ella waved a hand. "She doesn't need anything."

"Oh, come on," he said, "it couldn't hurt."

"You don't need to win her over. She'll be perfectly pleasant. I promise."

"I'm sure she will, but my mother taught me to come bearing gifts, especially when someone's not expecting you. I'll walk the two blocks to Harris Teeter and pick her up some flowers and wine and be right back. Then I'll go upstairs and change."

"If you insist. I'll be finished with this sauce in a minute, and then *I'll* change."

They needed to stop talking about changing clothes. He was getting very bad ideas in his head. They were alone. Totally alone. In the old days, they'd indulged in quickies all the time while they were getting dressed or undressed.

He suddenly remembered something. "Hey, this morning I was in the shower when your friends came over with those doughnuts. Next thing I knew, someone opened the door. When I got out, my bathrobe was missing. Maybe it was Pammy. But I swear she was still asleep at the time. I had to run upstairs in a towel in front of everyone. Miss Thing was pretty entertained."

Ella laughed. "The same thing happened to me. But it was because I forgot my robe."

"I know. I saw you from the kitchen."

"You did?"

He shrugged and grinned. "Sorry. At least you were covered up."

"True. I saw you in a towel too." Her cheeks turned pink. "I was in the bathroom upstairs putting on makeup with the door open and saw you behind me in the mirror, coming up the stairs and down the hall."

"Oh." He hoped he'd looked decent. He worked out with a couple of personal trainers. But this was *Ella*. He wanted to look like a god in front of her. Or close to.

She thought for a second. "It was Miss Thing. She's just naughty enough to have reached into the bathroom and stolen your robe. I'll bet we'll find it hidden behind the couch."

"I found it tossed over the back of the armchair," he said. "Miss Thing *is* bad."

"She is." Ella grinned. "She wanted a look at you in your towel. And she probably wanted me to see you that way too."

He paused a beat. "I like how she thinks."

A smile danced on Ella's lips, and in her eyes he saw the old heat. The old, familiar heat. Instantly, he could see in his mind's eye the Ella he'd made love to was the same Ella in front of him now. But she'd blossomed even more and was alluring in whole new ways.

"I promise you, I didn't forget *my* robe on purpose,"

she said, and backed away a step. She picked up the spoon and held it in front of her.

He swallowed. "No, that was simply sheer luck—for me. It brought back a lot of amazing memories. The best ones of my life."

She nodded, the spoon in her hand forgotten. It hung there sideways while she considered his words. He waited for her to say something.

And waited.

"Mine too," she eventually whispered.

Hank took the spoon from her. And then he kissed her.

# CHAPTER EIGHTEEN

*Hank.* Ella instantly remembered everything about him from the old days. He was still in there, that guy she'd loved on and given every bit of herself to. Not only that, somehow she felt like she knew everything that was going on inside of the new Hank—who somehow felt like the old Hank. But sturdier, more sophisticated, sexier.

Was he the new *and improved* Hank?

She didn't know. But he was Hank. *Hank!* And she was home again, back in his arms. She couldn't believe she was letting it happen, letting Hank kiss her, *really* kiss her, with a hot, exploring tongue that didn't bother with the preliminaries. He was all man, and he told her with his urgency that he found her all woman. And if they continued like this a minute longer, they would wind up in the bedroom. Or she might find herself on the kitchen counter.

She kissed him back: locked in, zoned out. And if she wasn't careful, her heart was going down.

One more kiss . . . just one more, she promised herself.

And then she pulled away.

*His* pupils were huge.

*Her* breath came in little hitches.

"We can't—" she said.

"We just did," he said back, and reached for her hand.

She put it behind her back. "Hank, no."

When she said that, he drew in a breath. "Okay. We'll stop. But it was fun while it lasted. And I want to do it again. Don't you?"

Of course she did. But she wasn't going to tell *him* that. "People do dumb things when they're stuck in a small house together."

"This is a *really* small house," he said.

She could tell he wasn't going to push. He was being respectful, tuned in to her needs, and she appreciated it. In that moment, they went back to normal. "Normal" meaning that they weren't kissing.

"We have to get out of here," she said quickly and looked around for the lid to the pot of sauce. She also wanted a few kitchen towels to wrap around it. "I'm going to get this ready, and you can go change, and then we can stop at Harris Teeter on the way and get my mom those flowers you wanted to get her."

"And wine," he reminded her.

"She'll be thrilled," Ella said, striving to sound warm and friendly, but not overly familiar. It was how she addressed people she didn't know well in social or business situations. She honestly didn't know how else to act with Hank at this point. She went back to opening drawers and trying to look busy.

The post-kiss era had begun. What did that kiss mean? And how could she forget it? She'd be thinking about it all night.

"Hey," he said, "I like being around you."

It was such a simple, wonderful thing to say. Ella was

touched. But she had to keep things real. "You know better than most that I have my moments," she said, "and they can get pretty dark."

"I know." His expression was serious. "But you face things head-on and work through whatever's bothering you. You don't let it win, and—and I envy that."

He was right. She didn't run. That was a huge strength of hers. *Except for that one time she ran away from New York after getting her heart broken by a man—and left her big dream behind.*

She had to think for a second how to say what she wanted to say. "You're right that I like to tackle my issues. But I've run before. Don't forget I ran away after we broke up. To this day, I regret that. As happy as I am here in Charleston, I have the occasional what-if moment about leaving my career dreams behind. So don't go thinking I'm doing everything right."

"But Ella—"

"Wait a minute," she said, and studied his face. "I've only just figured out in the last couple of years that it's less about getting things right, Hank, and more about getting things *done*. Taking action, moving forward, however messy it is, however many mistakes you make along the way. That's more important than getting things right because, honey"—she'd picked up a little of Miss Thing's Southern style of conversing—"life's too short for what-ifs. I still have to remind myself of that. It's probably a lifelong challenge to stay in the present and not worry about the past *or* the future."

"See?" he said, and took her by the elbows. "You're wise. And you help people around you."

"So do you, through your acting. What I want to know is why you don't give yourself more credit for hitting the big-time."

"Because I see talented people who never come close. It was luck. I know I'm not the most talented. I was in the right place at the right time."

"Wrong," Ella said. "You were in the right place at the right time, *prepared* for success. You got yourself ready. You weren't just twiddling your thumbs. It was more than luck, Hank. You worked your butt off, and you need to own your part in it."

His eyes gleamed. "I'll think about that."

"You'd better."

He saluted her. "Aye aye, Cap'n. Whatever you say."

She chuckled. He'd just channeled one of her favorite characters he'd ever played, a U.S. Navy ensign in World War II. "You're lucky you can get away with being a smart aleck," she said. "Not everyone can pull out diversionary tactics quite so unique."

"It's a big perk of my *superstardom*," he said with exaggerated effect, "which I had some hand in."

He winked at her, and he was so cute in that moment, she could hardly breathe. "You're a good pupil," she said, and turned away from him to compose herself.

"You're a good *friend*," he said back.

She turned to face him, surprised at the sweet compliment.

"Thanks, Ella," he added softly. "You did it again. You made me feel better. Just by being you."

"You're welcome, Hank." She could hardly get the words out. She was falling for him again. "You'd best get upstairs, Ensign, and change your clothes," she said. "Feel free to dress down for Mama's. Jeans are good."

So, of course, when he came back downstairs, changed into a summer-weight white button-down shirt, worn Levi's, brown Sperrys, and a belt embroidered with nautical flags—"They spell out my name in flag code," he said with a grin, "a gift from Mom"—he reported that he was ready to take on the Mancini clan.

"Let's get going, Charleston boy," Ella said.

"This is a Hamptons clam bake look," Hank insisted, and picked up the big pot of sauce. "It complements your hipster, Union Square farmers market in spring look, don'tcha think?"

She glanced down at her halter sundress. "This is not what I'd call hipster, Union Square farmers market in spring. I'm going for an Isle of Palms beach shack shop post–Labor Day sale look."

"Whatever it is, you look fantastic," he said.

She eyed him. "No flirting."

"No way." He eyed her back just as sternly.

Satisfied, she followed behind him to the front door, and tried not to look at his backside in those Levi's. But it was impossible not to. She indulged herself while she could, and then he opened the door and turned, the delicious view gone—for the moment, at least.

Ella shut the door behind her. It was still light out, the height of summer. It wouldn't get dark until after eight.

"I wonder how Pammy's doing," he said, and wedged the pot of sauce on the floor of the back seat between a few bricks they'd found in the potting shed behind the carriage house. The lid was on tight, but even so, the delicious aroma of a good meat sauce filled the car when they got in.

"I texted her to let her know where we are," Ella said, "in case her date is over before we get back to the house."

"That was nice."

"She wrote back that she was killing it." Ella laughed. "They're walking around the Market with all the tourists. The merchants know Reggie, of course, so they're saying hello. Pammy said she's being treated like a queen, especially at the food stalls. She's getting free samples right and left."

"I'm glad she's having fun."

"Me too. She's doing great. I think her nerves were more about being a little homesick. Maybe her parents can come out and see her soon."

"I'll fly them out." Hank sounded relaxed. Sort of like the old Hank who used to hang out with her on a blanket in Central Park, a basket of grapes and Saga cheese and good bread between them. They'd chug wine from a Thermos.

"You mean, like on a private jet?"

He shrugged. "It's a perk."

Ella enjoyed the companionable silence that fell over them as she navigated the narrow streets, so many of which were one-ways.

When they turned onto East Bay Street, she braked to let a couple of tourists with cameras cross in the middle of the street since no one was behind her. "Harris Teeter on East Bay Street is Charleston's biggest social gathering spot," she told him.

A minute later, they were at the door. Hank opened it for her, and they made quick work of getting a vase of Mama Mancini's favorite, gerbera daisies. She liked all colors of them, Ella said, so Hank got her red, pink, and orange. And then he picked up a couple of bottles of the most expensive red wine in the place. When they were almost to the register, he turned back around and got two cases of the same stuff. A clerk went in the back and grabbed two cardboard boxes and loaded them up.

"So everyone can have a taste," Hank said, "and then your mother can keep some for later."

"Really," Ella said, mortified, "you don't have to do this." She felt terrible. The bill was going to be around a thousand dollars. Harris Teeter prided itself on carrying good wine.

"I know I don't," Hank said in line at the register. "But let me get some pleasure out of making so much money. Most of it just sits there collecting interest."

"All right," she said, hating to cave in. She didn't want to feel beholden to Hank, and now he was spending a fortune on wine for her family. She hoped he wasn't doing it for *her*.

"Don't think I'm trying to buy my way back into your good graces either," he said, reading her mind. "I've gotten spoiled. I like nice wine, and I can afford it. This has zero to do with me and you."

*Me and you.*

"Got it," she said, feeling slightly relieved. And then disappointed. A secret part of her that she only reluctantly acknowledged wanted Hank to try to please her. The truth was, she was lying pretending she could be around him and not let romantic thoughts about him— about *them*—intrude.

She missed him. Plain and simple.

At Mama's, the curb on both sides of the street was lined with Mancini vehicles. There was a preponderance of old Dodge Challengers from the *Dirty Harry* era, mainly because in New York, no Mancini had needed a car. So when they'd arrived in Charleston, Uncle Sal had bought a fleet of first-generation Challengers, built between 1970 and 1974, from the widow of a collector in Myrtle Beach who sold them at a massive discount to him because she was moving to a nursing home. Uncle Sal had gifted them to the family because "I want you all to have wheels," he'd said. "But you need to get a license first. Even you, Mama Mancini."

The cars were a gift to everyone, a result of selling

their family restaurant in the Bronx at a tremendous profit, the one Papa had been a partner in. Ella was the only one with a "normal" car, a boring four-door sedan she'd bought when she'd first arrived in Charleston. It turned out that Mama loved her hot rod, adored driving, and was the best driver in the entire family.

"Whoa," Hank said, when he saw the cars, all the hoods striped, the bodies painted either cobalt blue, scarlet red, lemon yellow, white, black, or silver.

"People come by to look at them on Sunday afternoons," Ella said. "That's when we gather at Mama's for dinner." She told him their purchase history.

Hank laughed. "I want to meet this Uncle Sal."

"He's great," Ella said.

"I loved your family restaurant in the Bronx," Hank said, "especially the marinara sauce. So simple yet robust. I used to dream about it after you left."

"You did?" Somehow that got her right in the heart.

"Yes, but I was afraid to go back."

It was a shame, but she understood.

"Anyway," he said, "every time I was there with you, it never had an empty table."

"It was very successful." Ella was proud of Papa and her whole family. Everyone had played a part. "That marinara sauce is my great-great-grandmother's recipe. I've finally learned how to make it."

"You have?"

She laughed. "Yes, I was a haphazard cook when I was younger. But I'm starting to appreciate devotion in the kitchen."

"I always loved your cooking."

"Well, you'll get to see how much I've improved."

"I'm very lucky," Hank said.

She believed he meant it. Hank wasn't a person who

tossed out meaningless compliments. They walked up
the sidewalk side by side. She carried the pot of sauce.
He lugged the two cases of wine, one stacked on the
other. They must have weighed a ton, but he had the bi-
ceps and triceps to handle them.

"I'll send a nephew or niece out for the flowers," Ella
said.

She had the strangest feeling as they strode together,
their steps matching. It felt as if they were a couple. They
were in sync again. The pot of sauce was their mutual
offering, that and the wine and the flowers.

She stole a glance at his gorgeous profile, his stubbled
jaw and defined cheekbones. "You'll be fine," she said.
"Don't worry, okay?"

He chuckled over the top of the boxes. "I'm not worried. I'm excited."

"You are?" That made her happy.

"Very. These are *your people*."

He said it as if that made them special, which was
sweet of him. "Yes, they are," she replied. The Mancinis
weren't exactly polished. And no one would ever peg
them as being from Charleston. But this was the place
the Mancinis called home now—this Southern city,
which they'd embraced with utter faith that they could
make their contribution to the community and be happy
here.

They had made their mark in only a few short years,
and they were very happy.

The next thing Ella knew, she and Hank were swept
up in a crowd of loud talkers who whisked the pot of
sauce out of her arms, then kissed her and hugged her
tight without her even getting to explain Hank's presence.

"Wait," she yelled over the noise, and watched two
teenage Mancini nephews carrying the cases of wine

toward the kitchen. A younger sister—not Jill, who was still in New York with Cosmo—carried the pot of sauce. "I need someone to get the flowers out of the car—and to introduce someone to you!"

"We know him!" cried Nonna Sofia. "He's that lovely young officer from the World War Two movie!"

"And the other movie where he takes the queen as a lover even though his head might get chopped off!" shouted Nonna Boo. "*Abbiamo visto il suo culo nudo!*" she called to eight people huddled in a corner—the Sicilian relatives. *We've seen his naked butt!*

Ella and her three younger sisters in their twenties—two of them married with kids—and her fourteen-year-old niece giggled.

"*Abbiamo visto anche il suo culo nudo!*" called back one of the Sicilian relatives. *We've seen his naked butt too!* He was a skinny old man with closely cropped white hair, large blue eyes, and an unshaven face. He wore a faded coat and a shirt buttoned up to his neck.

"My goodness," Mama shouted. "We've all seen his naked butt—except the children. It's Hank! Hank Rogers! Ella's old beau!"

"The one who dumped her?" cried Uncle Sal.

Ella cringed.

"The very one," said Mama, but she didn't sound angry. She sounded happy. So very happy.

What was *that* about?

Ella wished Jill was here to ask. Sometimes she got Mama better than the other sisters. But Ella didn't have time to think about Mama at the moment. She tossed her keys to a nephew and told him to get the flowers from the car and put them in the kitchen. Then she caught a glimpse of her ex-lover out of the corner of her eye. He was surrounded by younger Mancini cousins, all of whom had seen him in a big Christmas movie the year before. He'd played Santa Claus's misunderstood brother in a screen adaptation of K. O. Cronkite's bestselling children's novel, *I Am Santa's Brother.*

"It's Derrick!" they were yelling. A few hopped up and down.

The youngest one, four-year-old Margaret, was crying. Tears of joy, apparently. "D-Derrick," she stuttered through her tears. "I love you soooo much. Can you call Santa *right now*?"

Poor Margaret! Ella couldn't help but laugh. It was funny to think of Santa having a brother named Derrick. Margaret certainly thought Santa did.

"My brother's busy eating cookies right now, sweetheart," said Hank. "Gimme some snow slaps." That was nerdy Derrick's signature greeting. Hank held out his hand. Every kid lined up and slapped his palm, then said, "Ice to meet you!"

"Ice to meet you too," he said back in his Derrick voice.

Oh, God. Hank was excellent with kids. Willing to look like an idiot in the name of getting a laugh, yet he also looked like a hero. The character Derrick learned that not comparing himself to his brother Nicholas was the key to finding his own happiness. The kids gazed at Hank with shining eyes. Yet another reason to fall in love with him again—

Which Ella definitely refused to do.

All night long, she refused, even when he shyly offered the vase of gerbera daisies to Mama, then took her hand and kissed the back of it and said how sorry he was that he never told her when he was dating Ella that he admired her strength after the loss of her husband. Ella refused to fall in love with him again when he told Nonna

Sofia she had the eyes of a screen siren, and when he told Nonna Boo she was funny and he wanted to call her every day for a new joke.

Ella also refused to fall in love with him when he caught her gaze across the table when one of her younger sisters, the single one, twenty-one-years-old, was telling everyone that true love did not exist, that every guy she went out with turned out to be a frog.

"You'll find your prince someday," said Mama.

"Huh," said Ella's single sister. Cara was her name. It meant "dear."

"And when you do, you'll know it," said Nonna Sofia. "But it won't be a big moment. It will be a quiet one."

"Don't knock those big moments," Nonna Boo said with a chuckle.

Nonna Sofia began to laugh with her, although more quietly. It was a knowing laugh from both of them, one that clearly had everything to do with the unbridled joys of sex.

"*Nonnas*," Uncle Sal chided them. "We've got company." He indicated Hank.

Hank grinned. "I'm enjoying myself immensely," he assured the table.

"He's enjoying himself," Nonna Boo said, and kept chuckling along with Nonna Sofia.

"Mama," said one of the nieces, age eight, "why are the *nonnas* laughing?"

"They've had a great deal of fun in life," said one of Ella's younger married sisters.

Ella looked at Hank and grinned. What the heck. It wasn't going to kill her to share some funny moments with him.

Mama repeated the snippet of conversation in Italian for the Sicilian side of the family. All evening, translations had been tossed around the table, and the Sicilians would nod and sometimes offer extended comments that Mama would translate for the younger crowd. Not everyone at the table was fluent in Italian. Not by a long shot, including Ella.

Now the Sicilian guests laughed and two of them rattled off some Italian, and laughed some more, along with Mama, Uncle Sal, and the *nonnas*.

"It's time," said Nonna Sofia, and took her knife and hit the long table that ran the length of the living room—the only room that could accommodate two long tables end-to-end, and a round cousins' table—with the bottom of the handle, making the nearby wine glasses filled with Hank's delicious wine rattle. "It's time for the story of my shoe." She stared at Ella. "Only *you* may hear it."

# CHAPTER NINETEEN

Ella tried to hide her sense of awkwardness with a smile. She didn't like being singled out. All her sisters and nieces, even Máma, would feel hurt that Nonna Sofia didn't want to include them in the telling of the shoe story. Why had Nonna Sofia brought up the topic in front of the entire family? She was acting very strange, even for Nonna Sofia.

"Nonna Sofia," she asked gently, "wouldn't it be nice if all the women in the family could listen to your shoe story?"

"*No,*" her grandmother said, her lower lip sticking out. "Only you. And if you tell it to anyone else, I will be very unhappy."

It was final. That face meant Nonna Sofia refused to budge. And Ella was stuck.

She exchanged a glance with her mother. *She's being difficult*, Mama's gaze said. *Just go along with her.*

"Very well, Nonna Sofia," Ella said softly.

"Not until after the tiramisu," said Nonna Boo, "which Daisy and Nina made this morning with their grandmother."

Mama smiled over at the cousins' table. "The girls did an excellent job."

"Thank you, Nonna Maria," the two girls said in unison.

"I know this shoe story," one of the Sicilian guests, Nonna Alberta, said in a voice that sounded as if it needed to be oiled, like a creaky hinge. It was the first time she'd spoken that night.

The tables went silent. Everyone had forgotten that Nonna Alberta spoke English. They rarely saw her, and whenever she talked, it was in Italian. But Ella remembered her mother telling her that Nonna Alberta was the only Sicilian relative who spoke *fluent* English.

Nonna Alberta was ninety-two. She'd spent three years in New York in her early twenties with her American soldier husband, who was killed in the Korean War. She'd then gone back to Sicily as a widow, remarried, and had three children. "I will tell everyone else this tale while Sofia tells Ella in private," she said. "It is not her story only. It is a story for the entire family. May all who hear it embrace it as a piece of precious family history."

Nonna Sofia turned bright red. But she said nothing. She couldn't defy the matriarch of the Sicilian branch of the family, who was a good fifteen years older than she.

"Go ahead, Nonna Alberta," Uncle Sal said. "Tell my mother's shoe story."

Nonna Alberta cleared her throat. "Once, back in the early seventies, a young lady named Sofia Brattorio arrived in Palermo from a nearby village, but her home was in Rome."

*Sofia Brattorio* . . . that was Nonna Sofia's name before she married, the children at the cousins' table quickly learned from their whispering mothers.

"Sofia was no more than seventeen or eighteen," said

Nonna Alberta, "and wore beautiful leather sandals with a very high heel when she got off the bus. They showed off her legs to perfection. In Palermo, women in high heels were not a common sight. My two sisters and I, all of us married with grown children, were shopping in the nearby market and were enthralled with these shoes. We wanted to meet this young girl to get a closer look at her. But before we could walk the short distance to the bus stop, where she was struggling with a very fat suitcase, a young man came up to her and began talking rapidly, moving his hands with some urgency. He took her suitcase, and she went scurrying after him."

Nonna Sofia sat stiffly while Nonna Alberta told the story. Ella felt for her. She could tell Hank did too, by the serious, concerned look in his eyes. They were very expressive, which was probably why, in addition to his good looks, the big screen loved him so much.

"And then what happened, Nonna Alberta?" Mama encouraged her to go on.

Nonna Sofia scowled at her daughter, and Ella remembered that she hadn't wanted Mama to hear the story, in case she became ashamed of Nonna Sofia, if she thought her foolish.

Nonna Alberta looked down the table at Nonna Sofia. "We thought Sofia Brattorio would pull off her shoes to keep up with the young man. But she kept the gorgeous sandals on her feet. We went running after her, and then others began to follow. Especially the men."

Everyone at the table chuckled. Except for Nonna Sofia.

"Sofia did not look back at the crowd," Nonna Alberta said. "Neither did the young man carrying her suitcase, whom we knew to be the son of a powerful vineyard owner in Palermo, a high and mighty man above our touch. Many of us worked for him, but he wouldn't attend any festivals with the townspeople. Nor would his son."

Ella had *no* idea where this story was going. But she would be patient. Most of her family's stories were long and circuitous.

"Eventually, we all got to the gates of the vineyard," said Nonna Alberta. "The big house was at the other end of the drive. The son of the owner opened the gates and let the young woman through, and then shut the gates in our faces. I asked him, 'What has happened?' and he said that the young lady in the fancy city shoes was the nurse from Rome who would help deliver the baby of the owner's favorite mistress, who had gone into labor a month early. The vineyard owner had kept her in a house in a nearby village to be prepared."

Nonna Sofia's face went redder than ever.

"And?" Uncle Sal asked Nonna Alberta.

"Sofia Brattorio told the son she would put one shoe outside the mistress's cottage window if the baby was a girl, two if it was a boy. If it was a boy, the baby was to be adopted by the vineyard owner. If it was a girl, the mistress and the baby would be sent away."

"To where?" asked a teenage niece of Ella's.

"Oh, probably to a convent near Rome," said Nonna Alberta. "Somewhere far away, never to be seen again in Palermo."

"That's not very nice," said an eight-year-old nephew.

"What's a mistress?" asked Margaret, her pudgy little hands folded on the cousins' table.

Her mother looked back at her. "A fine lady," she murmured.

Ella and her married sisters exchanged worried looks. Nonna Sofia had been right not to tell this story to the whole family. Mama, too, appeared nervous, her lips pinched thin. Hank, Ella saw, had a serious, calm expression on his face, but his eyes were alert. It was his protective mode. She remembered it from long ago. If he thought something was about to happen that could hurt Ella, he became guarded. She wished—inappropriately— that he were sitting next to, not across from, her.

Nonna Alberta went on. "Ten hours of not knowing passed. The sun was going down when one shoe finally appeared outside the cottage window." She looked down the length of the adult tables. "The new mother, who had been the owner's favored companion for twenty years, did not want to be sent away. Palermo was her home. So the nurse pleaded with the vineyard owner on the mother's behalf, and he let her and the baby girl stay on. The nurse, he said, must also stay for three months to assist the new mother. During that time, the son of the owner fell deeply in love with Sofia Brattorio and asked her to marry him several times. But she always said no."

Nonna Sofia's eyes filled with tears that did not fall. Ella's stomach tilted. This story was creating terrible tension in her grandmother. Ella was worried. So was Mama, who couldn't stop looking across the table at her stricken mother.

"What then?" asked one of the aunts. "Did the nurse return to Rome?"

"No." Nonna Alberta gave a crooked smile. "An eighteen-year-old young man in the crowd who followed Sofia Brattorio the first day she arrived in Palermo, a poor boy who tended the owner's vines daily, was secretly courting her, leaving offerings of grapes and small bouquets of fresh marjoram and thyme outside her door behind those big gates. It was *he* whom she loved. And *he* whom she chose to marry. That young man was my son Giuseppe, *your* late father, Maria."

Mama's face lost a few of its anxious lines. "Papa," she said, with a warm smile at Nonna Sofia.

But Nonna Sofia was looking at Ella. "He was *your* grandfather, which is why I wanted to tell you the story, as you are my only granddaughter to turn thirty and not yet be married."

In this traditional family, that was unusual. Ella was secretly amused, but she maintained a respectful posture. It helped that Hank, too, had a gleam in his eye—that protective one, which bolstered Ella more than she liked.

"I chose the man of my heart," said Nonna Sofia. "I want you, too, my dear Ella, to wait as long as it takes for your own Giuseppe. And if he never shows up, I want you to be a kickass single lady for everyone to admire."

*Kickass single lady?* Maybe Nonna Sofia wasn't so traditional, after all.

"I will, Nonna Sofia," Ella said. "I'll be one of those single ladies who goes out dancing and wears gorgeous shoes all the time."

Everyone laughed.

"I stopped wearing sexy high heels when I married," Nonna Sofia said. "Back in the old days, it was grape-stomping country in Palermo. Many dirt roads, stone walls, and high grasses too. Not a good place for heels, but you must keep wearing yours, whether you marry or not. Promise me, Ella."

"I will," Ella said with a smile. She was glad the story was over. Done. They could move on. It had been charming, very sweet. But she could only take so much singling out at the family table because she wasn't married.

"Mama," cried Ella's mother, "why would you not

want your own daughter to hear the love story of her parents?"

Oh, no. They were to go on, apparently. Hank caught Ella's eye. He was worried about her, and it warmed her heart. She smiled at him. *I'm fine*, she tried to say without speaking.

Nonna Sofia lifted her chin. "Because you might think me foolish."

"Why would I?" Mama asked.

"I turned down the rich man and married the poor."

"Why would I think that foolish?" Mama asked. "I believe in love. And without you and Papa together, I would never have happened!"

"We will discuss this later," Nonna Sofia said in a hard tone, her mouth thin, her brow drawn low.

Something shifted in that moment. A feeling passed between Ella and the feminine members of the dinner party silently and faster than the speed of light. It occurred to her immediately, and she could see the same thing happening to all the grown women in the room—her sisters, her mother, her aunts, and to Nonna Boo, whose eyes widened—that Nonna Sofia was suggesting Mama's paternity was in question.

*Nonna Sofia must have slept with the son of the vineyard owner before she married her Giuseppe!*

Ella was rocked. To the core.

But imagine how poor Mama must feel!

Mama laughed, but it sounded almost like a cry, which broke Ella's heart. "You're not saying, Mama . . ."

Nonna Sofia looked at her. "*Later.*" Then she turned to Nonna Alberta. "See what happens when you take my story away from me and tell the whole family?"

"Why did you bring it up in front of the whole family?"

asked Nonna Alberta. "Because deep inside, you wanted it to see the light!"

"No," said Nonna Sofia.

"You were playing with fire," said Nonna Alberta, "and you knew it, and you were tired of carrying this secret." She frowned at Nonna Sofia. "It is why we are here, to prove that Maria is indeed Giuseppe's daughter."

*Oh, my God*, Ella thought, her heart racing. Every single adult in the room stiffened.

"Of course, I'm Giuseppe's daughter!" Mama slapped her hand on the table, her bosom rising and falling rapidly. "How could you have kept this from me all these years, Mama?"

To Mama's left, Uncle Sal wrapped an arm around her shoulder. "Hush, Maria, no need to be upset. This changes nothing. We are family—you and I are brother and sister, united forever by blood *and* through love. As you are with the rest of the family."

Mama blinked back a tear. "Thank you, Sal," she croaked out.

Aw, Uncle Sal! Ella couldn't cry, even though seeing Mama cry made her feel terrible. She was simply too stunned, and she wanted to stay strong for Mama.

Nonna Boo sat on Mama's right. She reached over to Mama's flattened palm on the table and wrapped her gnarled fingers around it. "Don't you worry," she said. "Don't you worry, my daughter through marriage. Mine forever," she added fervently, which touched Ella's heart too.

She and Hank exchanged a look again. *I'm here for you*, his eyes seemed to say. And she was glad, *so* glad he'd come with her today. She lifted her half-full glass of red wine to her lips and downed the rest of it, thankful that he'd bought it, not only to honor her family but because he so obviously wanted to please her, however much he'd denied it earlier at Harris Teeter.

He'd brushed off his effort because of *her*, because he knew she would spurn his reaching out to her through thoughtful gestures. He'd been right too, and she wondered now why she'd been so willing to turn away a loving action. Of course, it was because she was afraid to get hurt by him again.

But look at her now. Alone, and hurting. No matter what, pain would come to her life. How much control did she have, really? How much should she try to exert to keep the hurt at bay, or was it part and parcel of loving? Of being in relationships?

"Thank you, Nonna Boo, for your sweet words," said Mama, "but of course, I must worry."

"No," said Nonna Boo. "This changes nothing."

Nonna Sofia sighed. "You were born five months after we married, daughter. We were never sure. But it doesn't matter. It doesn't."

"I thought babies took *nine* months to bake," said one of the nephews under age ten.

"Some babies take less," said his mother.

"Then why were you going to tell Ella?" Mama asked her mother.

"To get it off my chest before I die," said Nonna Sofia, "and not to burden *you*. Ella can take it. Especially if she never marries and has the additional worry of a family of her own."

Ella's heart hurt hearing herself spoken of that way. A quick glance around the table showed her that other people were taken aback by the bluntness of Nonna Sofia's remark too. But Ella, chagrined as she was at being so casually written off as a possible singleton for life, was also oddly touched Nonna Sofia found her competent to handle her personal secret.

"But we can find out the truth," said Nonna Alberta to Nonna Sofia, "and I want to before *I* die. The family of Giuseppe, my beloved son, deserves to know if all of his long, illustrious line carries his blood. We have brought strands of his hair I saved from his favorite comb. Sofia, you may also have artifacts that could aid us." She shot a laser look at Mama. "If tests reveal new facts, we are still family, bonded at the heart, child. No need to be upset."

A tear trickled from Mama's eye and she pushed up from the table. "I am far from being a child," she said. "I am much too old for this."

No one knew what to say. Ella jumped up from her chair too. She went to her mother. "It's all right," she tried to soothe her, and put her arm around Mama's waist.

But Mama ignored her. She was far too distressed to accept comfort. Even so, Ella squeezed her closer. She caught Hank's eye. *You're doing the right thing*, he said without speaking. *Hang in there*.

"This family doesn't need this sort of upheaval," Mama said. "Look at you, all in shock. And the children . . ."

"We're fine, Nonna Maria!" cried one nephew. "We don't know what's going on. But we don't like it if it makes you cry!"

"*Nonna Maria!*" Little Margaret said, her voice cracking.

Mama's smile trembled. "Don't cry, sweet Margaret, I am *fine*," she said to her youngest grandchild and to everyone at the cousins' table. She then seemed to notice Ella. "I'm okay," she said softly. "You go sit down, *preziosa*."

"All right, Mama," Ella said, and kissed her cheek.

"We can have this resolved within the week," said Nonna Alberta. "We simply need you to cooperate, Maria, with the testing. And Sofia must be supportive, as well."

Mama squeezed her eyes shut, then opened them. "So be it," she said.

Ella's sisters, her aunts and uncles, everyone at the table, including Hank, felt for Mama. It was evident in their drawn brows, the deepening lines on either side of their mouths.

Poor Nonna Sofia. She was swallowing hard, trying to keep from crying herself. "All right," she said to Nonna Alberta, "we will cooperate, but you could have told us what you were up to before you flew across the ocean to wreak havoc in our lives."

"You wouldn't have wanted us to come," Nonna Alberta said stoutly. "And it was meant to be. You yourself brought up the shoe story, in front of the entire family. *It was meant to be.*"

And that was that. The proclamation from the Sicilian matriarch, age ninety-two.

"Let's have dessert," said Uncle Sal.

"Yay!" the children all shouted.

Hank met Ella's gaze once more. He gave her a little nod, a discreet wink of encouragement. She was rattled to the core, but she had to be brave for Mama and the children. She had to carry on as if everything was the same—because it really was, if they wanted it to be. It really was.

Love didn't care about paternity tests.

# CHAPTER TWENTY

"That was more dramatic than any movie scene I've ever filmed," said Hank in the car. Ella let him drive. He grabbed her hand without asking. Squeezed it tight. "Are you okay?"

She nodded. "I think so. But poor Mama. I can't even imagine how she's feeling. Did you see her helping the girls scoop out the tiramisu? She kept praising them, acting as if nothing had changed. Which is good, because really, nothing has."

"Right," Hank assured her. "She's still your mother. And Sofia's daughter. And Giuseppe's daughter, whatever the test results are."

"But she was under such stress," Ella said. "I'm sure she wanted the gathering to end. But she stayed and acted cheerful for everyone."

"It was a massive shock, I'm sure," Hank said. "It would be for anyone. It'll take a while to process, don't you think?" He released Ella's hand, not wanting to take advantage of her wobbly emotions.

"Yes," Ella said, her voice breaking a little. "Mama is strong."

"She's a real trouper," Hank agreed.

"I wish Papa were here to support her."

"*You're* here, and all the family," Hank reminded her. He hated to see her so upset, but what could he do? Nothing, really, except be her friend.

"I'm counting on the test saying my grandfather Giuseppe was her biological father, and this whole crisis will pass."

"Of course it will," he said, turning her car into the driveway to the carriage house. They passed the Wilders' big house, the corner of it glowing under a street light, then moved into almost total blackness, save for the tiny porch light on the carriage house's front step. "It will pass even if it turns out her biological dad is the son of the vineyard owner. Your mother will have lots of loved ones to support her."

"I hope that doesn't happen."

"It won't be easy," he said, turning off the car engine. They sat in silence, listening to the engine tick as it cooled. "Change is hard. Especially, I'll bet, when you've believed one thing for fifty years or more, and you find out you didn't necessarily have all the facts."

Ella let out a gusty sigh. "I had no idea I was leading you into the lion's den today. I'm really sorry."

"Don't worry about me," Hank said, and dared to look at her. "I'm worried about *you*. Not only about how you're feeling about your mother and her situation. What Nonna Sofia said about you not being married—it wasn't an insult, but it's obvious that you're the odd woman out in some ways in your family."

Ella nodded. "I'm used to that. I've never been very traditional. But I think they're proud of me for stepping out, getting Mancini women to think about their options. Not that I don't want to be a wife and mother someday . . ."

I do—if I find the right partner. But marriage isn't the only way to be happy. I want my little girl nieces and cousins and my youngest sister—the one who keeps kissing frogs—to realize that they can have a full, wonderful life on their own, with friends and family. And if they're lucky, they might find a partner to lean on and love in return. So says the matchmaker."

She grinned and stole a glance at him.

He put a lock of hair behind her ear. "You're amazing," he said.

She smiled shyly. A beat passed. "I know," she eventually replied, and laughed out loud.

It was a relief to hear her do that. He laughed too. "I'm glad you realize you're the cat's meow."

She shrugged. "It took a long time."

"It was my fault," he told her. "When I left, did you think I thought you were lacking somehow?"

"I couldn't help but wonder that, yes," she said.

"I never did." He tried to maintain eye contact with her, but she looked away. "It was all on me. *I* had issues. Not you. You were wonderful then, and you still are. Better than ever, in fact."

Yes, he was talking too much. But guess what? He had to stop thinking so hard and simply be who he really was, whether he got rejected or not.

"We should go in," she said quietly.

"Okay." He wouldn't push it any further, and she obviously didn't want him to either. "I wonder when Pammy will be home?" It was nine o'clock. Her date had lasted a good three hours.

Pammy was a safe change of subject.

"I don't know," Ella said. The house was dark. "But it must mean she's having fun. And that makes me happy."

"Me too."

Things felt a little more normal, or at least less tense, between them. He wanted to win a second chance with Ella, but he hoped that somehow—if he maintained faith in what he believed they still had between them—she would move toward him too.

When they got inside, Hank flipped the light switch in the living room, and a lamp turned on in the corner, casting a yellow beam over a worn leather armchair with a matching ottoman, scuffed from lots of shoes being put up on it. He couldn't remember the last time he'd sat in a beat-up recliner with a couple of magazines or a good novel. He had plenty of downtime on movie sets, but he used those hours to call friends and business contacts, answer emails, and read scripts. He was usually in a trailer, which shouted *temporary* the same way a hotel room did.

"You okay?" he asked Ella. "Should we do something like go to the Blind Tiger and play some pool?"

She waved a hand. "No, thanks." She put her purse by the door and plopped onto the sofa. "This is heaven," she said, "Just sitting here. I love my family, but . . ."

"But they suck a lot of energy out of the room. Like a tornado." He tossed her car keys into her purse.

"You've described the Mancini clan well," she said. "Usually, though, I come home feeling revived. The tornado picks me up and puts me on fresh green grass. But tonight? No. That's not happening."

"Would a glass of wine help?"

"Sure." She sounded distracted, and no wonder. "I had plenty at Mama's, but it's one of those nights that another wouldn't hurt."

In the kitchen, Hank opened a bottle of red wine—not nearly as good as what they'd had at Mama Mancini's, but it would do. There was no TV, so everything was quiet. He realized they'd have to chat. Or play a game.

Maybe Scrabble would take her mind off things. "You want to get out the Scrabble board?" he called to her.

"Sure," she said again.

He could tell she wasn't too invested in talking or being social.

Under any other circumstances, Hank—who was used to tons of attention—might feel mildly insulted. But he couldn't blame Ella for withdrawing. He wanted to comfort her badly. But he had to remember his boundaries.

*No flirting*, he commanded himself when he exited the kitchen with two empty glasses and the open wine bottle. Ella was busy setting up the Scrabble board on the coffee table. He pulled up an armchair on the side opposite her, then poured them each a glass of wine. She pushed seven blank wood squares toward him, the letters facing down, and a letter rack to stand them on. She set her letter rack up too, an adorable squiggle on her brow.

He'd been right to remind her of Scrabble. She could forget for a little while what had happened at her mother's house that night.

His phone vibrated and he looked at it. *Date going well*, Pammy texted him. *Won't be home tonight.*

*Sure you're not moving a little fast?* he texted back.

*If you call taking the nine pm to six am shift at the homeless shelter's front desk moving fast,* she wrote. *Reginald asked if I'd want to hang out with him, and I said yes.*

*Good for you for volunteering,* Hank texted. *Can you take the day off tomorrow?*

*I'm the master wood craftsman, so I make the rules,* Pammy said. *But I'll probably come home, eat breakfast, and work until one. Then crash.*

*Sounds good,* he texted, and sent her a thumbs-up emoji.

She sent one back.

And then he sent her the emoji of an eagle. Pammy loved birds of prey.

She sent him a GIF of puppies.

Pammy was being mischievous. She knew he wanted a puppy but had never committed to getting one. He could ignore her teasing, but it was much harder to ignore Ella, who chewed her lower lip as she moved her tiles around, looking like a pouty sex goddess. He sighed inwardly. She was oblivious to the illicit direction his thoughts were taking as she prepped to take him down. He was determined to do the same—to focus on annihilating her at Scrabble.

Hah. Fat chance. Fat chance that he'd win—she was brilliant—and fat chance that he could stop thinking about her—

With no clothes on.

Yeah, he was a Neanderthal like that. Not that anyone would ever know. He was a sophisticated guy. A ladies' man too, but a gentleman, above all. He was proud of that fact.

"What exactly are you thinking?" She eyed him suspiciously.

He had to come up with something quickly. "Words."

"What kind of words?"

*Luscious.*

*Sexy.*

"Scrabble words," he said. "Like 'aardvark.' 'Meticulous.' And 'ostentatious.'"

"Right." She gave a short laugh.

Okay, so she didn't believe him. In fact, she saw right through him.

Which sucked. The whole night dragged before them. It was going to be difficult to think about Scrabble words and not Ella's beautiful form and her warm heart. Hank desperately wanted to bed her. But he refused to cave and admit that he was lusting after her. It was time to summon his best acting chops.

"May I go first?" he asked, pretending he was chomping at the bit. "I'd really like to, if you don't mind."

"Be my guest."

He saw that wary look in her eyes. He was almost positive it wasn't about him being a horndog but about Scrabble. She wanted to win, and she was worried he had a really good word. Thank God she was so competitive.

"Okay," he said, and started to panic. He *didn't* have a great word. The best he could come up with was "stove." La-di-da.

He put it down, picked up five new wooden squares to put on his letter rack.

"Stove," she said.

The clock on the mantel ticked loudly. He was determined to keep his poker face. Was that a twitch of her mouth he saw? Was she about to laugh at him?

"Your turn," he said, to take the heat off.

"Okay." She hunched over the board, her hands folded loosely and dangling between her legs. Her thinking pose.

The clock ticked. And ticked.

"Don't you have anything?" he asked, putting the pressure on. She'd appreciate that. If there was anything Ella hated, it was someone letting her win. She wanted victory fair and square. And she liked her opponents to be challenging, or the win meant nothing to her.

"I do have a word," she said.

"Bring it on." He watched her fingers hover over the little shelf holding the tiles.

She started with the *S* in "stove" and put an *E* underneath it. Then she looked up. "I'm going for a lot of points on this one." The next blank on the board was for a triple-letter score. She laid down the letter *X*, and looked up at him. The *X* was worth eight points. Times three.

What was that expression in her eyes? He couldn't tell.

"You're kidding me, right?" he asked her.

"Nope." She paused, then added three more letters—*T-E-T*—to spell "sextet." "Get your mind out of the gutter, Mr. Scorekeeper. That's twenty-nine points. Write it down."

He shook his head. Wrote it down. Looked back up. Saw her smile. It was a wicked one. Mischievous as hell.

"Sextet," she said, "as in a set of six people or things."

"Hey," he said. "Don't mess with me, all right?"

"We're playing Scrabble," she said.

"We'd better be," he said back. "You've had a rough night. Let's keep it simple."

"I am," she said. "Your turn."

If she was going to mess around with him, he'd mess around right back. He looked at the mix of letters he now had. Oh, she was going to regret that she'd ever started this!

He picked up an *O*. Put it next to the first *T* in "sextet." Added an *N* for "ton." A really crappy word worth almost no points. He paused and glanced at her out of the corner of his eye. She had that little smirk going. So far, so good. He wanted her to think she was winning in more ways than one.

"Well," he said, and sat back up. Looked at her as if he was done.

"That's it? 'Ton'?"

"I didn't say I was finished." His tone was casual. He added a *G*.

"'Tong,'" she said. "That's better. Although I always think of a pair of tongs with an *S*. I've never used it in the singular. But you could. You should have added it to the second *T* in 'sextet' so you could have gotten a double-letter score on *G*."

Such a smarty pants.

"I'm not done," he said, and took a sip of wine. He laid down a *U*. And then an *E*. "'Tongue.' *Now* I'm done. And by the way, by using the first T in 'sextet'"—he emphasized the word—"I managed a double-word score. More points this way."

She shifted uneasily. "Right. I didn't know you were going to spell . . . 'tongue.'"

"Now you do," he said. "You're still winning, but this game is far from over." Let her think any double entendres she wanted.

She looked at him over the rim of her wine glass. The air between them crackled with tension.

"Fine," she said, and started unbuttoning her shirt. "I agree. This game has only begun. Let's get it really started. You and I both know it was headed this way, didn't we?"

"*Ella*," he said, unable to take his eyes off her fumbling fingers. "What exactly are you doing?"

"You see what I'm doing."

"You've had too much wine. And a big shock."

"Not to mention you're my ex-boyfriend who dumped me when I thought you were about to give me a ring. I'd be an idiot to take off my clothes." Her expression was serene. Sexy.

She was the only woman in the world who could totally take him by surprise.

He jetted a breath. "We can't do this. You're in no condition. And if that's not enough to convince you, you never quit Scrabble before you win."

But she kept unbuttoning. "I haven't had nearly as

much wine as you think. And I'll grant you that the shock of what happened to Mama is making me a little crazy, yes. But it's also made me realize that life is short. Secrets suck. And the truth is, I've been lusting after you—against my better judgment—since I bumped into you when I was coming backward down the stairs with my suitcase. That kiss today didn't help. I'm not going to hide it anymore."

He put his head in his hands and groaned. "I'm in an awkward position here."

"You might as well give up."

He looked up. Met her eyes. She stopped unbuttoning. Her shirt gaped wide and her gorgeous breasts, encased in a silky bra, were a sight to behold. But it was her eyes that got to him. She was seeking something from him. That much was clear.

But she was also defiant.

"I told you," she said, "I go after what I want these days. And until someone stops me, I keep going."

"I'm going to stop you," he said.

"No, you're not." She shrugged out of her blouse and started working on her bra clasp.

He could feel his resolve weaken. "Just think about it, Ella. Seriously. I'm leaving when this week is over."

"Uh-huh." She was still fiddling with that bra. "I'm aware of that."

And then he heard the clasp release. The bra popped forward, the straps sliding down her arms. Her breasts were still covered. Just barely.

"You really want to get involved this way?" he asked.

"I've made it obvious. Do *you*?" She slid a strap off her arm.

Hank thought a few curse words so he wouldn't give in to temptation. She was more gorgeous than ever.

"Of course, I do," he said. "You're a beautiful woman. And . . ."

"And what?" she asked. She was now naked from the waist up. She leaned back on the sofa with her glass of wine. Her free arm was slung across her abdomen. She looked comfy lounging there on a sofa with her wine, her breasts unbound.

But he wasn't thinking comfy thoughts.

"You were saying?" She took a sip of wine.

"I said you're beautiful. And you know you're special to me." There. He got that out. "Which is why I'm not going to ruin things by getting involved this early."

"Meaning you were planning on getting involved before you left," she said, her unflinching gaze fixed on him.

"I wanted to," he said, admiring her confidence. "But I had no idea if we'd be in that place. I didn't want to force it."

"I've taken the first step, obviously."

"You have. In a big way. I didn't expect this, Ella. At all."

"But you're an international celebrity, Hank. This must happen to you all the time, women throwing themselves at you."

"You're not just any woman, and you're not throwing yourself at me. I feel distinctly unworthy. This half-naked-on-the-couch seduction scenario feels like you're intentionally reminding me of that fact."

"Maybe so."

"It's like waking up on Christmas morning after you've robbed a bank the night before, and Santa still gives you a gift. You feel guilty as hell when you open it."

She laughed.

"Well played, Ella." He said it with affection.

"Tell me this, Hank." She sat up a little higher. "You

could have come down to Charleston any time, so why'd you wait for a movie role?"

"It was a good excuse. Otherwise . . ."

"Otherwise, you would have nothing to hide behind," she filled in for him.

"You're right."

"What are you afraid of, Hank?" She swung her crossed leg. Took another sip of wine.

"Hurting you again," he said. "And never getting to touch you again. You can see I have a problem, and I don't see how it's solvable."

"It's not." She put her wine glass on top of the Scrabble board. And then she stood and unzipped her jeans, her eyes on his. "But venturing into that territory is a risk I'm willing to take. The older I get, the less inclined I am to run away. There's too much good stuff mixed in where hurt and fear reside. I don't want to lose out."

"I don't either." He stood.

"I'm getting naked. Feel free to join me." She got one leg out, revealing a pair of tiny silk panties that matched her bra. Back in the old days, she never had matching sets. She got her undergarments from discount department stores, five pairs of cotton panties to a pack and a bra on a plastic hanger, all for a song. The underwear she wore now was expensive, something a successful working woman could afford.

And then she started working on the other leg.

"If we do this, Ella, we're going to do it every day," he said, "until I leave."

She shimmied out of her panties. "We're on the same page."

# CHAPTER TWENTY-ONE

*Oh my God, what am I doing?* Ella thought as she pranced—yes, pranced—up the stairs buck naked on Tuesday night.

*I know what I'm doing*, she reminded herself. *This is what I want. And I embrace it.*

She *knew* her rear end was definitely bootylicious. Hank was a butt man, and seeing her from behind was probably driving him crazy in a good way that promised high sexual energy later. Hopefully, sooner rather than later. Hopefully, in about two minutes. Or less.

She threw herself on her bed.

Maybe in thirty seconds.

*Please! In thirty seconds . . .*

She started counting, and was at *twenty-seven Mississippi, twenty-six Mississippi* when he appeared at her door.

"Come on in," she said, leaning back on her elbows, her knees propped up, kept primly together.

That wouldn't last long.

That was the beauty of knowing someone already sexually. She was instantly comfortable. Hank knew her hot spots. She knew his—unless, of course, something had changed in the last ten years.

She'd had a few boyfriends over the last decade. One had lasted a whole year and a half. She'd even had two well-protected but steamy one-night stands with guys at conferences halfway across the world.

But nobody excited her and satisfied her the way Hank did. She was ready to join a convent after he left because she was sure she'd never want to have sex with another guy again. Luckily, she'd made the decision not to be so foolish and cut off her nose to spite her face. She was too young to swear off intimate encounters.

Yet she had to admit, not a single one had remotely reached the level of fantastic, mind-blowing lovemaking she'd shared with Hank.

He started unbuttoning and unzipping while she watched, and when she was at *four Mississippi* he landed on the bed next to her.

*Hank.* The man who'd left her, who didn't deserve to be with her, was now naked as a jaybird too, and a fine specimen of manhood he was. She raked her glance over him from top to toe. "Mmm-mmm," she said with the smallest shake of her head, to signify how intensely she appreciated his physique.

"That's a new Southern thing you've picked up," Hank said, almost grinning. But not.

She saw that he was torn between amusement and looking at *her,* appreciating her feminine form.

Well, let him look! Let him see what he'd been missing for a decade!

"I learned at Miss Thing's feet how best to show appreciation for something pretty, or remarkable," she said. "You're pretty remarkable."

"Not as remarkable as you," he said, and ran his hand down her side.

She closed her eyes and let herself enjoy the feeling of his hand on her flesh. "You feel amazing," she said.

He leaned over and kissed her breast—before he'd even kissed her mouth. And she let him. She jutted it higher, let him take more of her nipple into his mouth.

He grabbed her elbow, effectively making her fall on her back, and moved his mouth to her lips.

They kissed. With wild abandon. It was the only way she could describe it, and when she told the girls about it later—*if* she told the girls—that was what she would say. They kissed with wild abandon, their every inhibition gone. Then with the strength of a linebacker, she hooked his thigh with her leg and pulled him over on top of her. She had no idea how she managed that. She was petite, and he was a big guy. Her desperation to feel him covering her is what gave her the strength and agility.

When he was on top of her, she wrapped her legs around him and held him close, urging him toward union with her. And they'd barely started kissing.

But he was ready too. He was *so* ready.

And here she was. About to mess around with a man who'd done her wrong. What would her friends at Two Love Lane say?

She knew what they'd say.

But her survival instinct, which was really strong, wasn't as powerful as her desire for Hank. That eclipsed *everything*.

"You have protection?" she said. She was barely aware of the words they'd spoken. She was too lost in sensation, in remembering, in running her hand up and down his back.

Hank.

*Hank!*

They still fit perfectly together.

"Wait a minute," he murmured.

"You're getting something?" she asked. "I forgot. I don't have anything here. Aw, shoot. The Sicilian side of the family staying at my house might see my basket of condoms under the bathroom sink. I meant to move them." She paused. "They've been collecting dust."

She shouldn't have told him *that* part! Why did she do that? She had a tendency to get close too fast, say too much, believe in sunshine and unicorns.

*To trust too much.*

That was her problem.

"Don't worry about your relatives," Hank said, in between kissing her breasts, and then her belly. She knew where he was going, and it wouldn't require a condom. "You're thirty years old. You don't have to explain anything to anyone. And guess what? I don't have anything either."

"You mean you don't always carry something in your wallet?" She was shocked.

And then she had the magnificent—*stupid!*—thought that maybe he'd been celibate since he'd left her, that she was the only woman he'd ever wanted to have. And so he'd suffered without sex all these years.

"I'm not a teenager." He chuckled. "So, no, I don't carry a condom in my wallet. If I'm going to have sex with someone, I pretty much know when and where ahead of time. Sadly."

Oh. So he *had* had sex since he'd left her. Of course, he had. Too bad. She'd hoped—

No, she was a realist. Hank was a red-blooded, masculine male. And she wasn't actually a narcissist. She knew her body wasn't the only one in the entire world that could tempt him, especially over a period of ten years.

"Yeah, that's a shame," she said. "About the condom. But also about the fact that sex is scheduled for you."

"I said too much."

"So did I. About the dusty condoms." As if she needed to repeat that. She just couldn't stop herself.

They both laughed.

"I guess it's part of getting older," Ella said. "I mean, losing a sense of spontaneity. And wonder. Probably because we're very busy with our careers. And being grown-ups. Doing taxes and having to pay bills does nothing for my libido."

"Mine either, although I hire people to do that stuff." He pressed a deep kiss in her belly, and her pelvis rose up in response. She wasn't at all embarrassed. It was Hank. "And you know what? I haven't lost that sponta-neity with *you*."

"Maybe that's because we haven't had sex in ten years. It's new again."

"Maybe," he murmured. "But I don't think that's it. I really don't."

"You're kind to say," she said automatically, as if he'd complimented her on her dress. Or haircut.

"I'm not kind," he said. And before she could respond, he moved between the apex of her thighs, his face warm on her most delicate flesh, his hair sweeping over nerve endings that clamored for more. He burrowed there, kiss-ing every inch of her.

No tongue, though. Simply homage to a reunion be-tween old friends—him and her lady business.

She almost chuckled thinking about the Scrabble game, how the word "tongue" had sent her over the edge, and she'd practically ripped her clothes off. It was because she remembered . . . Hank had excelled at loving her this way.

"What hand of fate gave you those letters?" she asked him, barely able to speak. "The Scrabble gods?"

"You mean 'tongue'?" he asked, and then showed her what he was capable of with his.

"No, 'stove,'" she said. Even in the midst of this, she could crack a joke, heady with lust as she was.

He started to laugh.

The vibrations took her to the next level. "Oh," she said. It was sexy enough to make him stop laughing.

"Keep laughing," she whispered. "Please."

"No," he said low, which worked even better than laughing.

"Keep saying no," she said.

But he wouldn't. He wrapped her legs around his shoulders and took his sweet time, giving her the kind of focused, thoughtful attention he gave to everything in his life.

Within seconds, she was lost. Out of her mind.

*Why*, she managed to think right in the middle of it, *why did this ever go away?*

It was the best thing that had ever happened to her. If this happened to her every day, she would never want for anything more. She'd give up her special accounts at her favorite boutiques, her regular pedicures and manicures, her expensive perfume, and even her shoe collection.

"Hank," she cried as wave after wave took her. And was annoyed with herself. She shouldn't have called his name. Because no doubt he could tell from how she said it that *he* was the best thing that had ever happened to her.

Not the sex, great as it was. *Him.*

He was nirvana.

When the pleasure finally subsided, she closed her eyes and turned her head to the side, ready to melt into the sheets, to disappear so she could savor what had just happened.

His phone rang.

Her eyes flew open.

Hank cursed. The phone was across the room on top of the bureau. "I gotta get it," he said.

She followed him with her eyes. He didn't take his off her either. "Hello?" he said, grinning at her.

She smiled back and imagined herself taking a bath with him. In bubbles. With wine. . . .

She felt herself drift off as he spoke.

"Hey," he whispered close to her ear, what felt like a second later.

She came instantly awake. "Oops," she said. "I'm so sorry. That was the biggest—I mean, I haven't had something like that happen in a very long time. I mean, of that *caliber*. It kind of knocked me out."

"I'm flattered," he said. "It's fine. I had to take that call. I have to get to the set."

"You do?"

"Yes. In the next thirty minutes. They were able to clear the end of the Battery wall where we're doing that nighttime shot. We're supposed to do it tomorrow night, but it's going to rain."

She was still lying on her pillow. "Oh. Lucky I'm not in it." But then she remembered it was Hank's turn for sexual satisfaction now. He was ready. That much was clear. "We need to take care of you first," she said, "before you go."

"Nope."

She sat up on her elbows again. "What? That's crazy!"

And then she looked down the length of his body and couldn't stop looking. "That's actually criminal. I can't leave you like that."

"Sure you can," he said, and grabbed his jeans from the floor and slipped into them. "This is why they pay me the big bucks." He was wearing no boxers. She hadn't even noticed when he'd stripped earlier.

"You used to wear boxers," she said.

"Yeah, I know. I packed for myself this time and forgot them." He zipped up his jeans.

Good thing he wasn't outside around the paparazzi in the daylight. "What a shame," she said. *Not.* It wasn't a shame at all. She wished she could witness Hank in an aroused state in a pair of jeans and no shirt on all the time. "Are you going to go commando every day you're here?"

"Except on the set, I guess," he said. "They dress me from the inside out. In fact, I can steal a couple of pairs of boxers there."

"No!"

"Okay." He shrugged and pulled on his shirt, started buttoning.

"Why are you okay with not . . . being satisfied?" she asked, still resting on her elbows.

"Because I'm a professional actor," he said, "who's got a job to do."

"Oh, come on. I get that, but you're not even grumbling."

"It's because I had a great time," he said. "I feel lucky that I got to be with you. I'm counting my blessings. I could live off the visuals I have now in my head of you naked in this bed tonight for another ten years."

She blushed. "And why would I grumble when I know we're going to do this a lot this week?" he added.

"That's right!" She got excited at the thought.

He chuckled. "Besides, it was so obvious you were through."

She felt sheepish. "Really?"

"You were out like a light during that phone call."

"Sorry." She bit the edge of her thumb. "That was rude of me."

He laughed. "That's what happens when you interrupt a great moment to take a lousy phone call telling you to report to work."

She couldn't help laughing too. "Oh, Hank, I'm sorry."

"And to be honest," he said with a grin, "if you and I ever got back together, I'd owe you ten years' worth of sex to make up for my absenteeism anyway."

"Getting back together?" She swung her legs over the side of the bed. She felt light and happy. And she didn't take him seriously. She knew what he meant.

"I didn't say we *were*." He sat next to her. "I'm just saying if we *did*."

"We've only been in the same place together two days," she reminded him.

"Right. And we have a week. Not even."

"This is all rather . . ." She put her hands in the air, moved them up and down, palms up, not exactly sure what she was going for.

"This is all sudden."

"Exactly." She shook her head. "No one in their right mind—especially two people as smart as we are—"

"We know better than to—"

Neither one of them could finish the sentence. Ella didn't mind. She got the gist of it: they were crazy. This week was going to be wild and exciting. And then it would be over.

# CHAPTER TWENTY-TWO

Hank went to his room to get ready to head out.

Ella started dozing off again—she really had had the wind knocked out of her, in the best way—when her phone rang from the bureau. She groaned and jumped up to get it.

"Hello?" she croaked into it.

"You're asleep at nine thirty?" It was an English voice. Samantha.

"I had a busy day," Ella said.

"Well, I need you." Samantha sounded as if she wouldn't take no for an answer. "You're not in the shoot tonight. But I would love to run some lines with you before tomorrow morning's scene. I figured since your handsome roommate was coming, you wouldn't mind coming along as well."

Oh boy. Running lines. Ella was *not* excited, but she should be. This was Samantha Drake, world-famous, Oscar-winning actor.

"Sure," Ella said, and ran her hand through her hair to untangle it.

"By the way," said Samantha, "I think you two should be together. You and Hank."

Ella held the phone away from her ear. "*What?*"

"I said—"

Ella put the phone back. "No, I heard you, but it makes no sense. Why would you say that? Maybe *you* like him."

"He's not *nearly* good enough for me."

"He most certainly is." Ella huffed. "Not that I'm encouraging you to think in that direction."

"Good, because I'm not. But he's still quite the catch for someone else. So go jump his bones, or whatever you Americans call shagging."

"We're already halfway there," Ella said, "but you can't tell anyone."

"You *are?*" said Samantha.

Ella couldn't believe she'd admitted that. Maybe it was the wine, or the sex euphoria, lowering her inhibitions. Or maybe she wanted to lord it over Samantha, who only that afternoon had reminded Ella of all the sex scenes and kissing she'd do with Hank. "Yes, we are."

"Good for you. Is that why you sound . . . sleepy? Is that a post-coital drowsiness I'm sensing?"

"Please, Samantha," Ella said. "Let's not talk about it."

"If you insist."

"It doesn't mean anything anyway."

"It doesn't?" Samantha sounded doubtful.

"No."

"Then why do you sound like it *does*? You sound like it means the world. Which is quite a feat, considering you're rather out of it. I can hear your smile."

"You can't hear a smile." But it was true. Ella didn't even realize it. She was smiling.

"Have you been drinking?"

"A little. But that's not why I'm sleepy."

"I've heard of women like you. I'm the opposite. After a good shag, I'm rarin' to go."

"We didn't—"

"Oh, right. You didn't quite get there. Well, halfway is still not bad. It actually must have been damn good."

Ella didn't know what to say.

"More details, darling. I know you'd love to spill."

"We've only got a week together, but we're going to try to make the best of it," Ella confessed.

Samantha laughed. "Meaning you're hoping to shag all week long. Good luck. You two will be *working*, my dear. Grueling hours. And you're going to fall into bed each night exhausted. You'll be lucky to get five hours of sleep a night."

"Maybe we can rendezvous in his trailer," Ella said, "during the day."

"That's a pipe dream," Samantha replied. "People go in and out of there all day. Makeup, costumes, agents, producers. The caterer."

"We live together. Surely we can find time."

"Ella, have you ever been in a movie?"

"No."

"I promise you that the last thing on your mind when you get home will be making love. You'll collapse in bed."

"But he's so *hot*, Samantha." The truth must be spoken. "That won't happen."

"I hope not, too, for your sake, darling. He won't be here long. You must gather ye rosebuds while ye may, and so forth and so on."

Some old English poet had said that, Ella knew from high school.

The truth of Samantha's observations—and the

poet's—hit Ella hard. Something twisted in her throat, made her eyes burn. "So I'll see you tonight," she said, her voice cracking only a little.

Samantha sighed. "You don't want him to go on Saturday. Your heart is already involved."

"No," Ella insisted, "it's not."

"You might as well come to the set as often as possible," said Samantha, more gently. "It's Tuesday. The clock is ticking on Hank's departure. Mine too, for that matter, not that you care."

"Sure I care," said Ella, pinching the skin between her eyebrows as hard as she could. It helped her buck up. "You're a very interesting woman."

"Thank you. As are you."

There was a short silence on the line. Ella didn't know what to say. It was almost intimate, how they were speaking—formal, but as if they were veering toward becoming friends.

And they weren't. How could they be already? But look at what had happened with Hank already! Anything was possible.

"Okay, see you in thirty minutes," Ella said in a rush.

"Goodbye, Ella," Samantha said in her famous honeyed tones.

They hung up at the same time.

It was a bright, moonlit night when Ella and Hank started to walk to the Battery, only two blocks away from the carriage house. He grabbed her hand.

Ella let him. She savored the feel of her palm against his. Yet she couldn't relax into it. Not quite. "What does it mean, us holding hands?"

"That I like you," he said right away. "That we had fun tonight. . . . Didn't we?" He smiled down at her.

"We did." But she felt stiff for some reason. Unable to relax or to smile.

"I want to hold your hand," he explained further, "because you're coming with me when you didn't have to."

"I'm helping Samantha with her lines," she reminded him.

"I know." They walked on another ten feet before he added, "But this is how I see it: You're a generous person, and people don't tell you that enough. *I* didn't tell you that enough. I didn't want to leave the house on my own, and you came with me. Bada-bing. I'm a lucky guy."

Ella loved hearing those words. She loved feeling his fingers wrapped around hers. But she was worried, nonetheless. "Hank?"

"Yes?"

She kept walking. Somehow he sensed that she wanted to free her hand at the same time she took it back. There was no awkward pulling or grasping to hang on.

And then they were apart.

She couldn't tell what he was thinking. She felt sad. And mixed up. She needed to explain further, not only for him but for her. "I don't mind spending the rest of the week in bed with you," she said, feeling out her words as she walked. "It's private. But there's something very public, something very sweet, about holding hands. It means two people love each other. If someone saw us, they'd assume we were together."

"True," he said. "It's an awkward situation."

"It is. But I'm okay with it. As long as we keep talking about what's going on. I just don't want any surprises this time."

*This time.* The end was inevitable. Again.

"I don't either," he said.

Their footsteps alternated among loud, hollow, and gritty, depending on the sidewalk, the plant debris that had fallen onto it, the occasional steel gratings, the asphalt streets. But at least those footsteps were going somewhere.

*While we wander*, thought Ella. Theirs was a love that was doomed to haunt them—aimless, without form—not unlike the ghosts Charlestonians claimed roamed many of the historic mansions they were passing on their walk.

When they arrived at the Battery, Ella saw a small hospitality tent had been set up on the park grounds for the cast and crew who had to report so late to work, as well as for the police who had cordoned off the area and stood guard.

The residents of the Battery were putting up with the inconvenience of the filming, probably because Samantha Drake commanded a lot of respect in Hollywood and among American moviegoers. In fact, at the edge of the cordoned area, a contingent of fans stood waiting for both Samantha and Hank to notice them. Some carried signs to attract attention.

Samantha was already there, doing her thing, speaking to fans and winning them over by bringing her best Dame Samantha persona: lots of hair tossing, along with her distinctive, droll voice and witty comments. But Ella was more focused on Hank. She watched as he patiently signed a lot of autographs with little fanfare. He had such a beautiful smile. He stayed very busy. His fans adored him. One young woman was a visitor from China and didn't speak English, but her American friend told Hank that they both loved his movies, and her friend had seen almost all of them in Beijing.

*He belongs to the whole world*, Ella thought, and her

heart ached. He could never belong to her. Holding his hand had been excruciatingly painful because she wanted him back, and he couldn't be hers.

How could she feel that way after only two days?

All she knew was that she did. She simply had to come to terms with it. It wasn't realistic. There was something in her, obviously, that craved a happily ever after. Nothing wrong with that. But it couldn't be with Hank Rogers.

After the fans got their autographs, the police sent them home, and it was time to film the scene. It started with Hank driving up to the Battery wall in a blue Mustang. Samantha was a passenger in a black SUV behind him. He braked swiftly. Ran out of the Mustang, left the door open, and swiftly climbed the stairs to the sidewalk and steel railing fronting the harbor. Samantha exited the SUV, pulled a gun out of her purse, then ran up the steps after him. She pointed the gun at Hank, and that was when he jumped over the wall into the Atlantic.

Ella watched from afar as Hank leaped across the railing, over and over, to escape the character Samantha played. He insisted on doing the stunt himself. Every time, he landed on a hidden raft and had to crawl back over the wall again. Once he landed on the raft and then slid off into the water, and for a minute there was a lot of shouting.

Ella's heart was in her throat when that happened. Hank was an excellent swimmer, but it was close to midnight, and the water was black. The wind was starting to blow too, so a mild chop was forming on the harbor's glassy surface. Soon they'd have to pull the raft out of the water. Too much lifting and sinking on the waves.

In the movie, the scene would take less than thirty seconds. But it took the cast and crew until two a.m. to film it. They had to get Hank new clothes several times. Dry his hair. Redo his makeup. Isabel had him approach the Battery wall from two different directions, too, in his car. A few takes they played around with Samantha's approach as well. Should she pull the gun out as she was exiting the taxi? Or when she was climbing the stairs to the sidewalk and railing?

In between takes, Samantha, whose role in the scene wasn't nearly as taxing as Hank's, would call Ella over, and they'd run through Samantha's lines for the next day. One scene involved Ella. She had four lines in it. Of course, four lines—all of them easy enough—weren't enough to gain any sort of traction professionally. But they were satisfying to say, nonetheless.

"It's a small part, but you're good," Samantha said. "You've a liveliness about you that's compelling."

"Thanks," Ella said. Those were huge words, coming from such an acclaimed actor. But she didn't care as much as she cared about Hank.

*She was doing it again.* What was wrong with her? She should be holding Samantha's words close to her heart, writing them down in her journal when she got home, calling up an agent and getting work in commercials, or moving back to New York and trying again. She was young enough. Even if she got one juicy role to live on for the rest of her life, wouldn't that be reason enough to pull up roots in Charleston and try again on Broadway?

"See you," Samantha said at the end of the night. She sounded exhausted.

"Bye," Ella replied. She wasn't nearly as tired and Samantha and Hank. She was only depressed. Screwed up. And she'd been doing so well. . . .

Until Hank came to Charleston.

She was mad. *Really* mad. No man could or would

control her life. No man would throw her off-balance, especially in such a short time.

No man . . .

But when Hank walked up, a tired grin on his face, she lit up inside, despite all her self-talk. She couldn't help thinking how life could change so much in only a few days, how she could go from being strong, confident Ella with no real worries to this emotionally distraught, confused person—

*Who was also walking on air.*

She was happy when she was with Hank. That was the bottom line. How was she supposed to resolve the push-pull on her heart that she was feeling? Their intimacy, as wonderful as it was, had only made things more complicated.

"Ready?" she asked him.

"Am I ever," he said in a warm tone that made her blood hum and took her right back to their time in bed. "Thanks for waiting."

He sounded truly grateful. The way he carried his shoulders, a little low, let her know how exhausted he was.

They walked home through quiet streets.

"You okay?" she asked him.

Up ahead, Beau and Lacey's house loomed before them, silent, its windows dark.

"It was tough," he said, his voice a bit hoarse. "But I had a good time."

"You did? What happened when you fell in the water?"

He laughed. "Swimming at night in the harbor . . . never thought I'd do that. I felt more sorry for the guy tending the raft than me. He had to crouch out there all night. At least I got to walk around in between takes."

"He probably got paid well to do that," said Ella.

"Not really. Sometimes the hardest part of the business is knowing how unfair the compensation is."

"Think about it this way: You have a special gift—being able to draw millions of people to the movie theater. You deserve to be compensated accordingly."

"Thanks, but it's still too much. When I think of how hard everyone else works—"

"You're creating jobs for them. Don't forget that. The talent is essential to the making of any film." She reached out her hand to hold his. "Hey, I'm holding your hand."

"I noticed." He grinned.

"Friend to friend." She squeezed it tight, feeling emotional. "Because you're a good person, Hank." He was. His leaving her all those years ago didn't make him *bad*. Just not ready to be in a committed relationship. "You're too hard on yourself. Why is that?"

He released a huge sigh. And didn't answer the question.

Ella stayed silent and held on tight. He needed her. She could tell. And she was going to be there for him. Sometimes words couldn't comfort the way sheer human contact could.

When they got home, she pulled the front door shut behind them. It was two thirty in the morning. "What time do you have to be on the set tomorrow?" she asked him. "I report at noon."

"Nine, for me. It was supposed to be seven, but they're giving Samantha and me a few more hours because of tonight."

"Wow. So you have six and a half hours between now and then. To sleep, to shower."

"Not even. They're going to send a taxi over at eight thirty."

They stood looking at each other.

He put his arms on her shoulders, bent low, and kissed her on the lips—a slow, sexy kiss that lingered. A hungry kiss, one a hard-working man bestowed on the woman who could best bring him comfort.

"Your mouth is sweet," he whispered. "I want you. Badly."

She blinked up at him. "I'd like that." She couldn't help a smile curving her lips. He was adorable. And she wanted him right back.

There was another pause. He cupped her bottom with his hands and stared down at her as if she was his everything.

She could get used to that look.

"I'm a lucky guy," he said, "that you're here with me. In the same house."

"But we both know you need sleep," she whispered. "You're worn out."

"I know." He gave a slight shake of his head. "This sucks. But thanks for being here."

She snuggled next to him, her breasts flattened against his chest. He held her close, his chin on top of her head, his arms around her waist. If they were in high school, they'd look like that couple that was always joined at the hip.

"I don't know what's going on," she said. "But I'm just going to say how I feel and ask for what I want."

"Tell me."

"I want to sleep with you," she said. "For real. Or even sleep *next* to you. But I know if I do, we'll be awake too long."

"You're right."

"And we might be doing the wrong thing. I don't know."

"I know what *I* want." He held her back a little so he could look at her. "A second chance with you."

She didn't know what to say. To think. She was confused. Plain and simple. "But there's so much stuff in between us. Hurt on my part."

"And a ton of regret on mine."

"I don't know why it still hurts." She wasn't imagining the ache in her heart. "It was so long ago. And we had an agreement to pursue our careers."

"I shouldn't have chosen the movie in Hawaii over you," he said. "Whatever our agreement was, I should have chosen *you*, the way you chose me."

It meant so much to her to hear him say that.

"But honestly," she said, "I have huge misgivings about the choice I made. I put my own aspirations on the back burner for a guy, something my dad told me never to do. And that bothers me, not just because of Papa, but for myself. I never got to see how far I could have gone." She paused. "You were right to choose your career."

"But look what I gave up." He played with her hair. "*You.*"

"It's never wrong to do whatever it takes to be the person you're supposed to be," she said, her voice a little shaky. "There's no easy answer."

"But there feels like there should be," he said.

"If we're still wondering how to judge the situation after ten years, I think that proves both our points. We need to let it go."

"Let's think about starting over." His voice was rough with fatigue, but there was energy to his words too, something that made her feel hopeful.

But she had to be smart. "On what grounds?" she asked him. "That we're still attracted to each other?

We're brand-new people. We have ten years of experience behind us. It's *changed* us. Have you ever seen a huge ship try to turn around?"

"It's slow. It takes forever, actually. But it can be done."

"Not in a week, at least not *this* ship. It would take a heckuva lot longer than that."

"I get it." He ran a soothing hand down her back. "There's a lot of cargo to shift. But time passes either way. Why not spend it working on the thing that you want to make happen, however long it takes?"

They stood in silence.

"Let's stop thinking about it," Ella said, "and go to our own beds."

"All right. You go first. I'll wait until you're out of the bathroom. And then I'll come up."

"Okay." She walked upstairs ahead of him and looked over her shoulder. He was still watching, so she blew him a kiss. "Good night."

"'Night." His smile was distracted.

She could tell he was already worlds away, back on the set. "I'll get up in the morning to make sure you get out of here."

"You don't have to do that."

"I know." There was a half-beat's pause. "I want to," she added.

The corner of his mouth quirked up. "Thanks, Ella."

*Life was filled with small moments like this*, she thought as she turned her back to him. *Over and over, we choose how to live, who to love.*

Right now she was choosing Hank and everything that came with loving him, even the hurt she knew was inevitable.

# CHAPTER TWENTY-THREE

Wednesday morning Ella's alarm went off at eight. Her eyes popped open. Time to make sure Hank was awake. She tiptoed to his room, put her ear on the door. Didn't hear a thing.

"You looking for me?"

She nearly jumped out of her skin. Hank came out of the upstairs bath, smelling like aftershave and looking cozy in a light robe he'd stolen from Beau. "I'm already showered. You should go back to bed since you don't have to be at the set until noon."

She felt nervous at the sight of all that masculinity, but she refused to let him know. "I'm running to the office." Her tone was breezy. "I can squeeze in a few hours of work. And if *you're* up, I'm most definitely not sleeping in. Is Pammy back yet?"

"She is. She's sound asleep. She left us a note in the kitchen. She was up all night at the shelter teaching the mayor and a couple of residents English rummy."

"Oh, okay." Ella felt awkward.

Hank took a step toward her. "We might not see each other much today."

"You're right," she said. She could barely get the words out.

He came much closer, wrapped his arms around her waist. "You look pretty."

"Like this?" Her hair was a mess.

"Sure do. Want to come see my room?" He put on his most obvious Big Bad Wolf grin. "I was going to show you the portrait of those three boys, remember?"

She laughed and slipped away from him. She had to brush her teeth. At the very least.

"What are you running away from?" he called after her.

She looked over her shoulder. "Today's International No Sex Day. Ever heard of it? Established in 1982."

"Isn't that interesting. What happens to people who ignore International No Sex Day?"

"They, uh, have sex, I guess."

"They're making a mistake. They should consider the merits of being celibate on No Sex Day. What are those merits again?"

"Not being late for work is a big one," said Ella.

"Oh, yeah. It's good to arrive on time at your job. It's better than getting cozy under the sheets, that's for sure. What else?"

"Well, when you don't have sex, you definitely can't help recalling the times you did. And you develop an appreciation for it."

"That's right," he said. "It's better to imagine yourself having sex than actually having it. I'm going to imagine it right now. You might as well too, since you're not having sex today." He stepped into his room. "I guess I can show you the portrait later. See you in the kitchen, maybe. But if not, on the set. And if not there, tonight. Late. Here. Back where we started this loooong, no-sex kind of day."

"Okay," she eked out.

He winked at her and shut his door.

"Damn," she said aloud. She'd missed her chance.

Sure enough, she didn't see him at breakfast. She rushed to get ready, but she was still upstairs when he left the house at 8:30. Pammy was also asleep when Ella left for her job at Two Love Lane at 8:45.

Roberta dropped by the office at 9:15. "I've got the ingredients, and I'm heading to the commercial kitchen," she said. "I'm going to bake all day the rest of the week."

"Fantastic," Ella said. "Let me know if there's anything I can do."

"Thanks, but I'm ready to do it on my own," Roberta said. "Twenty-five hundred a day for four days. They'll take fifteen minutes to mix up, forty-five minutes to roll into logs, cut into pennies, and put on the baking sheets. Twelve minutes to cook. While they're cooking, I'll scoop the previous batches off the cookie sheets. It's going to take me about thirty hours all told, including meal breaks and bathroom breaks and me just losing steam. So I rented the kitchen for four days, but I'm shooting for finishing in three."

"Oh my gosh, this is going to be crazy! Can I come visit? I'll bring breakfast, lunch, and dinner."

"I've got that covered, and honestly? I don't want to jinx it. I want to be there all on my lonesome."

Ella shook her head. "You're awesome."

"I'm determined, Ella. Twenty-five years I've been living with this problem."

"I know things will be different for you after this is over."

"I feel it too," Roberta said.

"I love your spirit." Ella gave her a hug.

And then Miss Thing, Macy, and Greer had to, as

well. And they all ran up the cobblestone lane to Roast-busters to get Roberta a farewell coffee.

"I can't stay long," Roberta told Pete.

He was behind the counter running his little kingdom, tamping, pouring, calling out customer descriptions in his usual manner—he never used people's names. "Tall latte for the teacher who deserves a trip to Paris because she's so good to her students," he yelled out to Mrs. De-Mille, who taught French at the nearby high school. And "Double espresso to the young man in the green jacket with the charming grin and polite manner who'll go far in life," he said, and held out a cup to a guy with John Lennon glasses and a backpack on his shoulder.

"It has to be to-go," Roberta told Pete.

"Coming up." He gave her a thumbs-up. "And I already know what the Two Love Lane ladies are getting. But I won't make theirs until you leave, Roberta, seeing as you're in a hurry. Where ya headed?"

"I have to go bake ten thousand cheddar pennies," she said.

Pete never lost his levelheaded cool. He handed Roberta her coffee and said, "I'm not sure if you're speaking in secret code or what. What the heck's a cheddar penny?"

"Pete, you grew up on Long Island, so you have no idea," Miss Thing said, with utter delight.

They were old friends, but lately, Ella had noticed a heightened sparkle in Miss Thing's eye when she was with Pete that seemed directly Pete-related.

"Well, are you going to tell me or not?" he asked both Miss Thing and Roberta.

"I have to go," Roberta said. "Tell him, Miss Thing."

Which suited Miss Thing just fine.

But first everyone wished good luck to Roberta, who

exited quickly, determination written on her face and in her body language. The crowd around the register parted to let her through, and then she was gone, off to bake ten thousand cheddar pennies.

Miss Thing gave Pete a snappy summary of Roberta's situation. "The point being," she concluded, "Roberta wants to date a good man who's *fun*. And unless she bakes ten thousand cheddar pennies, that ain't gonna happen."

Miss Thing was doing her extreme Southern thing again, where her drawl got thicker, one hand landed on her hip, and the other swatted at invisible flies.

"*I'm* fun," said Pete, pressing a lid onto a coffee cup and turning to grab another lid. "She doesn't need to bake ten thousand cheddar pennies to get me to go with her to the Aquarium gala."

"So you're looking for romance?" Miss Thing asked archly.

"Nope," Pete said in his usual matter-of-fact manner. "I had my one love of a lifetime. But I'm a sharp dresser and a damn good dancer. She could do worse, let me put it that way."

Miss Thing took her coffee from him. But she didn't say a word. Highly unusual of her.

Ella jumped right in. "Do you mean it, Pete? You wouldn't mind being a backup date in case we need one?"

Miss Thing took a sip of coffee and studied the crowd with a wide-eyed gaze. But Ella sensed her friend was listening hard, waiting for Pete's answer.

"I've got my tux ready to go," the coffee-shop owner said. "Thirty years old and it still fits. I wear it every year to a Toastmasters banquet."

"Because you don't go out to parties," Miss Thing said. "You like bowling. And watching ESPN."

"So?" Pete shrugged.

"You could wear that tux at least once a week during the Season," Miss Thing said.

"The season? As far as I know, there are four," he said. "Winter, spring—"

"I know, I know," said Miss Thing, waving her free hand. "I mean *debutante* season."

"Oh, yeah," Pete said with a laugh. "That's right up my alley, T."

Greer, Ella, and Macy exchanged a look. They'd never heard Miss Thing and Pete getting testy with each other. And they'd never heard him call her "T." Was that for Thing? Or something else? Nobody knew Miss Thing's first name except for their accountant, who needed it for tax purposes.

"I'm only saying it wouldn't hurt you to go to parties," said Miss Thing, her chin lifted. Her voice was higher than usual. "The Charleston social scene has oodles of opportunities to make toasts."

"Oodles?" Pete asked.

"I'd say so," Greer interjected. "With the abundance of champagne that flows here."

"Fine," he said. "Maybe I'll go with Roberta to the gala if she can't find a decent date, and I'll make a toast. Will that make you happy?" He looked right at Miss Thing.

"It would be a lovely gesture," she said, and studied her nails.

Pete was obviously done talking about it. He said nothing else and handed Ella her coffee. "Enjoy," he said, with his usual good cheer.

"I always do." She smiled at him.

He winked. "You're looking extra happy today, Sunshine," he said, and then he was back at it, making more drinks.

*Sunshine?* Ella was honored. And embarrassed. Did it show? That she'd recently had a fabulous time in bed with Hank?

"I think you look extra chipper too," said Miss Thing. The girls all stared at Ella. "I'm fine," she said.

"She's more than fine," Greer whispered.

"I'd say she's pretty happy," said Macy.

Ella's three best friends giggled.

She rolled her eyes. "I've got work to do before I head to the set. See you later."

"We'll come with you," said Macy.

They all thanked Pete and streamed out.

They were walking over the cobblestones of Love Lane on their tiptoes, their coffees held out to avoid spilling, when Macy said, "How's it going with Hank?"

"I don't want to talk about it," said Ella. "Miss Thing, is something going on with you and Pete?"

"I don't want to talk about it either," Miss Thing answered. "Except . . ." She had a hard time staying quiet. "No, never mind."

"I get the feeling you like him," Macy prompted her.

"Hmmph," said Miss Thing. "Why would I like Pete? I've known him forever, and he always says how he's had one love in his life, and that was enough. Besides, he treats me like a little sister. And I treat him like a brother."

"I don't know," said Greer. "You and he help each other out a lot. He came to your house for dinner when the accountant was getting too flirty after you won *The Price Is Right.* Just to act as a buffer."

"As a protective brother would," Miss Thing said.

She'd won the Double Showcase, a rarity in *Price Is Right* history.

"And you held down the fort at the shop when he had that surgery recently," Macy said.

"I did, didn't I? Like a caring sister."

"But he called you *T*," Greer said.

Miss Thing stopped walking, so they all did. "Yes, he did. It's a nickname he gave me—the same way a brother would."

"Is it because he knows your first name?" asked Ella.

There was an extended silence on Miss Thing's part.

"And did you want to go with him to the gala?" Macy asked.

The silence went on.

"That's enough about Pete," Miss Thing finally said, and started walking again.

Ella, Greer, and Macy exchanged another look. Something was definitely going on. Miss Thing, who was usually so talkative, so willing to share, was clamming up.

"But since you're pushing on me," Miss Thing said at the front door, "I'm gonna push on you, Ella. Any smooches yet between you and Triple H?"

"Triple H?"

"Hollywood Hottie Hank," Miss Thing explained.

That was a good reminder. He belonged to Hollywood. Ella looked around at her three friends. "Yes, as a matter of fact. And you'll be interested to know that we've progressed beyond a sweet smooch on the front porch."

Miss Thing collapsed a shoulder against the door. "Oh, Lord. That makes me so happy."

"Don't get excited," Ella said. "I initiated it because he's afraid to hurt my feelings when he leaves. I don't want to talk about it yet. But I promise, at some point, I will."

"Before or after he leaves?" Macy asked.

What she really meant was, before or after Ella's heart broke again?

"I don't know," she answered. And she really didn't.

"Well, here's what *I* know," said Macy. "When two of my friends aren't up to talking, something big is in the works."

"Exactly," said Greer. "Like when the earth's plates move before an earthquake."

"Honey," said Miss Thing, "no earthquake is gonna be happening in my life. I promise you."

"Don't look so sad saying so," said Ella. "Earthquakes are dangerous."

"They certainly shake things up," said Macy.

Ella was nervous when she got back to her desk. She needed her old life back. Before Hank's return.

But like it or not, the earth's plates had already shifted for her. Just thinking about their time in bed together made her knees weak. She couldn't go back, no matter how much she felt she should. Hank was here. Hank was going to leave again.

And Ella's horizons were changed forever.

# CHAPTER TWENTY-FOUR

Wednesday was a good day for Hank—except for the major problem of not seeing Ella at all. He looked for her, but he always seemed to show up about five minutes after she'd left the costume shop or the break area. And her set was closed. It was a golf cart ride away, a bedroom at an old Charleston single home. The cameramen and director could barely fit in, much less visitors who had no good reason to be there.

When he got home at 11:30 that night, Pammy was sitting in the recliner in the living room, reading a book. "Hey, you," she said, and shut it right away. "I knew you'd be gone a lot. But this is *really* a lot."

"That's how it goes in the movie biz, unfortunately," he said, and sat down on the corner of the sofa closest to her. "How's it going with you?"

Pammy shrugged. "I had a good time with Reggie. I got home about six this morning, slept until noon, and then met some students at the main campus to talk about a woodworking project we're doing for some people with an old house down the street. And then I went to Beau and Lacey's and worked there. They have some issues with the old built-in bookcases in their library."

"Sounds like a good day." He was dying to ask her more about the mayor. But he didn't want to come across as nosy.

"Aren't you going to ask me about the mayor?" she said.

He laughed. "I wanted to. But I was going to leave it up to you to tell me what you want."

She chuckled. "He's adorbz. I'm in love."

"But you just met him." Hank paused. "I mean, that's nice. But—" He didn't know how to say it without insulting her. Pammy was thirty. She was smart and she could do whatever she wanted.

"You're worried I'm latching onto the first guy who shows an interest in me here in Charleston," Pammy said. "Because I'm homesick. And now . . . I'm not. Poof." She snapped her fingers. "Homesickness gone."

She'd hit the nail on the head. He *was* worried.

"You're not homesick?" he asked, trying not to sound skeptical. But a major romance couldn't happen that fast. No way.

"I'm not ready to hop on a plane back to Bend. And guess what? It's because I've latched onto the first guy who's shown an interest in me since I've been here." She chuckled. "Oregon? See ya later. Pammy's gonna be doin' the Charleston for a while. I mean, literally. The dance. Have you ever done that?"

"No." Hank was getting slightly confused, but he vowed to hang in.

"It's fun," Pammy said. "I did it last night at the homeless shelter. But I also mean, I'm gonna stick it out here. Love is in the air. I felt it when I first flew in and walked out of the airport and saw a couple of gorgeous police officers shooing people away from the curb. They were seriously hot. And again when I took a taxi downtown and got out and smelled yellow jasmine. It smells heavenly, Hank. Like everyone should be in love." She stabbed a finger on his knee. "Cupid's touch is strong here. But he wasn't shooting arrows at me. It's because I was too worried about being alone. I was sucking up all my own energy. But then Ella came, and she reminded me to let go and let love. Repeat that, Hank."

"Pammy—"

She raised her finger. "Say it: Let go and let love."

"Let go and let love," he repeated after her. What the hell. She was his cousin. And he hadn't seen her all day, and he was leaving soon.

"See?" Her face brightened. "You feel better already."

He kind of did, but he wouldn't tell her that.

"Once you stop trying, Cupid jumps in and goes to work," she said. "And he doesn't work on anyone else's time card. Love exists outside of time. Ask the late, great Stephen Hawking."

"He talked about that?"

"No, but it makes sense, right? Time doesn't matter with love. Fast, slow, whatever. Don't measure it on a clock, Hank. Let go and let love. Stop trying so hard to find it. It'll find you."

"I'm not trying," he said.

"Oh?" Pammy made a skeptical face. "*Oh?* Are you being a big liar? Or just someone in denial? I hope the latter. Because I take down lying cousins, Hank." She put on a very angelic face and cracked her knuckles.

Hank stifled a laugh. "Okay, so lately I *have* been trying. I mean, I wanted to see you, but I came down here to win Ella back. Not to be in a movie either."

Pammy drew in her chin. "Hank, my dear cuz, I knew all that."

"You did?"

"Yes. You've been trying to find your passion ever since you were little. You might think cousin Pammy is oblivious. But I know you better than you think. And you've *never* been satisfied with what you have. You are *always* looking. You want bliss, baby. Not *bland*, which is you being the tax lawyer your father wanted you to be. Not *bling* either, which is you in your Hollywood mode. The only *BL* word you want is '*bliss*.' Am I right?"

What could he say to that? She was right.

She took his silence as agreement. "And when you showed up here, it was written all over you. You were still searching for *da bliss*, Hank." She cocked her head. "You have this restless quality about you, you know? It comes across as a yearning on screen. Which is why you're a big star. It's sexy and raw. Chicks dig it. They think you're vulnerable. Guys think you're a badass."

"Um, thanks, I guess."

"And then I saw you with Ella. And you had that stupid hazelnut creamer incident." She chuckled. "It made me so happy. Because I realized then you'd finally figured it out. Who you love. Where your bliss is at." Her expression got serious. "If it works out for you, it might mean you'll suck on the movie screen from here on out. You won't have that natural yearning face anymore. You might look like this instead."

She made a happy face, the kind only Pammy could do. It combined the innocence of unbridled joy with her natural swagger. She grinned, but one of her eyebrows arched high. And somehow she waggled it, while the other one stayed still.

He would definitely lose ticket sales with that face. "How do you do that?"

"That's for you to find out on your own. Moving on." She was on a roll. "Let me tell you something, cuz, about me and Reggie."

"Okay." He sensed her fervor, burning bright. This was Pammy. Nothing was low-key with her.

"Reggie's the first guy I've really shown an interest in, too, not only since I've been in Charleston but since forever."

"Really?"

"Yes." She looked solemn and repentant. "I've been looking for any guy who looks good on my arm and can hang with the Pammy schtick." She tapped her heart. "I haven't been noticing that there's a place in me that needs to shut up and just let things be. It's a place where no one is good-looking or witty. It's a mysterious place, like Oz. Or the back corner of Walmart where all the clearance tools are. No one is ever there, but it's awesome, and I can load up my cart with sooooo many boxes of nails, it's crazy."

"Right," Hank said because he loved his cousin.

"I don't get to choose who hangs with me in this magical place," Pammy went on. "And I don't get to choose what I do. It's an enchanted circle I didn't know I had inside me. And that's where Reggie showed up. And I was like, holy shit. I had no idea this was in me. And the same place is in him. Don't think too hard about it—it'll blow your mind."

She leaned back in her recliner. Time to take a breath.

"You've only known him a couple of days," Hank reminded her gently. "I'm glad you like him so much, but aren't you a little worried you might be moving too fast?"

"Of course I am," she said. "But in Oz, you go with

it. So I am." She shrugged. "And it's the best place I've ever been. I can say that already, before we've even gotten to the bedroom wham-bam boogie business."

"Um, okay."

She lifted his hand from the sofa arm and slapped it against his face. "Wake up, cuz. Don't let Ella go. She's upstairs snoozing. Probably not hard. Probably waiting for you to show up and show her some rootin'-tootin' love moves." She stood. "I'm putting in my earplugs and heading to bed."

"Okay then," he said, standing up with her. She was way shorter than he was, but she looked up at him with that special Pammy look that promised many arm and leg wrestle fights if he didn't listen to her. "You rock, cuz," he said, and hugged her.

She squeezed him back. "Good night. I'm sorry your movie career is going to change drastically once you win Ella back. You'll be getting sensitive doctor parts now. But maybe that's a good thing. You've never played a doctor."

"True. I'm willing to play those kind of roles if—"

"If Ella goes along with your plan to capture her heart," Pammy interrupted him. "Here's my last tip, Hank. Take it from Pammy, who has had no experience with real love until now."

"What?"

"Don't leave Charleston."

"That's impossible. I have to go."

Pammy threw up her arms and dropped them. "Then get used to it, Hank. Without Ella, you're gonna be an A-lister movie star forever. No doubt you'll win *People*'s Sexiest Man Alive within the next couple of years. And you'll make buckets of money endorsing ultra-masculine products, like man-sized Kleenex, extra-hot barbecue sauce, and Old Spice. I'm sorry, but if you leave Ella behind, say goodbye to the doctor roles and all the sensitive products you could have endorsed if you'd follow through on your plan to surrender to love. Like Depends for Men and herbal tea. And anything to do with puppies. You're gonna hate that, Hank. You love puppies."

He did love puppies. And she was right. On his current career trajectory, no way in hell would Tracy ever let him be seen holding a puppy on camera. But he could still have a puppy if he wanted to. At home. Away from the paparazzi.

Which kind of sucked. If he ever bought a puppy, he wanted to cuddle it in a bistro. Or on the waterfront. In public.

But none of that mattered because Pammy disappeared into her room, taking her newfound Pammy wisdom with her.

Time for the rootin'-tootin' love moves she'd mentioned. Not that he wanted to remotely have Pammy on his mind once he started walking upstairs. So he took his time, stopping in the kitchen and opening the fridge.

His heart nearly stopped. There on the top shelf was a note that said, *I saved some for you, Hank,* next to a plate of brownies. *I gave the rest to the* nonnas *and Mama and the Sicilian relatives at my apartment. I stopped by after my scene today with Samantha to check on everyone. By the way, the scene went well. Working with S was a real treat (better than any brownie, haha!). Mama, the* nonnas, *and my Sicilian relatives say hello. Everyone hopes you had a good day, including me. I have to report to the set at six a.m. tomorrow. Samantha has some people coming in tomorrow afternoon, and she wants to get our scene done early. So I might not see you.*

Shoot. Ella knew he liked his brownies cold. In the fridge. She was the sweetest, most wonderful woman he'd ever met. And she had a life apart from him. A very full, rich life. And he was an idiot—*an idiot!*—to think that winning her over was going to be as easy as coming down here, crooking his finger, and having her leave her current life and come back to Brooklyn with him. And to LA. And to all his movie locations.

He wasn't Beau Wilder. Ella wasn't Lacey. Who knew why their marriage worked? Everyone was different.

Nope. He'd never fully thought it through. And it was because he hadn't had to strive for anything in his personal life for a long time. Not since—

Not since he'd been with Ella, and he'd ponder what flowers to get her at the neighborhood market. And think of ways he could show her he loved her at home, like lining up all her tea mugs at the front of the cupboard, for easy reaching. And giving her the best towel rack in the bathroom. And washing her hair for her over the kitchen sink when she missed her mother too much. Mama Mancini used to do that for her girls every Saturday night before church the next morning.

He grabbed a brownie and a glass of milk. Sat at the kitchen table. Savored that brownie and all that it meant to him. Ella cared about him. Ella put him in a category with her *nonnas*, her mama, and her relatives.

There was hope. She didn't have to leave him those brownies . . . or that nice note.

Was he over-reaching?

The imaginary psychoanalyst in his head said yes, he was grasping at straws, the same way he thought Pammy was. But Pammy knew her romantic situation better than he did.

And Hank knew Ella. She wouldn't leave him pity

brownies. How else could he put it? He leaned his fist on his ear and chewed. Could these be break-up brownies?

No. They weren't together.

He thought about it. Finished the brownie. Ate another one. Downed it with milk. If Ella wanted him gone, she'd straight up tell him, he decided. He'd get no brownies to pack in his suitcase to take back to New York.

No. These brownies meant something and he refused to let himself doubt. Now was not the time for doubt. Now was the time for action.

Hank was scared—he didn't know how to—what did Pammy call it?—let go and let love. But tonight he was going to try.

*Let go and let love*, he silently told himself as he walked up the stairs. He'd go to his room, get undressed, and then he'd knock on Ella's wall. He'd wait inside his bedroom door, and if she peeked out of hers, he'd ask to come visit her. In the bathrobe he'd borrowed from Beau, of course. He wouldn't make any assumptions.

When he got to his room, for some reason, he went straight to the portrait of the boys and lifted it off the wall. It was heavy. He looked at it hard and flipped the painting over. On the back were some words written in faint ink with a quill pen, in formal handwriting: *Michael, Frederick, and Thomas Griswold, 1822.*

"Who were these guys?" he murmured. At least he knew they were from the same family, likely brothers rather than cousins with the same last name.

He wondered if he could find out. He took out his phone and Googled them. Nada.

But maybe he could check with Pammy. She might know some historians from all the work she was doing on old Charleston homes. She'd at least lead him in the right direction.

That was what he'd do.

He turned the painting back over and studied the boys' faces. The paint strokes were fine. Whoever had labored over the canvas had rendered their expressions with loving care. Hank couldn't help but smile. He felt the artist had captured the essence of the boys. They seemed about to burst out of their skins, the way boys of all generations do.

He remembered when he was like that, first as a kid playing in Central Park with his friends, and then as he got a little older, busing tables at Serendipity 3, where he dreamed of big adventures while he picked up dirty ice creams dishes, cups and saucers, and glasses. Some days he wondered why no one could tell he was filled with big plans—he was the guy who was going to change the world. Yet at the same time, he didn't care what anyone else thought. Back then he believed in himself without even thinking about it.

And then things changed.

He grew up. The world intruded with its harsh realities, as it did to everyone. He had to start comparing his life with everyone else's. He saw his strengths. His weaknesses. He saw that no one, apart from his family and friends, cared more about him and his goals than he did himself. He would have to fight to be heard, to get what he wanted.

He'd learned to fight. He'd learned to be heard. But he had never known what he really wanted. Until now.

He wanted Ella. Everything else was gravy. But she was his center.

He hung the picture back up. Shut his window. Listened carefully in the hallway before he shut his door gently behind him.

He would let her sleep.

# CHAPTER TWENTY-FIVE

"So come over tonight for dinner and drinks," Samantha said to Ella on Thursday. "Some friends of mine from L.A. are flying in just to keep me company the next few days, and then we're all going to New York. They've never been to Charleston. I'll tell Hank."

"Sounds fun," Ella said. "Thanks for the invite."

They'd just wrapped their scene, which meant that Ella was able to spend her entire afternoon back at Two Love Lane. And she had only one more scene to go. So far, the movie had been a fun experience, but even working with Samantha, she hadn't felt that ambition to be a star pumping her up nearly as much as she thought it would.

She'd been thinking more about Roberta and how things were going at the commercial kitchen. And she'd been thinking about her mother. When she'd brought over the brownies the night before to Mama's house, it was obvious Mama was trying too hard to be cheerful. Nonna Sofia was also markedly quiet, knitting away, ignoring Nonna Boo when she made her usual disbelieving comments about the women in Hollywood from their favorite reality show. "Look at her bazoongas!" Nonna Boo cried at one point. "They're falling out of that dress! Someone needs to tell her. Ella, write a letter to Bravo."

But neither Mama nor Nonna Sofia said a word.

And then Pammy, too, was on Ella's mind. Ella had seen the mayor that very afternoon, touring the set, and she could swear he'd been flirting with his tour guide, the girl with the Bluetooth earbuds who carried the iPad. He'd put his arm around her. She'd whispered in his ear. And when he left, he went out of his way to walk through a crowd of crew members to kiss her on the cheek. And the girl had grabbed his elbow and whispered in his ear again.

Ella wasn't sure what to think. But it gave her a bad feeling, especially as the night before, Pammy had come home from work and said the mayor had to cancel their dinner date at the last minute because he had work obligations.

Did he really? Or was the mayor a player?

If so, Ella was really worried. Because Pammy had told her she was already falling in love.

Ella believed real love could happen that fast. It had with her and Hank, long ago, when they'd had their first date at Serendipity 3, four years to the day after he'd asked her out when she'd gone to Serendipity 3 with Papa. So she wasn't discounting Pammy's feelings.

But what if the mayor didn't love Pammy back?

And . . .

Ella hated to admit it, but more than anything, she was thinking about Hank and their sexy night together, and she wondered when it would and could happen again— she thought it would the night before, but she'd fallen into a deep sleep and she never heard him come in.

But that morning she'd seen he'd eaten some brownies.

He'd even left her a note thanking her, which she was now carrying in her purse. She'd already re-read it about ten times. *Dear Ella, your brownies are amazing. Like you. Thank you very much, and I hope I get to see you today. Hank XO*

It was so sweet. And polite. And then there was the *XO* at the end. What did that mean? Did he really love her and want to hug her? Or was he just being friendly?

"It's no wonder you're not feeling all gung-ho about the movie," Greer told her at the office. She was sitting on the edge of Ella's desk, in her new lavender Stella McCartney pantsuit and a frothy white blouse, both from the Junior League Thrift Shop. Roberta had inspired her to go there. She was holding Hank's note in her hand. "And I think the *XO* is a sign of genuine affection." She smiled at Ella as if she was slightly pathetic, which Ella knew she was. "You can't read too much into it. But it's definitely nice." She handed it back. "I think the most important thing about the note is your reaction. It's very clear you're head over heels for him."

"Did you say head over heels?" Miss Thing called from the outer office.

Greer had forgotten to shut the door all the way. "Sorry," she whispered to Ella.

They both laughed quietly.

"You might as well come in," Ella called out to Miss Thing.

Miss Thing did just that, her pink-and-white polka-dot sheath a miracle of fine tailoring and a testament to her cheery nature. She left Ella's office door wide open. "I couldn't help overhearing," she said. "Those words are like candy to a baby. *Head over heels.* Are you that way about Hank?"

"What's going on?" Macy walked by with a few file folders and peeked in.

"Come on in." Ella gave up. You couldn't say anything at Two Love Lane without everyone eventually contributing an opinion.

Macy looked extra sexy in a fitted white dress with a low cowl-neck collar that showed off her tanned collarbone. Her smile was bright, her blonde ponytail high. "I sense tension. Which could be love brewing. And saying that reminds me of coffee and Pete at Roastbusters. Are we talking about Miss Thing and Pete?"

"Absolutely not," said Miss Thing, her cheeks turning even pinker under her generous application of blush. "We're talking about Ella being head over heels for Hank."

"Are you?" Macy asked.

"Yes," Ella admitted. "I am. It's terrible because I'm doomed to heartbreak. Again."

Macy and Greer looked at each other, their eyes wide.

"Miss Thing, are you head over heels for Pete?" Greer asked.

Miss Thing's eyebrows drew together. "Yes, sugar. I'm doomed too. But there it is." She looked up to heaven. "I hope my darling departed husband won't hold it against me."

"Of course he won't," said Macy. "He'd want you to be happy."

Miss Thing wiped away a tear. "It's hard moving on," she whispered.

Outside, a mockingbird sang its song. The house itself, steeped in the comings and goings of generations, seemed to sigh. Time moved on, but within its walls, love lasted. Love was what gave Two Love Lane its heart.

Greer held Miss Thing's hand. Macy put an arm around her shoulder.

"It's okay," said Ella, feeling her friend's sorrow. "It really is."

The older woman sniffed. "Even if I get over that part—which I'm not sure I can—I don't think Pete likes me back. He said he's already had his one love. I did too. I'm awful for thinking about getting a second chance."

"No, you're not," Macy insisted, and hugged Miss Thing closer.

"You can't stop living," Greer reminded her, and squeezed her hand harder.

"Everyone deserves a second chance, and a third, and however many they need," Ella told her. "You have to live and love until the very end. You can't just quit."

Miss Thing smiled. "'Live and love until the very end.' I like that."

"And *you* need to take your own advice," Greer told Ella. "You're not doomed to heartbreak. This is an opportunity."

"You may be in for a wild ride," Macy said to both Ella and Miss Thing. "But that's life. At least you can look back later and say you never chose boredom. Or giving up."

"Right," said Greer. "The risks you're taking are worth it. You deserve to love and be loved. Period."

Miss Thing shook off her friends gently and went to the door. "I'm not giving up on life and love. And I hate to be bored. But I sure as sugar ain't gonna run after Pete. Love's a two-way street."

"Fine," said Macy. "But don't you pull off that street into a parking lot. Ya hear?"

"I hear." Miss Thing gave a shy smile, but then she pointed a finger at Ella. "And you—you'd better rev your engines. And speed through a red light. You can't let Hank get away. He's obsessed with you. I could tell when we brought over the doughnuts."

"How?" Ella was highly skeptical.

"The way he looked up the stairs when he told us you were there in your room."

"That's all?" Ella twirled a pencil and tried not to be drawn in.

"It's the little moments, honey," said Miss Thing. "It was written all over his handsome face. You're the woman he adores."

Ella couldn't help feeling delighted to hear that. But she'd been burned ten years ago—and it had happened overnight—so she wasn't going to buy into Miss Thing's fanciful daydreams a hundred percent. Maybe five percent. Or twenty, after what had happened between her and Hank in bed. Any more than that, and she was setting herself up for disappointment.

Then again, she'd just told Miss Thing she had to live and love until the very end. . . .

The love game was all so risky, Ella thought, and was still thinking that when she got to Samantha's rental that night. It was a condo in a big mansion on South Battery. The owner lived in Connecticut and only came down several months a year. On the sidewalk outside, Ella made a quick phone call to Roberta.

"I'm leaving for the day," Roberta said. "Ella, I don't know about this. I am so exhausted after baking three thousand cheddar pennies. And I have to do this for at least two more days. I can't spread out the baking because I need to get moving on those dates you've arranged for me with stellar men! The gala is getting closer and closer."

"I know." Ella wished she knew what to do. "I feel for

you. Maybe taking off one day between bakes is a good thing."

"No, I won't do it," said Roberta. "I'm going to push through. The sooner I can get back on the dating circuit the better."

"How do the pennies taste?"

"I'm afraid to try one," she said. "I need to eat the ten thousandth one I bake, right?"

"That's what Miss Thing said."

"So every one counts toward that number. I put the ones that break in a plastic bag and number exactly how many are in there."

"Good going."

"But they smell delicious. And it's a great family recipe. I'm thinking about selling them. I could hire a team to do the baking, and I'd market them to all the tourists."

"I think that's a wonderful idea," Ella said. "But save some for the locals too."

"Don't worry," said Roberta. "I've got nine thousand nine hundred and ninety-nine to pass out to all my friends."

"Yay!" said Ella, and looked up at the windows of Samantha's condo. Dusk had fallen, and all the lights were on. It was a welcome sight. "Gotta go. Keep me posted. I've got five potentially awesome Aquarium dates lined up and ready to go when you are."

"I can't wait," said Roberta. "Where do you keep finding these men? Charleston isn't exactly Atlanta or Charlotte."

"Two are men who want to try again with you. And the other three are guys you don't know. They're businessmen, but they don't go to the Chamber of Commerce meetings or any of your usual places. Two are brand new to town, and one commutes between New York and Charleston every week."

"Oh, they all sound appealing," Roberta said. "This is giving me more energy for the next couple of days. Thanks, Ella."

After they hung up, Ella had a warm feeling inside. Roberta sounded different. Ella had no idea if that tarot card reader had been blowing smoke. She also didn't believe in magic, per se, or spells. But she did believe that people could convince themselves of something or pick up on stray bad vibes looking for a place to land. Maybe this crazy idea of baking cheddar pennies was exactly what Roberta needed to get her out of her long-standing rut. It was certainly the wildest piece of advice Ella had ever given one of her clients.

She had a pan of homemade Huguenot torte, Charleston's signature dessert made with brown sugar, chopped walnuts, and Granny Smith apples, cradled in her left arm when she rang Samantha's doorbell. She'd beat some heavy whipping cream in Samantha's kitchen to serve as the topping. She'd already asked her hostess to pick some up when she went to the store. Samantha loved to cook, was doing all of it herself, and told Ella to add whatever she needed to her shopping list.

Samantha answered the door, a martini in her hand. She was in a blue silk caftan and looked gorgeous. "So good to see you," she said, and pulled her inside. A great Frank Sinatra tune was playing somewhere.

"I'm excited to be here," Ella said, not at all intimidated anymore by Samantha's celebrity status.

"Come meet my brilliant L.A. friends," Samantha said, "although they're originally from all over. That's how it is in L.A."

"Of course," said Ella. It had been like that in New

York too. It was a place that attracted talented people from all over the world who wanted to be at the epicenter of American culture, a place where they could make a difference.

She'd been like that once, but now she saw how she could be fulfilled and make a big difference in a smaller city too, like Charleston.

The foyer and living room were fantastic: all modern paintings mixed with beautiful old furniture. And seated on the two sofas were three men, who stood when Ella and Samantha entered the room.

Ella was taken aback by how good-looking all three were, in different ways, and how fascinating their jobs were. These were accomplished men with creative sides, which would have been hugely attractive to her just last week. All of them were in their thirties. Dating age.

But she wasn't interested. Not one bit.

*You love Hank*, a little voice inside her said.

She wasn't going to lie to herself. But how could she be in love with a man who had no intention of living in Charleston? Not that she was adamant about living there all her life—

But she pretty much was.

*Wow.* She hadn't realized that until right now. Charleston was home. Charleston was forever for her. And it felt good to know that.

"Hank will be a little late," Samantha said. "Let's get some drinks and take them up on the roof. It's nice out, and it's all lit up."

So they did. It was a charming space, with comfy chairs and big potted plants, strands of lights hung from the walls, and an amazing view of the harbor. Ella got to talk to all three men alone without a lot of interruption.

Every time one started up a tête-à-tête with her, Samantha would somehow manage to wrap the other two into conversation.

Ella was highly suspicious that her hostess was trying to play matchmaker. But Samantha knew Ella was crazy about Hank. Why would she do this? Was it because Hank was leaving soon? Maybe Samantha was hoping these men would serve as a distraction for Ella after he left.

"So tell me more about yourself," said the guy Ella was currently talking to. He was her third out of three.

He ran an observatory on a remote mountain in New Mexico four months a year. The other eight he taught astronomy at UCLA. During his free time, he played with a group that adapted pop music to the cello. He also liked to run half marathons and cook. He specialized in Cuban dishes.

Samantha had been sure to outline all the guys' wonderful qualities before they each had their own little interview with her. Ella was trying her best to put up with the obvious set-up. Later, she'd take Samantha to task.

So far, the first one, the CEO of a major tech company in Silicon Valley, had been extremely egotistical. He actually admitted it, but he said it was because when you're in the world's top one percent, how else were you supposed to feel but extra good about yourself? The second guy was relatively humble. He ran a huge nonprofit that benefited runaways on the streets of L.A., a very worthy cause, so he was in contact with a lot of celebrities who wanted to help. But he had a thing about wanting to date only tens, he said.

And left a big silence.

"Do you think I want to date you?" she asked. "And

that's your way of deflecting me? Because guess what, I don't want to go out with you."

"Uh, are you sure?"

"I'm ninety-nine percent positive," she teased him.

"Okay." He grinned. "Good to know."

"And I'm a hundred percent positive I'm done talking with you," she added.

His face fell, and she moved on to guy number three.

"You've heard I'm a matchmaker," Ella told him.

"Oh, yeah," he said. "I love that."

"Thanks." She waited to see if he'd ask her more about herself.

"You get desperate people together," he said.

She disliked him. Instantly. "I'd hardly call any of our clients desperate."

"Anyone who needs help dating is pretty desperate." He chuckled.

"I think you're extremely judgmental," she said, "and I'm going downstairs to fix another drink."

"How about one for me too?" He held out his glass, and she walked right by him.

"Samantha," she said pleasantly, "I'm not sure I can stay for dinner."

"But—"

"I'm ready to go."

"But Hank's not here yet."

"Give him my best regards."

"Ella—" Samantha followed her to the roof door.

Ella stopped long enough to say under her breath, "Not one of these guys can hold a candle to Hank. So why on earth would you be trying to set me up with them? I'm not interested."

"I know," said Samantha. "They're awful. I only wanted you to see that Hank is one in a trillion. He's the guy for you. I sense that. The way you two look at each other—"

Ella shook her head. "But he's leaving."

Samantha sighed. "I know. Don't let that happen."

"I can't stop him. And this sort of game is not the way to get us together." Ella strode down the rooftop stairs and into the kitchen, where she deposited her glass with a slightly trembling hand. Those men had been jerks, and she was more than a little annoyed that she'd been manipulated by Samantha, even though the Englishwoman's heart had been in the right place.

Matchmaking was an art. Not a mere skill. There was nuance to it. Intuition. A little bit of luck, too, but you had to be prepared for that luck. And preparing involved years and years of analyzing potential dating scenarios.

"Darling." It was Samantha, sounding concerned.

Ella turned, and she couldn't help her face setting into lines of annoyance. To be subjected to those three men and their stupidity was something she didn't deserve. "They were horrible," she said.

Samantha threw up her hands. "I wanted you to meet them and see how lovely Hank was in contrast."

"Oh, Samantha." Ella leaned against the counter. "You didn't have to do that. I already know he's wonderful. And I-I have no way to control this situation. If he goes, he goes."

"You can tell him you love him."

Ella's eyes burned. "I've done that before."

Samantha sighed. "Sometimes things don't take the first time around. They need time. Like breads that need two risings. And a good wine. And my special coq au vin. My mother's recipe. She was French. Did you know that?"

"No, and it smells delicious." Samantha must be a

good cook. Ella was impressed she didn't cater every meal, even though she had the funds to. And she loved that Samantha was proud of her mother and her family recipe.

"Hank's coming," Samantha reminded her. "He'll be disappointed if you go."

The Sinatra music continued, but now it felt less jaunty and fun, especially because Frank was singing "My Funny Valentine," which was sad.

Ella was nobody's Valentine.

She put a lock of hair behind her ear, and tried to think what to do. "I know you meant well, but I don't know if I can sit down to a meal with those guys."

Samantha drew herself up. "I had every intention to be aboveboard about this, and I obviously failed. I want you and Hank to be together," she said, "and to your face, I'm telling you right now that whatever I can do to make that happen, I will. I'm putting you next to him at the table. I'll focus on my three terrible guests as much as possible. And you and Hank talk. How much have you gotten to do that this week?"

"Hardly ever," Ella said. She perked up. "You'd do that?"

"Of course," said Samantha.

Ella hugged her. "Thanks. Will Hank feel manipulated, do you think?"

"Absolutely not," said Samantha. "I told him the same thing—that I'd love to see you two together."

"That's really generous of you."

"Don't believe it. The only reason I didn't go after him myself is that he's too good for me. But not for you. You've spent your adult life helping everyone else find love. Let me help you. In my own stupid way."

"You're not stupid," Ella said, and hugged her.

A knock came at the door.

"It's our boy," Samantha said. "Trust me for the rest of the night. And then you two can head home."

"But Samantha"—Ella had a hard time saying it—"he's leaving soon."

"I know," Samantha said. "Remember what I said. Sometimes the second time around is the *right* time."

They looked at each other, and Ella realized that people had to decide on their own whether or not to embrace love when the inevitable conclusion was separation.

*She* had to decide. No one else could do it for her.

# CHAPTER TWENTY-SIX

"Whether you choose to go all in with Hank or not," Samantha said, reading Ella's thoughts, "just know either way, I'll be here for you. On the phone, that is."

"You'll have to come back and visit," Ella said.

"And you'll have to come visit me."

"I think we're friends." Ella smiled at her.

"I think so too." Samantha smiled back. "I don't have a lot of female friends. Only a few girls from my youth who knew me before—and my makeup artist."

The doorbell rang again.

When Hank came in, Ella's world turned bright again. She could put up with those three guys. And now that she knew what Samantha had been up to, she was mildly amused. She could talk to Samantha's L.A. posse and save up some of their ridiculous statements to share with her girlfriends later.

Dinner was incredible. Samantha was a woman of many talents. And she was true to her word. She kept her three guests from the West Coast entertained so that Ella could snatch a few minutes here and there to converse only with Hank.

"You look so pretty tonight," he said.

"Thank you." She'd gone out of her way to dress up, knowing he would be there. She'd done a little something different with her hair too, putting rhinestone-studded bobby pins at her temples. "You look good yourself." He did. He always did. Tonight he wore a navy blazer and an open-necked, pale blue button-down Oxford. "Did you have a good day on the set?"

"Great," he said. "After you left, Samantha and I ran through one scene that had been giving us trouble, and we got it right after two takes. Then she left, and I had to do several scenes with her character's henchmen. You know, when they kidnap me."

"Oh, yeah, that's a scary part. But you look good for a guy who had a knife held to his throat and then is put into a freezer."

"Thanks," he said, but she could tell he wasn't really listening.

She wasn't either.

They were under a spell—just being with each other was enough.

She loved him.

Oh, how she did!

He managed to take her hand under the table and give it a squeeze before the astronomer asked him a question. From that point on, Ella and Hank were diverted from talking to each other the rest of the dinner, which drove her crazy.

"Let's go up to the roof again," Samantha said, "while my film cousin whips up the cream for dessert. You good with that, Ella?" She stood.

"Of course." Ella grinned. "Y'all disappear. I'll get coffee going too."

Everyone stood. The three visitors were fighting over who had better fans: the Lakers or the Dodgers.

*Y'all?* Hank mouthed to Ella silently.

"It comes naturally these days," she whispered.

"I'm staying down here to get the dishes off the table," Hank announced, not that the three guys from L.A. were really listening. They were already moving to the door leading to the roof. "We'll let you know when dessert's ready."

"Very well," said Samantha, looking pleased.

As soon as the door to the roof shut, Ella went straight into Hank's arms, and he kissed her. It was like being wrapped up in a fine cashmere sweater on a cold winter's day and sipping hot chocolate before a fire—but about a million times better.

"I missed you today," he said. And kissed her again.

"I've missed you too." It was a huge understatement, but sometimes saying what you really meant was impossible. *Showing* it, on the other hand, did wonders for getting the message across. . . .

He backed her into the kitchen. They kissed all the way.

She pulled back. "I need to whip the cream."

"Fine." His eyes were warm with lust and affection—a look she remembered well.

His gaze followed her every move as she fumbled for the metal bowl and two beaters she'd asked Samantha to put in the freezer. Hank stood behind her the whole time, ran his hands down her hips, over her breasts.

He kissed her neck. "Why is the equipment in the freezer?"

"Whipping cream whips better and faster if you use a cold bowl and beater."

"Ah."

She kept going, grabbing the carton of heavy whipping cream from the fridge and pouring it into the bowl. It was thick and rich.

"This is going to be good," Hank said.

She connected the beaters to the hand mixer Samantha had left out for her. Plugged it in. The beaters spun into a blur, and the cream swirled and formed a rapid whirlpool. Ella added a pinch of sugar from a sugar bowl on the counter.

Hank wrapped his arms around her waist and watched over her shoulder. "How long does it take?"

"Not long," she said. "Just a few minutes."

They watched together, saying nothing, his body pressed against hers. She leaned hers into his. *This is where I belong*, she thought. *With this man.*

When the cream formed stiff peaks, she reluctantly turned off the mixer. "It's ready," she said. Sadly. And looked up at him over her shoulder.

"I forgot to do the coffee!" he said.

She grinned. "Good!"

They bustled around, looking for the coffee, the filters, pouring water into the Mr. Coffee machine. They would have a few more minutes to themselves until the carafe filled and the aroma of coffee infused the air.

"So are you excited about finishing up here?" she asked him.

"I'm glad my scenes are done," he said. "They were the hardest ones to do, the Battery wall ones and the kidnapping stuff. Nothing else comes close. Up in Montreal, we're doing mainly office and outdoor urban scenes."

There was a tense silence. The coffee was ready.

"I want to go home," Ella said.

"Me too." Hank went to the door at the base of the

staircase to the rooftop and opened it. She heard him run up the stairs and open another door. "Hey, everyone. Dessert's ready. So is the coffee. Ella and I have to go."

"You're going before the torte?" Samantha asked.

"Afraid so," said Hank. "Ella's already gone. She got a call from her mom. Everything's fine, but they want her to come over for something. And I'm heading out because I don't know my lines for tomorrow."

Ella smiled, alone in the kitchen. Of course, he knew his lines.

"Wow," one of the guys said. "Well, good to meetcha, man."

Farewells were exchanged.

Samantha was quite amenable. "Tell Ella thank you for dessert, and I will see you both tomorrow."

Ella opened the front door and slipped out, racing down the stairs to the sidewalk. Hank appeared a minute later. He grabbed her around the waist and spun her.

"It's just you and me, kid," he said.

And it was. It was wonderful.

"Did Samantha know you were lying?" Ella asked him.

"Of course. At least this way her guests' egos won't be dinged."

They walked home along the Battery wall and then down Legare Street, which Ella told Hank was her favorite street in all of Charleston.

"Then why didn't we come this way before?" He made a funny-cute face.

She laughed. "Because we've hardly had any time together. There is so much more I'd love to show you."

They walked hand in hand—swinging hands—and she didn't think twice about it.

At one point Hank stopped and texted Pammy. "I want to know where she is," he said.

Ella knew why. It was because he was hoping she wouldn't be back at the carriage house. Ella was hoping the same thing. She waited expectantly.

Hank's face registered some sort of shock. "Well, I'll be. She just answered a question I texted her this morning about some names I found on the back of the portrait in my room. I thought it might be the names of the three boys in the painting. She checked with her historian friends at the Charleston Library Society and found out the names belonged to three brothers who used to live in the big house and go to the carriage house to visit with the servants. They were all three swept out toward sea on a raft they made from scraps, a raft they floated in Charleston Harbor, near the piers. Two of them made it back in and went on to become important indigo merchants. The brother who didn't has a marker in the St. Philip's graveyard on Church Street. They never found his body."

"That's so sad."

"It was in the papers. A big story." He read some more. "She's with the mayor."

"What are they doing?"

"They're finishing up playing pool at the Blind Tiger, and they're headed to dinner."

"Oh." Ella still felt some misgivings about the mayor.

"What?" Hank's eyes crinkled around the corners these days whenever he was concerned about something.

She shrugged. "I saw him on the set today. He was very cozy with the girl who carries the iPad everywhere."

"Mariah," Hank said. "That's his niece. She went to UCLA film school."

"She did?" Ella laughed. "I thought maybe he was flirting with her. I saw him kiss her on the cheek. And he put his arm around her, and she whispered something in his ear."

"She was probably telling him to be quiet when he visited the set."

"I was worried Pammy was being taken for a ride."

"No way. In fact, Mariah's with them right now."

Ella breathed a sigh of relief. "I'm so glad," she said, and swallowed hard.

"Do you think it's possible for people to fall in love at first or second sight?" Hank asked her. "I mean the kind of love that can last? Because Pammy thinks that's what's happened with her and the mayor. I guess I should start calling him Reggie. Just in case, you know, they stay together."

They started walking again.

"I think so," Ella eventually said. "I have a hard time accepting it in my brain. But in my heart, I do believe it's possible. I think love is bigger than time. Time can't control it. Love sets its own pace."

"I think so too." He squeezed her hand. "Pammy told you that you told her to 'let go and let love.'"

"I did," she said. She thought about how she'd first seen him Monday morning and then would have to say goodbye to him less than a week later.

He stopped again, pulled her off the sidewalk into a narrow alley between two Charleston single homes. It was lined with hot pink azaleas. He wrapped his arms around her. "Can you do that with me? At least until I leave? Can we just . . . let go? And let love?"

Her eyes brimmed with tears. "Yes," she said. "I'm willing to do that."

He kissed her then, and something new and fragile

blossomed between them, something that had nothing to do with anything that had happened between them a long time ago. It was fresh. And it felt bigger than the both of them.

"Let's go home," he whispered.

And they did. The last half block he picked her up and carried her.

"You're crazy," she said.

"Crazy in love," he said back.

At that moment she was so happy, she leaned her head on his chest and closed her eyes, let the rocking motion of his carrying her home lull her senses into something she could handle. Otherwise, she was heading to the moon. She was crazy in love herself.

He put her down at the carriage house door so he could unlock it. But then he picked her up again and carried her all the way upstairs to his bedroom and laid her gently down on the bed.

He opened the window, turned to face her, and started to slip off her shoes. She let him, and then she hopped right up.

"Hey," he said, "I'm trying to be romantic here."

"This is plenty romantic," she said, and started unbuckling his belt.

He undid her dress, helped her shimmy out of her panties, and unclasped her bra while he kissed her neck. They made love on the bed, fast and hard the first time, her arms flung above her head, Hank above her and then in her, her legs wrapped around his back, the window wide open, and a cool breeze caressing their naked bodies.

And when that wasn't enough, she rolled him over and teased him with her mouth until he was almost ready, then she slid on top of him and made him cry out her name before she took him all the way to bliss and back.

# CHAPTER TWENTY-SEVEN

Hank didn't want to leave Ella Friday morning, but he had to report to makeup at seven thirty. She was done on the set. She'd told him she planned on working at her office that day. She was going to check on Roberta, who would be finishing up her cheddar-penny baking hopefully that night. And she was going to prepare some notes for a talk on matchmaking and the skills one needed to find true love. She was giving it to a woman's group up in Manhattan in a few weeks. They'd already decided that she'd stay with him—and then he realized he'd be in Montreal, on the set for *Forever Road*.

They'd woken up once in the middle of the night and made love again and then snuck down to the kitchen and had some brownies and milk and talked about her family, and his, and how they were all doing. They knew Pammy was home because her combat boots were by the front door. She liked to take them off and leave them there rather than make a lot of noise crossing the hardwood floors.

So when Hank left Ella sleeping in his bed at seven,

he knew she was short on rest. She sat up, though, when she saw him trying to sneak out.

"Hey," she said with a sweet, sleepy smile. Her hair stuck up every which way. He desperately wanted to make love to her again.

Instead he came back and kissed her. "I wish I didn't have to leave."

"Me either." She kissed him back, her hand caressing the nape of his neck. He felt wanted. Strong. And loved. There was no better feeling in the world. "What time will you be done tonight?" She stretched, giving him a peek of the belly he'd lavished kisses on the night before.

"I hope by eight," he said. "Then I have to come back and pack. I wish I didn't have to get back to Brooklyn, but I promised my agent I'd go to her birthday party tomorrow afternoon. I could cancel, but—"

"You can't do that to your agent," Ella said.

"Well, she's a real friend. It would be hard."

"I understand." Ella smiled. "I'd feel the same way. And you have to go at some point."

"I do." What could he say? He took her hand. "Thank you for being you."

She gave a gentle laugh. "I am that."

"I mean, thanks for understanding me."

She looked down at their joined hands. "Thanks for loving me," she said.

Somehow their fingers clasped harder.

"Tonight I have to be with Pammy too," he said softly.

Ella nodded. "Of course."

"I want to ask you something," he said, "but I have to go now. But tonight, okay? After Pammy goes to bed."

Ella's gaze bore into his. "All right," she said. She didn't look at all happy.

And he didn't feel at all happy. He felt a deep dread

that made his stomach nauseous. Somehow, this moment felt like . . . the end. Like what they'd had the night before was only a dream. And when he came home tonight, they'd be back to what they'd been to each other all the past decade—

Ex-lovers.

He couldn't bear it if he couldn't lie with her again and show her with his body how much she meant to him. And he suddenly realized that when he'd told her he was crazy in love with her, she'd never said it back.

All day on the set with Samantha, he comforted himself with the knowledge that Ella had consented to "let go and let love." Wasn't that the same as saying she loved him?

He hoped so.

He asked Samantha what she thought.

"I think you and Ella have some issues to work out," she said. "Big ones. You're leaving. She's staying. That's pretty much a deal breaker if you're thinking about a relationship. I mean, some people do long-distance, but can you really? Don't you have a full schedule the next two years? Long-term work that takes you all over the world?"

"Malaysia, Australia, Chile, and northern Alaska." He'd told her about it earlier in the week. But he wished she didn't have to sound so practical. Then again, that was what one had to do if one wanted to stay an A-lister in Hollywood, look at the bottom line.

And follow it.

Samantha's expression had never seemed so sad to Hank. "I will say this," she said in a quiet voice right before they each left the set—and promised to meet up in Montreal for dinner the night before they were to report to that set. "Doing what we do isn't easy. You're a nomad a lot of the time, if you want to stay relevant. L.A., New York—these are your places to rest. But a lot of the time, you won't be around to hang out with your loved ones. Have you talked to Beau? He lives in Charleston, and he's still doing really well."

Hank scratched his head. "He's filming in England. And he took his wife and son with him. But yeah, I could talk to him."

Samantha's smile brightened. "Good. Maybe he has the answer. I wish *I* did."

But Beau didn't have much to say on the matter. "It all depends on the couple," he said. "Lacey can take her work with her. She's a writer. So that's made it fairly easy for us. I don't know what I'd do if she had a job in Charleston where she couldn't leave without losing a big part of her identity. I'd have to quit my job, I guess. But I do love my work, and luckily, I haven't had to give it up. Maybe someday that'll change. Good luck, man."

"Thanks," Hank said.

That night Hank had a lot of fun with Pammy and Ella. They got pizza from Uncle Sal's delivered—mushroom, sausage, and red peppers—and played all their favorite games. First, for Pammy, English rummy, which she won hands down. Then, for Ella, Scrabble. After Ella killed both Pammy and Hank in that, they went to the Blind Tiger for pool, which he loved. But he was off his game again, and Pammy won.

On the way home, the dread he'd felt that morning came back. Pammy seemed to sense his agitation—and Ella's. Ella had gotten very quiet at the Blind Tiger.

"I'm gonna go spend the night with the *nonnas*," Pammy said when they got back to the carriage house. "Reggie offered to have me stay over, but I'm playing hard to get—only because I *am* hard to get."

"Whatever you say," Hank told her, and kissed the top of Pammy's head.

Ella laughed, which was a good sign. She was showing more spirit. "You'll have fun with the *nonnas*."

"They're binge-watching eighties movies like *The Breakfast Club*," Pammy said. "I'm so there. They said I can sleep on the couch. The Sicilian relatives have the guest room."

She went straight to her room to grab her toothbrush and pajamas, and Ella stood in the living room, her arms wrapped around her middle, which Hank thought of as her sick posture. In the old days, she did that whenever she was nervous. Or extra tired.

"You okay?" he asked her.

"Fine," she squeaked.

Pammy came back out. "See you guys."

And then a rush of wind swept through the living room, although no windows were open, and the curtains flew up.

All three of them stood there, eyes wide.

"So," Hank finally said. "That was very weird."

"Yeah." Pammy swallowed hard. "I'm glad I'm getting out of here."

Ella released a pent-up breath. "What *was* that?"

"Reggie told me Charleston has a lot of ghosts," Pammy said.

"It does," Ella said, "at least according to the locals. Buxton Books runs a ghost tour each night. The owner wrote a book on Charleston's ghosts."

"I want to go on that tour soon," Pammy said. "How about it, Ella? After Hank leaves."

"Sure," Ella said, sounding sad.

Their life apart was starting very soon.

Was she ready?

Was he?

"So going out on a very long limb, if that, uh, disturbance was something paranormal," Hank said, "I wonder if it could have been the child in the picture, the one who didn't make it back to shore."

"Or maybe it was the groom who helped the boys make the raft," said Pammy. "He must have felt terrible when the disaster happened."

"Maybe it's the person who painted the boys," said Ella. "There's no signature on it. But I can tell it was someone who adored them." She'd looked closely at the portrait after she and Hank had made love the last time.

"We're never gonna know what that ridiculous blast of air was," Pammy said, "but if it's not screwed-up duct-work in the heating and cooling system, it was a ghost—obviously someone filled with regret. And they're sticking around to let us know they're frustrated about it." She cupped her hands around her mouth. "It's okay," she yelled to the house. "Life goes on." She paused. "Or not," she whispered to Hank and Ella and made a comic grimace. "Maybe I *should* sleep with Reggie tonight."

Ella grabbed Pammy's hand. "Whatever you decide, send the *nonnas* and Mama—or Reggie—my love."

"Will do. Wherever I wind up, I'm staying for a big breakfast, so this is it, cuz. Instead of 'Bye,' I'm gonna say 'Boo.'"

They hugged. Made promises to see each other soon.

"I want you to know something," Pammy told Hank at the door. "You don't have to worry about me getting homesick. If this thing doesn't work out with Reggie"—she slapped her heart—"I got me. I got my mad woodworking skills. And I got friends like Ella."

"Love you, Pammy," he said. "I'm not worried. You got this."

She winked and pulled the door shut behind her.

Hank turned to Ella. "So," he said. The feeling of dread was still there, but he'd ignore it. "I told you I wanted to talk to you alone. And now's the time."

She shook her head. "I can't."

"We can stay somewhere else," Hank said. "We can get a hotel room."

"I'm not scared of whatever just happened."

"Maybe it was a freak-out of the central air system," Hank suggested. But he wondered—it had happened right after they'd talked about the boys in the painting.

"Maybe it was a messed-up air duct," Ella conceded. "But if it wasn't, it makes me sad more than anything." She swallowed and sat on the couch. "If it was a ghost, they wish they had a second chance. But it's too late. They don't want to accept it, and so they can't rest. It's sad."

Hank sat next to her and put his arm around her shoulder. "You won't be that person. You're not going to come back and haunt people." He allowed himself a small smile.

She folded her hands in her lap and looked down. "I'm afraid to hear what you're going to say to me, Hank."

"But Ella—"

She stood, forcing his arm to drop away. "I'm not so sure it's a good idea."

He stood too. "I really want to say it."

She closed her eyes, took a breath, and opened them. "Okay."

He took her hands. "I want a second chance with you, whatever that means for us. I want to commit to you and work this out. We should be together."

She looked at him a long time. "I'd like that too. But"—she paused a beat—"it's too late."

"It's never too late," he said. "You told that to Pammy. You have to live and love to the end."

"I *am* living and loving, Hank." She sounded so earnest. And bright. And true. She sounded like the love of his life. "When you showed up Monday, I was already doing that. And I always will. Which is why I'm not going to throw it all away—what I have here in Charleston— to follow you around the world. I don't want to be an appendage of you, consigned to the shadows while you're a big movie star. I'm happy for you. I really am. But doing this movie made me realize I don't care about pursuing that kind of career anymore myself. I get to indulge my creative side right here at the Dock Street Theatre, and as a matchmaker, as a wannabe cook, and as a woman who has to juggle being part of a large family. I want to be the star of my own life, Hank. I *am* the star of my own life, and it feels right to hold onto that. I hope you understand."

Everything she said made sense. But he didn't have to like hearing it. "I love you, Ella." His entire body felt heavy with sadness. And fear. How could he continue living his life without her? "I never stopped."

"I love you too, Hank," she said right away. "I never stopped either. But life got in the way. And we forged new paths. Are you willing to change yours?"

"I don't know how to answer that." He really didn't. It was like looking down a deep, dark well without a flashlight. He couldn't see.

"Let's pretend you do know," she said. "Let's say you're willing to bend over backward to accommodate the fact that I'm not going to change my life for you. Don't you think you'd resent that after a while? That you'd be doing all the heavy lifting?"

"No," he said, then quickly amended that to, "I don't know."

Because he didn't know. He had to be honest with her.

A small, sad smile formed on her lips. "You were right, all those years ago. Loving each other isn't enough. Papa taught me we have to listen to our hearts and our own passions that have nothing to do with anyone else. They're part of who we are. I loved acting way before I knew you, Hank. And I loved my family. I also loved how much my parents loved each other and knew that somehow that love would guide me, and it did, toward my career as a matchmaker. What did you love before me, Hank? Or maybe after? Whatever it is, let it guide you too."

He was devastated. But everything she said—it mattered. It made sense. How to respond? How to respond when the love of your life admits she doesn't *need* you?

And did he need *her*? He'd been acting like it. Maybe that was his problem. Maybe he still had learning to do.

"I don't know what it is," he said. "I've been looking. When we first met, I was looking. And . . . then you came."

"It has to be more than me," she said. "I hope you find it. It's in you somewhere. You just need to find it. Everything you've done so far in your adult life points toward acting being your passion. You're so good at it, Hank."

"It doesn't feel like enough." He felt empty inside, saying that.

"Before you say another word"—she put her fingers on his lips—"I'm leaving. I wish you all the best." She dropped her hand and grabbed her purse from the coffee table. "I don't need anything. I'll come back after you leave tomorrow." Her eyes were bright with unshed tears.

At the door she said, "Goodbye, and good luck with the movie. Thanks for getting me that role. It really helped me see what matters to me the most. And you know what? It doesn't take long to figure it out. You don't have to take another ten years. Maybe it will happen in a week."

And then she was gone.

# CHAPTER TWENTY-EIGHT

The last time Ella had been to her mother's house, she'd been crying. Pammy had been there, too, out in the living room with the *nonnas*, watching their eighties movies. Pammy cried, too, and said Hank was a lost soul, like that maybe-ghost at the carriage house.

And Ella said, "No, he's not!" And then she cried, and said, "Maybe he is."

She didn't know.

"He's looking for something," Pammy said, and as she often did when she was agitated, she took her level out of her pocket and put it on the coffee table. "This isn't level."

Nonna Boo reminded her that most old houses in Charleston had floors that weren't quite level, and that they liked it that way. And that life wasn't level either, and everyone had to deal with it.

Even so, Pammy insisted on quitting the eighties binge movie marathon and going back to the carriage house to be with Hank, but when she texted him to let him know, he texted back that he was already in a taxi heading to the airport. His pilot was willing to take him straight back to New York. He told Pammy he was okay, and he wanted her to keep binge-watching eighties movies and to stay with the Mancinis, who were a very wonderful family. Unless she wanted to wind up at Reggie's that night. Hank approved. He thought Reggie was a very good guy and an excellent mayor.

Mama put Ella to bed in *her* bed, the one she used to share with Papa, and assured her that she herself would do fine staying with Nonna Sofia, who didn't move when she was sleeping. Mama knew this because when Papa had died, she'd flown back to Italy and slept with Nonna Sofia in her tiny apartment, the one she got after she was widowed. Nonna Sofia had had only one bed there. Mama had stayed for two weeks, and by the end of it, she was ready to go back to the States and start again.

But then Ella told Mama she wanted her to sleep with her. And Mama said, "Maybe sleeping with Nonna Sofia helped me too." So Mama slid into bed with Ella, and Ella wrapped her arms around her, and they fell asleep together.

Ella did that for two weeks. Not just for her, but for Mama. Because in that time, Mama found out her beloved papa—Guiseppe—wasn't her biological father. The vineyard owner's son was. They consulted with Nonna Alberta, who told Mama and confessed that as hard as it was to hear, she was relieved to know the truth. Together the three women decided Nonna Sofia wouldn't be relieved at all, and it might devastate her, probably because Nonna Sofia kept saying over and over, "I will be devastated, daughter, if your papa is not your father."

So Mama kept the secret of her ancestry hidden from Nonna Sofia but not from Nonna Boo, nor from her

brothers and sisters. She also told them the news that
Nonna Alberta had held back until she knew the truth—
that Mama was heir to a vineyard. Mama didn't care. But
Nonna Alberta said someday she would.

So Mama decided she would send Ella over to check
out the new family property in Palermo as soon as Ella
felt up to it—"which might be never," Mama said hopefully. "Who cares?"

But Ella told her mother that while she was there, she
would lay flowers on the grave of Guiseppe, Mama's beloved papa, who would always be Mama's papa and Ella's grandfather, no matter what. And she told her mother
that it would be nice to have the vineyard, the site of
Nonna Sofia's and Guiseppe's love story, in the family.
She reminded Mama that Guiseppe used to lay grapes
and sprigs of marjoram and thyme outside Nonna Sofia's
door.

Mama had softened a bit at that, and Ella booked two
tickets to Palermo, which she would visit after the big
Aquarium gala with Uncle Sal, who was a rock to her
after her own papa's death and still was.

The night of the gala, Ella was in no mood to go. She
hadn't wanted to socialize since Hank left. She'd thrown
herself into her work. Even Jill, her sweet sister who'd
arrived back home with her husband Cosmo, couldn't
convince Ella to do anything, not even walk the Ravenel
Bridge with her, which was something they'd both liked
to do together for exercise.

The only reason Ella was going to the gala was
because she had to be there to see Roberta on her date
with a fabulous guy she'd met after eating that ten thousandth cheddar penny—which she did at a big "Champagne and Cheddar Penny Party" at Macy and Deacon's
house, where all Roberta's friends gathered to wish her

well and take home boxes of cheddar pennies their friend had packaged and tied with a beautiful ribbon that said TRUE LOVE CHEDDAR PENNIES, the name of her new baking company.

This man wasn't any of the dates Ella had chosen for Roberta through Two Love Lane. Roberta decided not to go on those dates. Nor was he Pete, who wound up asking Miss Thing if she needed an escort to the gala after Miss Thing ignored him for a week, which was very hard on her because she'd gotten used to drinking her *Price Is Right* coffee every day, the one where Pete yelled "Come on down!" to whoever ordered it, in honor of Miss Thing's Double Showcase win.

This date of Roberta's was the owner of a taco food truck who had used the same commercial kitchen Roberta had. While Roberta was baking her cheddar pennies, he was making taco filling and his homemade salsa on the other side of the kitchen. They'd become fast friends, and Roberta had had no trouble chatting with him while she was mixing, rolling, chilling, slicing, and baking her cheddar pennies.

"Because we were just friends," she explained to Ella. "It's easy to talk to someone who's just friends. I was able to talk to him after he asked me out on a real date because I'd eaten that ten thousandth cheddar penny."

Ella decided to let Roberta decide for herself why she was talking to her new man, who happened to be called Robert.

"I always vowed never to date a Robert or a Bob," Roberta said, "and look at me now!"

Yes, things were going well for Roberta, but the real test was tonight. She'd only been out on five dates with Robert, and while they'd gone spectacularly well, she retained a bit of nervousness about the Aquarium event.

"This is the realest date of all," Roberta told Ella. "Because I'm wearing a gorgeous gown, and he's in a tux. We'll be like a prince and a princess, and I have a feeling that after the night's over, Robert might ask to stay over and maybe say nice things to me." She blinked a million times. "I'm afraid I won't be able to speak because I really, really like him. And then he'll be hurt when I just stare at him, and he'll go home and never call me again."

Ella assured Roberta that her other dates with Robert counted as real dates, and she'd been speaking on those just fine. "If you can't talk on *this* date, it might be that you're overcome with an emotion like happiness, not just nerves." Or a spell. But she wouldn't say the word "spell" out loud and jinx Roberta back into her old silence. "Being overcome with emotions like happiness happens to everyone."

You could also be overcome with emotions like sadness, but Ella knew that she could get through it with the help of her family and friends. She wouldn't lie to them. She was sad. But she also knew she'd made the right decision to let Hank go, to let him figure out what he really wanted for himself, deep inside, apart from her.

She thought she'd done a good job of reassuring Roberta, but she wanted to be at the gala just in case her client needed a boost. So when she was in the limo on the way over with Deacon, Macy, Greer, Ford, Miss Thing, and Pete, she was shocked when the limo stopped at a red light and someone opened the door.

"Miss Ella Mancini?" It was a rough-looking man in bib overalls and a squashed hat. He smelled a bit funny too, like fish. But she didn't want to say that. He was wearing sunglasses at dusk too, which didn't make sense. She wasn't worried that he was a carjacker or anything.

He knew her name. And she had Mace in her purse, which she always carried, as well as a whistle, along with the emergency twenty-dollar bill she always kept with a tampon, a condom (useless to her!—she'd never have sex again!), and a peppermint in the side zippered pocket most purses have. She'd been so blue getting dressed, she hadn't even attempted to choose from among her evening bags to carry to the gala. She was in a scarlet red dress with crisscross straps that boosted her décolletage, and she was carrying her daytime white leather handbag big enough to hold a frozen turkey breast from Harris Tee-ter, if she needed to. (She'd actually done that the week before; grocery shopping held no joy for her; she bought things willy-nilly and functioned, post-Hank's departure, mainly on Ritz crackers and pimento cheese.)

Of course, she wasn't so depressed that she didn't wear elegant high heels that bordered on ultra sexy, with rhine-stones flashing on the toes. The *nonnas* had told her she must continue wearing strappy sandals, so she'd made sure she did, although she took no joy in donning them.

Okay, just a little. Good Italian leather shoes could help carry one through hard times.

No one in the limo reacted, which Ella found strange. Miss Thing was the only one who looked remotely con-cerned. Her face was red. She was biting her left thumb too.

The man took off his sunglasses and grinned.

She suddenly recognized him! "Carl! What are you doing here?" He was the captain of a local shrimp trawler called the *Megan Casey*.

"I'm here to kidnap you," he said.

And at that moment, Macy and Greer reached over, pulled on Ella's hands, and yanked her toward the open door of the limo.

Ella pulled back. "I'm not going!"

"Yes, you are," said Macy, her voice calm and sweet.

Carl waited with his hand stretched out. "Come on, little missy. We're not going to let you escape."

"*No*." Ella dug in. But inch by inch, she was moving toward the door, thanks to various hands pushing and pulling her that way. She might have let a few curse words fly.

"Come on, Ella," Greer said. "We wouldn't steer you wrong."

"I know what's happening," Ella said, "and it's a terrible idea."

"If you go, I'll tell you my name!" cried Miss Thing.

For a split second, everything stilled.

"Okay," said Ella quietly.

"You tell her, Pete," said Miss Thing, her voice thin.

"Tatyana," he said proudly, "but I call her *T.*"

And before Ella could register any reaction, Carl grabbed her right hand and finally yanked her onto the street.

The limo took off.

"Let's go, Miss Ella," he said, and pulled her over the curb, then around to the passenger side of a pickup truck idling there.

"This is a bad idea, Carl," she said. "There is no one I want to go on Operation Shrimp Trawler with."

She remembered Miss Thing—Tatyana!—referring to it as one of their matchmaking agency's collection of romantic dating scenarios that they saved for special occasions. Miss Thing (Ella couldn't imagine calling her Tatyana) had bragged about it in the kitchen at Two Love Lane, when Samantha, Roberta, and Hank had been visiting, and most of them ate Miss Thing's giant pink cookies with sprinkles.

"I think you'll change your mind in a minute," Carl said.

"No, I won't." Macy and Greer were involved, Ella knew. And Miss Thing. Ever since Hank left, they'd been throwing men in front of her. Which was hard to do since she didn't want to socialize. But they'd found a way. What if one of them was on the trawler tonight?

Macy had a favorite: his name was Kevin, and he was really cute and fun. He played the banjo and was on the Spoleto Arts Festival board. Greer's favorite was Tomás, a Spaniard who'd recently moved to Charleston to study sea turtles with the Aquarium. Ella ruled him out because he'd be at the gala tonight, repping the turtles' cause. Miss Thing's favorite was Pete's youngest brother, who lived in Scranton, Pennsylvania. He was in town staying with Pete for a month because he could afford to leave his local thriving sports store chain at will. He wasn't going to the gala because he didn't care for the ocean, he'd told Miss Thing. (*Who didn't care for the ocean?* Ella remembered thinking). So no way would Pete's brother be on the trawler.

No. It had to be Kevin. Dear God, if he brought his banjo and tried to serenade her with it, she would die! "Please, no banjo," she said to Carl as they drove over the Ravenel Bridge to Shem Creek, where his trawler was docked.

He cast her a sideways glance. "Banjo?" And then gave a short chuckle.

Ella groaned. "It's Kevin, isn't it?"

"I'm not saying a word," said Carl.

Ella resigned herself to going to Shem Creek and boarding his trawler and chilling with Kevin. She had a fleeting thought, *If only it would be Hank!* But she knew it wouldn't be. She hadn't heard a word from him since he left, but she did stalk his Twitter page, and as of yesterday he was in Montreal filming *Forever Road*.

She knew Operation Shrimp Trawler well. First, the couple would meet up on the trawler—which Carl would clean up, of course. He'd take the *Megan Casey* out into the harbor; hand the couple an iced bottle of tequila; give them a styrofoam bowl of sliced lemons, a shaker of salt, and two red Solo cups. Then he'd go back to the wheel and circle around the harbor a few times. After a while, a chef belowdecks would bring out a splendiferous meal of boiled shrimp, fried catfish, some of Carl's incredible cocktail sauce (which had a lot of Tabasco in it), his homemade tartar sauce (which was really sweet pickle relish, dill, and Duke's Mayonnaise), and bread and butter, and the couple would eat it looking at a nice sunset over the Ashley River Bridges.

Not at a nice table either. They'd eat their bounty on paper plates. With their hands. And no napkins.

"It's primitive," Miss Thing would always say. "They'll have to lick their fingers a lot."

At this point, the tequila would be kicking in. Carl would cruise up the Cooper River to a sweet little farmhouse stocked with wine, beer, liquor, and breakfast food. It had a fantastic tree house on one side—with a queen-sized bed in it—and a nice pool on the other. When they got to the dock, Carl would give each of his passengers a bag holding a bathing suit and a toothbrush and toothpaste. That was it. And then he'd say he'd return in three hours, unless someone texted him and told him not to. At that point, he'd chug away from the dock.

Only once out of the four times they'd used Operation Shrimp Trawler had Carl had to go back, and it wasn't because the couple didn't like each other. It was because they'd accidentally broken their bottle of tequila when they were climbing up to the tree house and the guy had cut his hand pretty good and needed stitches. That couple wound up getting married. Three out of the four had. The fourth couple settled for becoming best friends and started a Charleston tourism package company together that was going gangbusters—but the ladies of Two Love Lane refused to let them use their Operation Shrimp Trawler idea. They had to sign an agreement not to.

"Because Operation Shrimp Trawler is worth its weight in gold," Miss Thing always said.

And it was.

But it wouldn't work on Ella. She wasn't a big tequila person. She'd eat the shrimp and fried catfish, and before Carl started moving up the Cooper River, she'd tell him to head back to Shem Creek, and she would thank Kevin for being such a lovely dinner companion.

The end.

She felt a little better imagining what she would do, so when she walked up the gangplank of the *Megan Casey* and saw Hank there at the bow, sitting on a chair with his legs spread and his hands between his knees, a game of Scrabble prepped and ready on a table, she nearly fell overboard.

"You're in Montreal," she said.

"Nope," said Hank, and stood. "I'm here."

Ella shivered. She was in that elegant gown with the thin straps and she was teetering on her heels. It was a balmy evening, but the shock of seeing Hank made her wish for a light wrap.

Which Carl provided. It was one of her own shawls. "Miss Thing sent this over. Why don't you take off your shoes, though."

She hadn't taken her eyes off Hank. "Okay," she said. She leaned against the front of the cockpit housing, a big

window behind her, and pulled off her shoes. Carl
scooped them up for her and stashed them under his arm.

She didn't care if she ever saw those shoes again, honestly.

All of her attention was on Hank. He was wearing a
tux. She just now noticed. What was up with that?

He stood. "Come on over," he said. "Take a seat and
let's play some Scrabble."

"Oh, no," she said, her eyes filling with tears. "I'm not
a tequila fan, really. Operation Shrimp Trawler is all
about tequila."

"I know," he said. "Your besties told me. We've got
wine tonight instead."

"I like wine," she whispered. "Operation Shrimp
Trawler's also about seduction. After having a meal that
you have to eat with your hands."

"We're sticking with that." He grinned, and her knees
nearly buckled. He was *Hank*.

"I hope it's boiled shrimp and fried catfish," she said.

"It still is. Captain Carl doesn't mess with success. Not
unless he's ordered to by the admirals at Two Love Lane."

His smile warmed the cockles of her heart. She didn't
know what cockles were, but Mama sometimes said it
when she was extra moved by something, and that expression fit better than any other Ella could think of.

She barely noticed, but the engine started and Carl
cast off the lines.

"Come sit down," Hank said.

So she padded over to the table in bare feet and sat
down.

The bow of the *Megan Casey* made a sharp left turn,
and they headed out Shem Creek and into Charleston
Harbor. The salt breeze felt amazing.

"Thanks so much for coming tonight," he said.

"You're welcome," she said, and remembered being yanked out of the limo. She could smile about it now. "I had no choice. I was kidnapped."

He winced, but on him, it looked good. All raw man. "You're right," he said. "There was some deception involved. I'm sorry if that annoys you. The last thing I want to do is offend you."

"It's okay," she said softly. "I think."

"You're a good sport." He reached across the Scrabble board and took her hand. "You look beautiful."

"You don't look so bad yourself." She squeezed his hand back.

He smiled. "The board's Velcroed to the table. And so are the racks. Captain Carl thought of everything."

"Amazing," she murmured. Scrabble was the last thing on her mind.

"But the letters might slide around," Hank said. "Let's hope we don't hit rough seas."

She laughed. The harbor was calm. The horizon held no clouds. "We'll be okay."

A young man in khaki shorts and a faded Shem Creek Trawling Company T-shirt appeared with two red Solo cups and handed them off to Ella and her unexpected date, which meant they had to release their handclasp. "Enjoy," he said. "The shrimp and catfish will be up in about ten minutes."

Ella took a sip of the mellow rosé and wasn't sure now she could eat. Her stomach felt nervous. As did the rest of her. What could Hank want? She was sure he'd reveal all. But meanwhile, she wanted to enjoy simply sitting with him, the harbor waters falling away on either side of the trawler, the bow gently moving up and down—and the sun, a melon-colored ball setting behind the Ashley River Bridges.

"Should we play and talk at the same time?" he asked her.

"Sure." They each picked up seven tiles turned blank side up that were clustered in the overturned cover of the board game.

"You go first this time," Hank said.

Ella laid down a harmless word, "hamper." "How have you been?" she asked him.

He laid down a boring word of his own, "timer," crossing her word vertically at the *M*. "I've been doing a lot of soul-searching," he said.

"You've had time for that in Montreal?"

"I didn't have to get there until last week. So I had a couple of weeks at home in Brooklyn. I saw my family a lot."

They each took sips of wine. It wasn't awkward, but things felt completely different between them. Ella wasn't sure why. "That's nice," she said. "I've been spending a lot of time with mine too." She told him the results of her mother's paternity test, and how Mama was coping well, considering the shock of having to reframe her personal history.

"I think not telling Nonna Sofia was a wise call, even if it meant you had to fib to her," he said. "Maybe someday she'll want to know, like Nonna Alberta. But obviously, she doesn't right now."

"Yes, it's kind of awkward. But it's for the best. When I go to Palermo, I'm just going to tell her Uncle Sal and I are visiting the Sicilian branch of the family. It's time."

"She'll get that."

They'd forgotten about Scrabble. Ella couldn't stop looking at him, and Hank couldn't keep his eyes off her.

She wrapped her shawl closer. "It's such a nice treat, seeing you."

She immediately regretted saying "treat," which was a Southern woman's way of describing someone or something utterly delightful in polite company. But Hank was way more than a treat. And he was more than polite company. His presence on the trawler was a gift. A very personal one.

"I mean to say that you're coming here means a lot to me," she said. "More than I can express in words." She glanced down at the game board. "Sometimes words aren't enough."

"I know what you mean," he murmured. "But I'm going to give it a shot, if you can bear with me."

She nodded, took a sip of wine. So did he. And then he looked out at the horizon for a few seconds. She'd have to be patient. He was clearly trying to get it together. To do this the right way, whatever it was.

"There's no right way," she blurted out. "No matter what you say, or how you say it, I'm always going to"— she took a quiet breath and braced herself—"I'm always going to love you, Hank."

Hank's expression then reminded her of how he used to look when they'd lie on the couch at their old apartment and listen to songs from *Les Misérables*. It made her sit up, her heart race, and her whole being light up from the inside out. Something big was happening. She sensed an impending earthquake. As Macy and Greer had said, plates shifted, and then, bam—

You were looking at a whole new world.

He lowered his chin for a second, then looked back up, his bow tie not even askew. It was a sexy move that also showed how vulnerable he could be. She didn't doubt for a second that it was authentic. "Thank you for saying that," he said. "I will always love you too, Ella."

They didn't touch. The purr of the boat engine was

almost peaceful. A seagull dove nearby, searching for its supper.

"I know what I want," he finally said. He sounded happy.

Ella couldn't help but grin. "You do?"

He nodded. "Apart from wanting *you*," he said with exaggerated playfulness, "I want to do something that makes me feel the way I did when I worked at Serendipity 3 as a lowly busboy."

"You do?" she practically squeaked.

"Yep. I didn't need that job. I was the son of a wealthy man, but Dad made me work all through high school so I could appreciate how hard it is to earn a dollar. I think he wanted me to see, too, how lucky I was to come from a family as blessed as ours. Some of the guys in the kitchen at Serendipity 3 weren't so lucky. They worked paycheck to paycheck."

"I can imagine," said Ella. She remembered a few times when Papa and Uncle Sal were worried about keeping their own restaurant open and having to lay off employees. Owning a business wasn't easy. She knew that from Two Love Lane. But being a worker—having no control at all over your future at that business—was an even more precarious position to hold.

"At Serendipity 3," Hank said, "I got to see a lot of customers find joy in the little things. In this case, ice cream. You didn't have to be really rich to come in and enjoy a scoop. I saw families like yours—parents with their kids—pay us a visit and find each other again over a frozen hot chocolate."

A sweet tenderness overwhelmed Ella. "Papa and I certainly connected that way. I always felt like a princess."

"And I used to like watching these little family scenarios unfold," Hank said. "A lot of couples had dates there too. The common denominator was that almost everyone came in after a movie or a Broadway show."

The memories Ella had of her and Papa at their Broadway shows would stay with her forever. "So what does this all mean for you?"

"It means I went into acting to be a part of that dynamic." He shifted, and a pained look crossed his face. "I have great parents. But we never did things like that together. I craved having family time. But Dad has a really strong work ethic and he was almost never home. And Mom, she was busy with her social life. The honest truth is, she was simply too self-absorbed to notice us that much. She left a lot of the rearing of her four children to nannies."

"I never knew you had nannies!"

"It's because I was embarrassed to tell you. Your family sticks together so much. Mine is more formal. We love each other—don't get me wrong—but my childhood, apart from playing with my brothers—felt a little disjointed."

"So acting brought you into that sphere of connection. People could talk about you over their ice creams. Kids and parents could bond. So could couples."

"I think so. When Dad tried to push me to law school, I pushed back so hard because I was trying desperately not to recreate his life. I wanted to be a part of a warm conversation. Not be assessed all the time."

"Assessed?"

"My parents were always trying to make sure their kids' accomplishments met their high—and fairly narrow—standards."

"Oh." She felt for him. Deeply. And she was upset they hadn't had a talk like this ten years before. She'd sensed that when she'd shared Thanksgiving dinner with Hank and his family that long ago day, there had been some tension, but she'd been worried about the pregnancy scare, and he'd not been ready to talk about his family after that dinner. So they never really tackled his relationship with his parents head-on.

"So you've never felt quite that acting was your thing," she ventured to say, "because you were getting into it not for the love of the dramatic arts but because it was a way to rebel against your dad and enter into those conversations families had to connect with each other."

"Exactly. I became a part of pop culture, anathema to my dad. And it also meant I was sort of embraced by a lot of people."

"Did you talk about this with your parents while you were home?" Ella hoped he had.

"Yes," Hank said. "We had a brutally frank talk, and there were a lot of apologies on their side. And I said I was sorry too, because the truth was, if I had talked openly to them ten years ago, my career trajectory might have stayed bumpy for a while longer, but I might have been more true to myself."

"Don't beat yourself up," Ella said. "You felt a lot of legitimate pressure from your dad. And you were young."

"I know. I'm not going to have any regrets. Acting has given me exactly what I hoped it would. I became part of the worldwide family conversation." He grinned.

"That's very cool."

"It is. It also made me wealthy. I can take time off. I can quit—if I want."

"Do you?"

"I'm not sure yet. I have obligations over the next two years that would be tricky to get out of. And in a way, I don't want to, now that I see myself more clearly. I can ponder my future while I'm acting. How much do I really like the actual art? And how much of this career was about fighting my personal demons?"

He stood and held out his hand to her. She grabbed it and they walked to the very front of the bow, let go of each other, and gripped the railing. What a gorgeous view of the historic peninsula city of Charleston lay before them! The antebellum homes on the Battery were stunning. The panoramic sight really hadn't changed much in more than two hundred years.

"I love acting," Ella said, her hair blowing out behind her, "but I realize I can practice the craft anywhere and still be happy. Which is what I love about community theater." She wrapped her fingers around the bronzed knuckles of Hank's right hand. "I'm really happy for you." She felt a lump in her throat as she said it. He'd had a huge breakthrough, and she was honored he'd shared it with her.

Of course, she wanted to know how she fit into the picture, if at all.

He turned toward her, and she toward him. Leaning on the railing, he wrapped his arms around her waist. "I want to be based out of Charleston," he said. "I'll have to travel a lot over the next two years, but if you can put up with that—and join me whenever you're free—I'm convinced we can take our second chance, Ella, and run with it. Whatever I decide about acting, I'm going to get involved in the business from Charleston. But I suspect"—he swallowed hard—"I suspect I'm going to find other things to do. Somehow I want to get involved in connecting families through exposure to the arts, especially families who have a hard time making ends meet. I feel I can honor your father that way too, and all the sacrifices he made to help his little girl find her dreams."

"Hank, this makes me so happy." Ella was crying. She was laughing somehow too.

"Me too." Hank wiped away some tears from his own eyes. But he was grinning. He was a new man.

And Ella, loving him, was a new woman. She'd never been happier.

"I'm dressed to go to the Aquarium gala," he said, "if you need a date."

"I do," she said. "I'll need a date for the rest of my life."

*Bring him home, Bring him home* . . . those short words from the song in *Les Misérables* came to Ella then. The trawler lifted on an ocean swell and a breeze, its bow pointed toward the Battery, Charleston's church spires rising high behind its historic homes to a coral sky.

"I want to be that guy," Hank said, and kissed her.